The Tough Guy Guy Falls

A Happy Montana Novel

I0532811

By
Zanne Sweeney

Dedicated to my sister Beth.
Thank you for your support!
This guy is for you!

Acknowledgements:
Jude - Lone Wolf - you are the best!
Cover by: Elm Street Design Studio
Cover Photo: Jasminko Ibrakovic

Prolog

Will MacPhearsons gut weighed heavily with the ball of turmoil that had been festering inside of it since he decided to quit. This was the last match that he was contracted for and then he was going to tell Mr. Aguilar that he was done. Money was no longer an issue, he had accumulated so much that he could probably live off good investments if he wanted to, but that's not what he wanted. He and his best friend Davey, also a cage fighter, wanted to open their own Engineering firm.

He and Davey had met as freshman at FIT. They became fast friends and Davey's family had welcomed him into theirs for every holiday and vacation they had taken. Will had lost his parents when he was young and the summer he had graduated for high school he lost the only family he had left, his grandfather. His grandfather was a tough man. He had never married, was a carpenter by trade, and he had been a Marine. Well, once a Marine always a Marine. His grandfather had taught him a great many things, for instance Will could build a house, do the wiring, and even the plumbing. He also taught Will how to fight and although Will valued all the other things his grandfather had taught him, learning to fight had become the most valuable.

In the spring of his freshman year Will needed some extra money, so he answered an ad that led him to Mr. Aguilar and into the brutal sport of cage fighting. Will was good at it. He was big and strong, but what set him apart from other fighters was his smarts. Will fought every month and soon his bank account was flush. The next fall Will introduced Davey to Mr. Aguilar. The two best friends hid their cage fighting personas from Davey's family and their other friends. The fought their way through college and even while they continued at FIT while getting their Masters. Now that he and Davey had completed their Masters they had both decided to quit the cage fighting circuit. The only foreseeable problem was that Mr. Aguilar was probably not going to like his number 1 and number 2 cage fighters leaving him, especially at the same time. The two young men decided it was in their best interest to leave without telling anyone.

Will and Davey had planned out every little detail. They were planning to leave, after tonight's fights. They would attend the party as usual and then jump in Will's truck that they had already packed and head as far away from Miami as possible. Their plan was to head north and travel for a while, avoiding large cities, until they reached Seattle, Washington. There they would lay low, living on cash for a couple of years, until they thought they were safe from Mr. Aguilar and his well connected family. Then they would start up their engineering business.

Davey had been the undercard to Will's fight and he destroyed a kid from Atlantic City, New Jersey. The crowd was buzzing and wanted to see a good fight. Mr. Aguilar motioned Ramos, his bodyguard to him and then Ramos repeated his words to Will. Mr. Aguilar wished for Will to stretch out his fight. Will knew that he wanted the spectators to feel that they had gotten their money's worth.

Will jogged into the center of the small warehouse towards the cage. There were cheap aluminum stands on all four side of the 15 by 15 foot enclosure. In front of the stands velvet ropes attached to gold posts stands separated cushioned folding chairs where the VIP's sat. Colorful assorted women's panties were being thrown at the gray metal bars much to the delight of the crowd. It all was because one darn woman decided to toss her panties at the cage one night, which in turn had more women doing the same. Then Tito would make a big production, after the fight, of picking up one of the tiny thongs and that lucky woman would follow him and Tito out of the ring where she would become a guest at the after fight party that Mr. Aguilar always hosted at the hotel down the street.

Tito turned it into a big Public Relations ploy that a national news Network had even covered one night. The women were led to believe that if their underwear was chosen they would be 'Romeo's' date for the evening. Will quickly let Tito know that was not going to happen. It didn't matter though. Women continued to toss their panties at the cage. Tito continued to pick one up and make a big production about it as he escorted her to the back hall, and Will continued to avoid the women and leave the parties as soon as possible.

Will really didn't like attending the glitzy after parties, but Mr. Aguilar was not a man you said no to.

Chants of 'Romeo!' 'Romeo!' filled the warehouse as the fight was announced. Will hated his nickname. His opponents taunted him with it and when Davey was pissed at him he even used it.

Will summed up his opponent quickly. He was a retrained south-paw. He had a good right leg kick, but when he kicked out with his left leg he leaned too far to his right and that was how Will knew he would beat him. The only dilemma was putting on a good fight before he could take the man out. This was dangerous. Will knew more than one good fighter that had fallen prey to a lucky punch or kick. In the fifth round Will was done playing around. The man he was fighting had gotten in a good right hook and Will had felt his lip split. He spat out blood, readied himself for the kick that he knew would come, and then bam the second Will saw the right leg lifting from the canvas he turned sideways and landed an upper cut so hard on the mans jaw that he heard the bone crunching. The man was out before he hit the padded floor.

Davey met Will in the back room they used before and after fights. Davey was already showered. He had a butterfly bandage pushing together the skin above his left eye and it was already starting to color. Will let the Doc look at his lip, but it wasn't anything they could stitch so Will showered and met Davey back in the room. A tall leggy redhead was teetering on the highest heels Will had ever seen and when she saw him she squealed and headed towards him. Will gave Tito the stink eye and Tito stepped in front of her before she reached him. Tito whispered to the red head in Spanish and whatever he said appeased her because she immediately calmed down and was content to simply walk with the four of them down the street to the hotel.

Davey kept looking at Will and Will knew he was as uneasy about seeing Mr. Aguilar as he was. The man headed a major crime family and he could smell trouble. The man had an uncanny knack for knowing things before they even happened. Will and Davey knew they had to act normal, and leave the party when they normally would. The truck was parked around the corner, packed, fueled and ready to go. They knew they'd never be paid for tonight's fights, but they had already pulled their money from their bank and had re-deposited into another one with branches up north. The party was the same as always lots of booze, plenty of women and every kind of drug you could possibly ask for. Mr. Aguilar was playing host as if he was a Massachusetts blue blood. The two friends accepted the congratulations of fans and each held a beer, for appearance sake. Mr. Aguilar made his customary toast praising his fighters and thanking his patron's and then the party began. Will stood next to the bar and Davey remained uncharacteristically at his side. Davey liked women and often found a willing female ready for anything. Will did too, but he hadn't been with a woman in awhile. They were a distraction and he needed to be focused.

Tito was talking to them about a fight he had just booked for them that would require them to travel. Will was to fight an unbeaten fighter who was tearing up the lower level competition. Will was to be his first big time bout. Will knew this was not good news because Mr. Aguilar would now see them leaving as a breech of contract, even though they had not signed the papers yet.

Ramos appeared at the bar and told Tito to take Davey and Will to the back room because Mr. Aguilar needed to speak with them. Will saw Davey beginning to panic so he slapped his best friend on the back pretending to be intoxicated and said, "Lets go see the boss." in the cheeriest voice he could muster.

The back room turned out to be the hotel manager's office. Mr. Aguilar sat behind the desk looking like he owned it. He motioned for the two men to sit down. Davey took the seat right in front of the desk and Will chose the one at the right.

"Will, you did good making that fight last." His accent was thick and Will could tell he was high by how glassy his eyes were and the slight slur in his speech. Will nodded.

"You though." Mr. Aguilar glared at Davey. "You make it so my customers think they are getting cheated. You do not make the fight last." Will could see Davey's adams apple bobbing nervously.

Tito jumped to Davey's defense. "He was facing a good man. It's better to put him down early than to get beat."

"Quiet!" Mr. Aguilar yelled.

Tito shut up and again Mr. Aguilar looked at Davey. "Did we not have this conversation before?"

Will looked at Davey nervously. Davey had never said a word to him about stretching out fights.

"I cannot have this disrespect."

A soft pop sounded and Will watched in horror as his best friend slumped lifeless in his chair, the blood turning his dress shirt crimson as it bloomed like a rose from his chest.

Will jumped out of his seat and Ramos tried to push him back down but Will was stronger than him. Then all hell broke loose.

One of Mr. Aguilar's men ran into the room yelling that the party was being busted, that cops were everywhere. Mr. Aguilar came around the desk quickly barking orders. Will saw the gun being leveled at him and he reacted on instinct. He kicked the gun out of his hand, punched Ramos in the nose and followed that up with a kick. He then he grabbed Mr. Aguilar's wrist pulled him against his body ready to snap his neck and that's how the DEA found him when they came through the door.

1

It was unseasonably warm for late May in Montana. The bright afternoon sun crept steadily towards the Elkhorn Mountain Range where it would soon sink behind, amid colors that made even hardened men stop and stare. Grease Prentiss had left his clubs Harley Dealership in Townsend and was now riding his 1999 Harley Heritage Springer, which he had personally customized, through a curvy mountain pass towards Happy, where he summered.

His long braid of dark brown hair whipped at his back, his signature bandana headband held back any escaping loose strands. Mirrored aviator sunglasses hid his brown eyes and protected them from the wind that blew across his beard covered face. Grease's Heritage Springer rumbled loudly on the last asphalt road he'd be on as he traveled to Happy. Happy was aptly named for a small rural town located between the Montana towns of Helena and Townsend. It boasted one good-sized mountain, called Happy Mountain, of course, and it was to that mountain where he was headed.

Grease was a member of the Steel Horse Cowboys, a motorcycle club. Ten years ago his best friend, Tank O'Brian, had shook the clubs roots by disentangling them from any illegal endeavors and creating legal job opportunities for its members. Many of the old timers had balked and some had even left to join other clubs, but most of the members had remained and they were now reaping the rewards that Tank O'Brian had promised them.

One of those rewards was a camp located on Happy Mountain. Tank owned the camp now, courtesy of his sister-in-law, Breezy, and he was constantly upgrading it, so his club members and their families would have a safe and fun summer place to vacation at. The property had at one time been used as a children's camp. When that went under the large piece of land had been rented out seasonally to the club, until Tank had bought. Since then Tank had been converting the camp to meet the needs of the motorcycle club. He had upgraded the cabins that had come with the property. These cabins were used by Tank and his wife Tess, Sweets and his wife Lolly and then there were two others that were used by guests.

A large, prefabricated, two - story cabin was the latest edition to the camp. It had been put up last summer. On the first floor was a huge dining room with a bar, and an industrial sized kitchen. Upstairs there was a meeting room and guest bedrooms. Outside of the prefab cabin the men had built a large stone patio and the entire cabin had also been winterized to hold up against the cold Montana winters. Tank's older brother Toby, who was the local Game Warden and married to Breezy, lived further up the mountain all year round. Toby was not a Club member, but he was still considered family. They had a little boy named Gus, that they had adopted, and Breezy also had twin daughters that were now college graduates and job hunting.

Grease's other friend, Joe, also not a club member but a good friend, just the same, had been married last Thanksgiving. Like Tank and Tess, they too had held their ceremony and reception in the newly erected cabin. Joe, a veteran, was now a Deputy in Happy and on track to become the next Sheriff, once

Liam Ross retired. Joe had married CC, an FBI Agent that he had met the summer before.

Grease still had a few friends that were single. Not that any of his married friends, or their wives, would ever make him feel as if he were odd man out, but it was nice to have a single guy he could hang with. One of his better friends was Dak, short for Dakota. He owned a gun shop and firing range outside of Townsend. He and Dak had begun to hang out more since their other friends had all tied the proverbial knot.

Grease turned off the highway and onto the road that led into the center of Happy. His thoughts turned to memories that he often repressed since they were from years ago and needed to remain concealed. Grease had been in Witness Protection for the last thirteen years. No one, not even Tank, his best friend, knew. In fact even his real age was not known by any of his friends. They all thought he was older, closer to Tank's age, but the truth was he was thirty- seven. He looked older, especially since he had allowed his face to become covered with a bushy full beard that reached his chest.

Grease's birth certificate name read Will MacPhearson, but when he was placed into Wit Sec his name was changed to Thad Prentiss. The first notable event that happened to 'Thad' when he was placed into Wit Sec in Townsend, Montana was that he stopped to help a lady who was having car trouble. It was Mrs. O'Brian, Tank, and Toby's Mom, but he didn't know that at the time. He fixed her windshield wipers that had quit on her in the middle of a snowstorm by applying a little grease to the pivot shafts.

Mrs. O'Brian was so grateful that she sent the unemployed young man to her husband's garage and her husband nicknamed him 'Grease-boy' and gave him a job. Grease-boy was soon shortened to Grease and it stuck. Grease didn't think anyone even knew what his Wit Sec given name was and he didn't really care because he actually liked the name Grease.

While working in Tank's dad's garage he soon became friends with Tank and he joined the outlaw motorcycle club that Tank rode with. He had to be careful in those early years not to be arrested or tangled up in any business that would take him back to Miami where he might be recognized. His US Marshall pleaded with him to not become a member, but Grease liked the men in the club, especially Tank. His thinking was that he was safer being a member of the club, than on his own. When Tank took the club legit Grease breathed a sigh of relief, as did his US Marshall.

The crime family that had sworn revenge against Will MacPhearson, aka Romeo, was still in control in Miami, but Grease felt safe in Townsend. The Marshall's office kept tabs on him, but now he only checked in with them once a month. It had not been as difficult to leave his old life behind, as Grease had thought it might be. When the ten-year renewal date came up, Grease chose to keep his new name and new social security number and remain hidden in the program.

Grease drove past Pete's General Store and saw the owner Pete, outside sweeping his front porch. It brought a smile to his face. The town of Happy did not have a stoplight in it, that's how small it was. The town consisted of Pete's General, a gas station, two churches, and an ice cream parlor, that was only open from May to September. A 24-hour Emergency Care Center, Hawkins Real Estates Office, a pizza parlor, the Sheriff's office, and a few other small businesses. Grease saw the newest edition to the town as he rounded a corner. It was a doublewide trailer that had been placed onto a vacant corner and converted into a local Post Office. He knew that the year round townies would be happy about that. Grease turned the corner and headed up the dirt road that the camp was on.

Driveways that branched off the small mountain road led to various rental cabins that were occupied in the summer and during the hunting and fishing seasons. One of those cabins was the one that Breezy had rented when she first found her way to Happy, two summers ago. It was the last cabin on the remote mountain road. Grease had been thinking about putting in an offer to buy it. He had not told that little nugget of information to anyone. He knew his friends thought he was a bit of an enigma, they called him Tough Guy, but he was what he was. Years of watching his back had made him an observant man. His years as a cage fighter that no one knew about had toughened him physically and emotionally, and the years of living alone had turned him into a quiet man.

Grease wasn't handsome like Tank, Toby, Dak and Joe were. He wasn't ugly either, but no one had really seen his face in thirteen years. Sometimes he wondered what he looked like under his hair covered face, ZZ Top like beard, and long hair. He knew he had an ominous look about him, but it tended to serve him well. He was very rarely fucked with. He was a little over 6'0" and he was broad. He wasn't fat; he'd been blessed with a muscular physic that often brought him unwanted attention, from both men and women. His shoulders were immense and his thickly muscled arms led to noticeably large hands. His wide chest tapered into athletic hips and his strong thighs stretched the fabric of his jeans. His typical dress consisted of his bandana, of course, jeans, tee shirts or flannels. He wore black motorcycle boots, even in the summer. Lolly, Sweets wife, would often tease him, when they would go swimming that his legs could belong to a vampire they were so white.

Grease turned down the camps tree-lined drive and when he drove into the clearing he was met with friendly waves and beer can salutes from the club members who were already kicking back enjoying camp life. Grease pulled his bike up in front of his cabin and dismounted. He took the leather sack off from his bikes frame and tossed it on his cabin stoop before he strode over to Sweets' cabin, where Sweets and Lolly were sitting in wooden Adirondack chairs and Tess stood leaning against the porch.

"Hey, took you long enough." Sweets said as he threw Grease a beer from the cooler sitting at his feet. Grease caught it, opened it, gulped half of it down, and smiled broadly. He loved summer!

"Yeah, Mr. Tully came in with a broken shift lever. Luckily the gearshift shaft wasn't broken too. I had to do the welding myself because I let Rusty leave early."

"Why did you let him leave early?"

"He's working until I get back, so I did him a solid. He wanted to take his family swimming and since I now have three wonderful months off it wasn't a big deal."

"We were wondering what was keeping you." Lolly added.

Grease looked over to Tess. "Where's Tank and Tommy?" Tommy was Tank and Tess' little boy.

"Tank is trying to put him down for a nap. He was a terror on the ride here."

Grease laughed. He knew that Tess had driven the family SUV and because Tank wanted his Softail in Happy for the summer he had rode that.

"He wanted to ride with his daddy?" Grease guessed.

"Screamed the whole ride." Tess admitted with a grin. The group of friends chuckled sympathetically knowing that Tank had probably been waving at his young son during the entire ride thinking he was calming him but most likely inciting him to cry harder. As if on cue, Tank walked out of his cabin and down the cabin's wooden steps. Sweets tossed him a beer when he got close. After he opened it and took a long pull, he tenderly put his arm around Tess who leaned back into his large frame. Tank gave the top of her head a sweet kiss.

"He's down?" She asked.

Tank nodded. "Yup, two books and he finally fell asleep."

Tank looked to Grease. "What took you so long?"

"Had to fix a shift lever."

"Where was Rusty?"

"I let him have the afternoon off."

Tank cocked his head quizzically and then smiled. "I think you're getting soft in your old age my friend."

Grease laughed. "Nah, just helping him out."

The group of friends moved to sit by the fire pit that someone had already piled wood on and lit. Even though Grease was alone, woman wise, his friends never made him feel like a third wheel, or in this case a fifth wheel. Being in Happy made him happy.

He had always felt safe at camp. Nestled up the mountain and set back in the dense forest, it was the only place he truly let his guard down. At camp he was surrounded by good friends, that he considered family. He knew every one there and they knew him. He was considered to be the 'strong, silent type.' His reputation as a ladies man baffled him though. He had hated the 'Romeo' persona back in his other life and he was surprised when someone joked with him about his love life now. He rarely worked to gain a woman's attention. They came to him. The last time he had been the first to flirt was when he and Tank had been drugged and Tank had been kidnapped. That was the summer Tank had met Tess. Thank goodness for silver linings, it could have been a disaster. Although no one knew it, Grease still blamed himself for that mess.

He had uncharacteristically approached three young ladies at The Pen, the local bar, and he had ended up getting wild with two of them in the back hallway. Meanwhile, the third lady had roofied Tank. When his two ladies had finished with him, he too had been drugged and when he had regained consciousness he was alone, and to his horror Tank was missing. Fortunately Tank had gotten free from his kidnappers and he had freed Tess from them as well. Grease was happy for Tank and Tess, they were really good for each other, and he was glad they had met, but he still wished the whole sordid ordeal had never happened.

As the sun continued to slip behind the tall trees surrounding the camp, more club members came in and soon the camp was buzzing with pre-Memorial Day weekend fun. The horseshoe pit was cleared of winter debris and for Grease; the clanking of the metal shoes on the steel rod was a calming background noise. Tank had pizza delivered from the one pizza place in Happy. It took them an hour and half to deliver them though because Tank had ordered 20 pies and by the time they got to camp half of them were cold. No one complained though. Tommy had gotten up when he heard the commotion of the party and wanted to join in for the fun. It was the start of summer, a weekend kick off party was in full swing and Tank had supplied them with dinner on their first night at camp for free. The booze was flowing and the jovial mood around camp was contagious.

The bonfire was cranking out some serious heat and Grease had moved away from it to sit in a chair further away from the tipsy revelers. A few of his lady friends, one he shared benefits with, had tried to cajole him to join them in doing shots, but Grease knew what that would lead to and he just wasn't interested, at least not yet anyways. After eating some pizza Tommy crawled up into his fathers lap and was soon asleep, again.

The young parents reluctantly removed themselves from the party to put their little ones to bed. Grease watched as Tess peeled a sleeping Tommy off of Tank's large chest before heading towards their cabin. Grease watched as Tank hesitates for a few seconds before standing up and following behind them. When Tess got to the cabin door she turned around to find her husband standing behind her. Grease viewed them as Tank pulled her gently to him and over the head of their slumbering son; he gave her a heated kiss. Tess smiled up at her man and they both disappeared behind their cabin door.

Grease heaved a sigh after witnessing the tender family moment. He was happy for Tank, for Joe, and even for Sweets, who had already been married when Grease had landed in Townsend. Being married hadn't changed them like he had so often heard it would. His friends were the same, but now they seemed content. They still drank and rode their bikes together and there had been a few times that they had mixed it up against men that had chosen to fuck with them, but still, Grease knew his friends loved going home to their wives.

Grease didn't know if he wanted that or not though. He had a complicated past and he knew from talking with his friends that secrets tore marriages up and he had a doozy of one. He also loved not being tied down. He didn't have to check in with anyone when he was out. He could just get on his Harley and ride. His friend Dak and he would meet up on their days off and just ride without even having a destination in mind. Usually they'd end up at a bar where they'd have a few drinks and watch a game. One thing Tank was adamant against and was vocal about, with all members of The Steel Horse Cowboys, was drinking and driving. The men knew how many they could have and still drive responsibly. You did not want to get on Tank's bad side in this serious matter and really, having a beer or two then switching to soda wasn't bad. Of course there were times the guys got lit up, but between wives, girl friends and of course the Prospects, a club member always had someone they could call to transport them safely home.

Bettina, a leggy blond with large firm breasts that Grease knew the young boys fantasized over plopped down on his firm lap wiggling provocatively. "Hey baby what 'cha doing here all alone?" Grease put his beer on the ground before he spilled it. The little vixen had her hands all over him.

"Bettina, when did you get here?"

"A couple hours ago. You look lonely over here Grease. I think I should just keep you company and wipe that sad look off your face." Bettina whispered huskily rubbing him in all the right places.

Grease gave her a mischievous grin. This girl knew how to rev him up.

"My trailers a little crowded." She murmured into his ear, her breath warm and seductive.

Grease stood up placing Bettina on her feet and with his large arm around her slim shoulders he walked her to his cabin. Sweets nodded at him as they passed by and Grease acknowledged him with a nod of his own. Bettina was playfully nipping at his neck and by the time they reached his front door his cock was already reacting to what would be a pleasure filled night.

2

Grease awoke to a tangle of arms and legs lying atop his naked frame. He lifted his head and looked at his disheveled bed and the two other persons that were in it with him. He had started the evening with Bettina and then there had been a knock on his door. Before he could get out of bed, Bettina had hoped up and ran out of his bedroom giggling. When she returned she had Gretchen in tow.

Gretchen had hair that was so blond it was white. She was not as tall as Bettina and she was a stunner to look at, however her attractiveness ended as soon as she opened her mouth. Gretchen was the epitome of dumb blond, but as long as she didn't talk, the sex was great. As Bettina had undressed a willing and giggling Gretchen, Grease sat back against his headboard and enjoyed the show. The women were clearly into each other and it became heated quickly. Gretchen loved that Grease was watching them and knew just how to move so that Grease was privy to an erotic show.

Then they moved to join him. Grease had been with multiple partners before so this wasn't anything out of the ordinary for him. There were two things that women loved about him during sex; one was his mouth, the other was his cock. Grease knew how to drive a woman senseless with his mouth. He enjoyed loving a woman with his tongue and the time he spent showing his partners this often left them boneless before they even got to the main event. When they did get to 'having sex', Grease did not disappoint anyone. He was endowed with a long cock, but its thickness was what set him apart from other men.

Even his own large hand could not completely encircle his wide shaft. Most men would love to have his girth, but it did pose problems; like when women tried to give him head. He was just too wide for it to be done with any finesse. He also had never deflowered a virgin. He knew he would hurt someone if he was their first time, so instead he satisfied them with his mouth and fingers. Although his unusual size had these snags there were also many positives. For example, he was pleased to have given many women their first vaginal orgasm. Under his large domed head he had a quarter inch rim that he would rub against their elusive g- spot driving his lovers crazy. Grease knew just where to position himself and precisely how to move it to send a woman into a back bowing avalanche of pleasure. Tonight was no different. Grease took control of orchestrating the ménage, and the three of them were pleasured multiple times before they succumb to sleep.

Grease got out of his bed and threw on his jeans before heading to the bathroom. When he looked back at his bed he saw that Bettina and Gretchen were spooning each other and Bettina had her hands covering Gretchen's fair-haired mons. He grinned, thinking about the unexpected turn of events and shut the door behind him.

After using the bathroom he made coffee and dug out a tee shirt from his large duffle bag that Lolly had brought up for him in her truck. Grease then took his coffee and headed outside. Sweets and Lolly were already sitting in their Adirondack chairs. Steam wafted from their coffee mugs and the rich aroma of Lolly's special blend filled the air around them. Grease sat down in a nearby chair and Sweets gave him a knowing smile.

"Good night?"

"Yup." Grease responded with a grin.

Lolly gave her husband a shove with her elbow and Sweets chuckled and pretended that it hurt.

"So Grease what have you got planned for your three-month vacation? Are you spending it all in Happy?" Lolly was like the clubs den mother. She cared for everyone with equal enthusiasm and she could keep many of the younger men in line with just a sharp glance. When Tank needed help with the women he went to her.

"I'll be here most of the time. I do have a couple things I want to do though."

When Grease didn't explain further Sweets knew not to press him. Sweets liked Grease. He was a good man, who was all about the club and he always had their backs. Sweets had the utmost respect for the younger man. He had watched him brawl with three men once and come out the victor.

The three of them enjoyed the peacefulness of the sleepy camp and watched it slowly come to life. While enjoying their second cup of Lolly's wonderful home blended coffee they watched Tank emerge from his cabin carrying Tommy. The second he set the young boy down, he went running towards the children's area, a grassy section in the middle of camp. Tank remained next to him, mindful, yet not hovering. Grease liked that about Tank. When the kid fell he just told him that he was fine, and he was. Tommy would stand back up and keep playing.

Grease's front door opened and the two beautiful blonds emerged. Grease stood up still holding his mug and walked towards them. Lolly and Sweets were smiling knowing exactly how he had spent his evening.

"Morning Grease." Bettina greeted him. Gretchen smiled at him contently. Grease wasn't sure, but the girls seemed to be keeping a secret, his thoughts were confirmed when he saw the blush that stole through their cheeks.

"Ladies." he returned the greeting.

"Thanks for last night." Bettina said totally unfazed by the unconventionality of it all.

"My pleasure." He assured them with a gentle grin.

"We are going to be here for most of June. Maybe we can, you know, do that again?" Grease watched as Gretchen gave Bettina a slight shove. "Or just one of us, hint, hint." She said giggling looking directly at Gretchen who was clearly flustered at her friend's lack of subtleness.

"It's a definite possibility ladies. Thank you for the lovely evening." Grease said in his most charming voice, treating them both to a wide mouthed sexy smile.

Bettina laughed knowingly. Grease didn't date. If you ended up with him at the end of the night just count your lucky stars and enjoy it. Poor Gretchen was totally smitten with him. She grabbed Gretchen's hand and they took off towards the area of camp where their camper was parked.

Grease thought about returning to Sweets and Lolly's porch, but Sweets would only tease him, and he didn't want to give him any fuel so he just went back to his cabin and showered.

Today he had things to do. First he wanted to go to Hawkins Realtors and see if the last cabin on

Happy Mountain could be purchased and he also wanted to ask who owned the property that The Pen sat on. The Pen was a bar at the edge of town that the club used to visit regularly. Then it was discovered that the new owner of the bar had a connection to Satan's Army, an outlaw bike club located in northern Montana. The owner had been put in jail for his part in drugging Tank and he and the property had now been sitting empty for over a year.

Grease had been working for an O'Brian since he had first arrived in Townsend. First for Tank's old man at the garage, and then for Tank, who had taken over the garage when his mother and father had retired to Florida. A few years ago Tank had bought a small Harley Dealership in Townsend, and he had placed Grease and Rusty in charge of running it. They sold Harley's and they serviced them.

About a year ago Grease started a side business, one not connected to the dealership or club, which Tank had given his approval for immediately. It began as an outlet that let Grease use his engineering degree, that no one even knew he had, and also his creative side. Grease began a business in which he rebuilt and overhauled motorcycles. Ever since the show Orange County Choppers had become popular, more businesses and regular Harley loving folk wanted their bikes to be a one of a kind machine. Grease was slowly making a name for himself by filling these requests.

Grease worked on the bikes during his off time and he had tried to give Tank and the club a percentage of his profits, but Tank would not accept them. He told Grease that he should use the money for something that he wanted. Grease had led a very simple life since entering Witness Protection and the money he had accumulated fighting, all those years ago, was still sitting in a bank collecting interest. He had a decent amount saved up. He would be using that money to hopefully buy the cabin and The Pen. He had agonized over whether or not to do this major change to his life for the last few months. He finally decided he wanted to move to Happy, year round and open up place where he could sell motorcycle accessories and rebuild motorcycles full time.

Grease left his cabin and sent Sweets and Lolly a quick salute wave as he turned on his bike and kick started his Harley. He turned his bike in a wide circle and saw Tank with Tommy in his arms striding towards him so Grease slowed to a stop, but left the engine running.

"Where you headed, man?"

Grease never wanted to lie to Tank, other than to keep his identity a secret. He blew out a deep breath and hoped his friend would understand what he was about to tell him.

"I probably should have discussed this with you first." Tank looked concerned and he nodded for Grease to continue.

"I've been thinking of buying the property at the top of the mountain."

"Breezy's old place?"

Grease nodded. "Yeah."

Tank put Tommy down, but kept a watchful eye on him.

"You unhappy here?"

"No, not at all." Grease cut his engine. He owed it to his best friend to explain his plans in detail. He swung his leg over his Harley and Tank backed up to allow him the room to do so.

"We better sit down." Grease told him.

Tank headed towards where the children were playing. Grease walked with him, both men contemplating what the other would say. The men sat down on a bench near the children and Tank let a squirming Tommy out of his arms.

"What's going on Grease?"

"It's not a done deal. It's just something I've been thinking about, a lot. I don't want you to misinterpret this. I love the club, you're my family."

Tank nodded, the knot in his stomach clenching tighter.

"I'm thinking of opening my own shop up."

"Grease'd Hog?"

"Yeah."

"You've been doing that for a year now."

"I know, but I want to open a shop up here in Happy."

Tank was quiet for a few contemplative moments.

"Why here?"

"I love Happy, the small town vibe, the way the population explodes in the summer and then dwindles to only a few hundred in the winter. I love this mountain."

Tank nodded and smiled. "Yeah, I do too."

"If you give me the okay..."

"Hold it right there man. I don't own you. We are part of a club and we all take care of each other, but I never want you to think you can't do what you want to. That's not what this club is about."

"I appreciate that. You're my best friend Tank. This club's my family. I wouldn't do this if you had a problem with it."

"Why open up here in Happy though?"

"Happy is between Helena and Townsend. I'm hoping to draw business from both areas. Tons of bikes travel that main road from spring through the fall. I think I can pull in some business. I'm going to find out who owns the property The Pen sits on. See if I can buy it. It's perfect for what I want to do. I can convert the bar into a retail space that sells mechanical parts, helmets, apparel, you know, stuff like that. Then I'll make the back barn into a garage where I'll do the rebuilds."

"What would you do with apartment upstairs?"

"Don't know yet. I don't want to live there. I like the mountain. I want to stay close to camp."

Tank smiled. "Good."

"So what do you think?"

"Grease you're an intelligent man. I know that. Your silent demeanor may fool some people, but I know you're way smarter than you let on. I've seen you work on cars and bikes; you're talented. You put in that sliding glass door last summer in my cabin and it took you two hours. I'll hate like hell replacing you at the dealership, and I won't lie and tell you that I won't miss you when we all head back to Townsend for the winter, but I get it. I just hope you want to remain in the club?"

"I do. I just want to explore this business opportunity. I think I can make a go of it. I've been thinking about it for a while now. You know I hate the managerial part of my job. I like working with my hands."

"I know. I get it."

"So we're good?" Grease asked.

"We're good."

"Can we keep this between us for now? I don't even know if I can buy The Pen or the cabin yet?"

"Yeah, but I will tell Tess. I can't keep anything from her and I want you to think about telling Sweets. He needs to know before he hears it from someone else. Once you walk into Hawkins the rumors will fly. You know Nancy and her mouth. She'll tell Pete and then the entire town will know."

"Yeah, I'll tell him when I get back."

"Good man." Tank stood and yelled at Tommy who was trying to follow an older boy up a tree that he was climbing. He then looked back to Grease.

"Good luck man." Tank was sincere in his wishes but Grease could tell his friend was inwardly downhearted. They'd been through a lot together in the last thirteen years. Leaving Townsend and the security of the dealership would put physical distance between them. Grease just hoped the gap did not extend to their friendship. Tank was his best friend; his brother and he'd do anything for him.

3

The town of Happy was bustling with Memorial Weekend tourists. Pete's parking lot was full and the circular, grassy green across the way was lined with cars as well. A craft vender fair was underway and judging by the people walking around the small booths, it was going to be lucrative for the merchants. Grease turned away from the center of town and drove to Hawkins. The real estate office had two cars in the lot. One of them, Grease knew, belonged to Nancy the owner. He pulled his Harley into a space and walked inside; a small bell over the door signaled his arrival.

Two heads turned towards him; one of them was Nancy. She excused herself, leaving a man, who was in his fifties, sitting in the chair that was opposite her desk, as she walked to personally greet him. Grease had on his usual attire, plus his leather cut. He knew he looked bad - ass and that set many men back on their heels. They either wanted to get the hell away from him, fast, or prove that they weren't afraid of him by doing or saying something stupid.

The man looked apprehensive and Grease knew he could place him in the 'want to get away' category.

Nancy showed no uneasiness though, she knew him, and had a genuine smile on her face as she held out her nail polished hand to him.

"Good Morning. You're one of Tank's friends?" She cheerfully greeted him.

"Yes, Grease." He replied, shaking her hand.

"What can I do for you?"

Grease looked to the man sitting back near the desk, pretending to occupy himself by reading a paper.

"How about if I sit over here and wait until you finish with this gentleman first?" he replied loud enough and with enough practiced charm in his voice that he hoped it would put the guy at ease. Yeah, he knew how to play the game.

"That would be fine. There are some listings in that binder over there." Nancy pointed at a large three -ring book sitting on a coffee table.

Grease picked up the book and made himself comfortable while Nancy finished her business with the man. Grease leafed through the book. He already knew what he wanted, but it was good that he was able to check out what the current market prices were of comparable properties.

After fifteen minutes the man left and Grease put the book back on the table, stood up and sat back down on the chair that the man had vacated.

"So what can I do for you, errr... Grease?" Grease chuckled.

"Yes, Grease." He smiled. "I'm interested in two properties actually. I'd like to know if the cabin at he top of Happy Mountain is for sale, and I'm also wondering about the property that The Pen is on."

Nancy tapped a pen thoughtfully against her blotter. "Honestly, I think I can get the owner of the cabin on the mountain to sell. He and his wife never come up here any more and if the price is right I bet they'd sell."

"And The Pen?"

Nancy heaved a sigh. "That could be difficult. I know you're aware of the owner's history?"

Grease nodded.

"Well the new owner of the property is a Mr. Flynn." Nancy said the name slowly. When Grease didn't

speak she added. "He goes by the name of Shooter."
She watched for Grease's reaction.
"Shooter owns The Pen?" Grease knew who he was,
all too well.
"Yes, I received the change in ownership notice a
couple of months ago."

Shooter was the vice president of Satan's
Army, an outlaw biker group that Tank had tangled
with the summer he had met Tess. The two clubs
generally steered clear of each other. Satan's Army ran
drugs, prostitutes, gambling, and they were known to
be involved in human trafficking. Tank didn't want his
club associated with them at all, but he'd never back
away from them if they encroached on his turf. This
was not good news.
"That's not news I was hoping to hear." Grease
admitted honestly.

Nancy leaned in towards Grease as if she was
going to tell him a secret and she actually lowered her
voice even though no one else was around.
"I told Sheriff Liam when I found out who the new
owner was. From what I understand Mr. Flynn knew
the previous owner."
Grease nodded. Yeah, Shooter knew Ditch, the owner
and since Ditch was literally, in the pen, he must have
sold the property to Shooter. Grease also knew that
Liam and Toby were close. There was no way Liam
wouldn't tell Toby about Satan's Army buying The
Pen.
"So Mr. Grease," Nancy said wanting to get back to
business. "I will contact the owners of the cabin and
get back to you. As for the other property I don't have
a number or I'd call on your behalf. Do you have a
cell?"

Grease shook his head. "No. I'll just check back with you every couple of days if that's all right?"

"That's fine. If I hear anything I'll tell Pete. Your friends are always stopping in there."

Grease thanked her once again and left the office. Satan's Army owned The Pen now. Why was the property in Shooters name? As a general rule, clubs like Satan's Army put their property under the names of club members that could stand up to scrutiny from the IRS and the law. This was so not good. Clubs had turf and Happy, Montana was theirs. He knew this wasn't something he could keep to himself. He'd have to tell Tank.

Grease sat on his bike wrangling with the information he'd just been given. Perhaps it was the guilt that he still harbored when Tank had been kidnapped last summer, he didn't know, but he came to a bold decision, one he knew would piss Tank off. His reasons for not heading to camp and telling Tank what he had just learned were sound though. Grease wanted to buy the property but he didn't want to stir anything up between the two clubs, and more importantly, he didn't want Tank, his best friend, who now had a wife and son, anywhere near the notorious outlaw club.

Grease shook off the portentous feeling that snaked through him. He was simply going to go find Shooter and ask if he'd consider selling him The Pen, man to man. Maybe Shooter wanted to sell it. The property had been sitting empty for a year now. He'd be a fool to think Tank would let him run a bar in Happy. There was only one way to find out, even if it meant dealing with an irate president, slash, best friend afterwards.

Grease kicks down on the lever and felt his bike thunder awake beneath him. His Springer was equipped with an electric start but there was just something so cool about kicking it old school. Grease headed out of the lot and towards Norwalk, Montana, which was a four-hour ride upstate. He had been to Norwalk before. He, Sweets and Tank had been looking for the guys that had kidnapped Tank and Tess and their one lead had been the prefix Mc, the partial name of a dive bar where the kidnappers had let slip to Tess that they frequented.

Tank, Grease, and Sweets had found the bar, McDives, and they had eventually found the kidnappers too. One of the men involved had been the owner of The Pen, Ditch, who was now serving time in a state pen. Grease chuckled at the irony of it.

Grease headed towards McDives, the bar that he knew members of Satan's Army hung out at. He didn't like doing this behind Tank's back. His best friend was going to lose it, and he hoped it wouldn't come to blows. They'd never mixed it up, but Grease knew they were evenly matched and it would be ugly. As he rode the two lane highway towards Norwalk, he reasoned with himself again, that if talking to Shooter alone saved his club from a turf war then it would be worth it.

4

Grease stopped once on his way to Norwalk for lunch. He had taken off his cut, he wasn't traveling as a Steel Horse Cowboy, and he didn't want to draw any more attention to himself than he normally did. This business was personal. Besides, it was considered a sign of disrespect to ride into another clubs territory wearing your colors.

Grease reached McDives in the late afternoon. The choppers lined up in the gravel lot alerted him that there were Satan's Army club members inside. Even without his cut on Grease knew he looked like a biker. That would put the men inside on red alert as soon as he entered the place. Grease hoped to state his business quickly. Either way he was prepared.

He paused for a moment on the cracked cement steps leading into the grungy establishment and shook out his stiff arms. Then he walked through the door like he belonged there. He fought to get his eyes acclimated to the dim room quickly. Even before his eyes had completely focused, he could hear the ominous hush that had settled over the patrons.

Grease's eyes finally adjusted to the lighting. It had only been a few seconds, but to Grease they had felt like minutes. He had been listening intently for sounds that would let him know that someone was approaching him and he was glad when he could finally see clearly.

Grease walked through the quiet room to the bar and ordered a beer. The bartender looked off to his left and Grease saw a biker sitting there who gave the bartender a nod telling him it was okay to serve him. Grease nodded a thank you at the man letting him know that he knew who was in charge.

A beer was placed in front of him and Grease threw a twenty on the counter top before he even lifted his mug. When he did drink he covertly surveyed the room. He'd never been in the bar before, Sweets had though. When they were tracking those men Tank had made Sweets go into the bar to get information. There hadn't been any bikers in the bar then and Sweets had to play up to one of the bar whores to get them the information they needed. Sweets had hated it. The woman had been all over him. Grease had teased him that he was going to tell Lolly and Sweets had almost taken his head off.

The bar was dingy and Grease counted twelve men. A shuffleboard table, a dartboard, and a pool table were in an adjoining back room, but Grease didn't see anyone back there. There were a few tables in the front room where he was, and an antiquated jukebox sat near the door filling the testosterone-laden room with an old Alabama song. There were five men at the bar, all eying him suspiciously, and he saw two barmaids with short skirts, low cut blouses, and grimy, white half aprons hustling to keep the patrons at the tables plied with drinks.

Grease kept hold of his beer, left his change on the bar, and sauntered down to the man in charge. When he got closer he could see the man's leather cut had a Secretary's patch sewn on it. Yup, this guy was large and in charge. Grease didn't sit on the empty stool next to the man, but remained standing. The clubs burley
Secretary looked up from his beer.
"You lost?"
"Nope."
"Not a good place to wander into."

"I didn't wander in. I have business."

That peeked the man's interest and he gave Grease the okay to take a seat.

"What's your business?"

"I'd like to get a message to Shooter."

The man stilled and now looked Grease over thoughtfully.

"I can take him a message."

Grease reached back to pull out his wallet and the man stood abruptly as three other men surrounded him.

Grease remained calm and quickly held out his hand signaling for the men to stop. "Hold on, just reaching for my wallet."

The four men remained around him as he took his wallet from his pocket and opened it. Grease reached into the money section of the wallet and produced a business card.

Grease'd Hog
Motorcycle Overhauls and Rebuilds
Grease Prentiss
555 210-6696

Grease turned the card over crossed out the phone number and wrote his email on the back of the card. He then handed the card to the man next to him.

"I rebuild motorcycles. I want to buy The Pen in Happy for my business. If he's interested tell him to contact me.

One of them men standing next to Grease spoke, "I heard of you. You did a rebuild on my cousins Harley. It was good, but aren't you a member of Steel Horse Cowboys?"

The men around him stilled uneasily and Grease held his hand up to them once again. "I am, but I'm here on my own."

"Does Tank know you're here?" The Secretary asked.

"Nope, this doesn't concern him."

"Seems like anything one of his members does should concern him."

Grease nodded. "Yeah, I'll probably get my ass kicked, but I didn't want to cause any trouble and I wanted to ask Shooter if he wanted to sell."

Grease had decided to be honest, because he really had nothing to hide. The man was right though, Tank was going to kick his ass and damned if he wasn't one of the few that probably could.

"Well Grease." The burley leader said looking once again at his card. I'll give Shooter your message.

"I'd appreciate that." Grease said and stood up.

"What's your hurry?" One of the men said standing next to him. Shit! Now they were going to fuck with him.

"No hurry, going to the head." Grease was toe to toe with the man before the man turned sideways allowing Grease to pass by.

Grease headed towards the bathroom remaining vigilant about the men around him. Out of one corner of his eye he could see one of the barmaids being pushed under a table. He knew what she was going to be doing soon. The other barmaid was boldly slapping another mans hand off her large breast. Grease used the bathroom and when he reentered the main room, sure enough, barmaid number one was giving the man at the table head while his friends watched. The biker continued to talk to his friends like it was an ordinary occurrence. Grease looked for the other woman and saw her standing next to the Secretary at the bar. Grease sent a small salute to the man hoping that would suffice for a goodbye.

He headed towards the front door and he was a mere step away from the exit when a huge man stepped in front of him. Once again the bar quieted down. Fuck!

The burley man from the bar spoke up. "We decided we didn't like that you rode into our town unannounced."

The big man in front of Grease was grinning like a crazy man. His eyes were darting back and forth and he was actually licking his lips like he was about to eat a meal.

"Like I said," Grease said tersely. "my business here was personal." He then sighed heavily. "But if you want to try to put a hurt on me." Grease paused for effect. "Then bring it."

The giant in front of Grease swung a meaty fist in his direction and Grease easily dodged it. However, a few men had stepped behind him and one of them shoved him back towards the giant who was preparing to swing again.

Grease regained his balance and turned sideways so that the blow caught only his shoulder, but shit if that didn't sting. This man was strong.

Grease started trading punches and when Grease didn't go down after a solid blow landed on his cheek, the giant grunted and then grinned eerily. The door behind the mammoth opened as an unaware biker strode into the bar and Grease saw his opportunity. He charged the gigantic man and pushed him out the open front door and over the steel bar handrail.

Unfortunately, Grease toppled over the bar with him and they both landed on the gravel below.

Grease jumped up and while the big man was attempting to right himself Grease used his knee to slam the man in his chin. Club members had followed them out the door and Grease knew he was about to be jumped by the entire lot of them so he ran towards his Harley. Two Satan's Army bikers reached him at the same time he got to his bike so Grease turned and punched the one man in his face. That guy was out before he hit the ground. The other man used his friend's misfortune to clocked Grease hard under his eye. Grease knew how to take a punch though and he also knew he'd feel that punch later, but he retaliated immediately with a roundhouse kick that the man had not been expecting. His cage fighting experience had simply taken over. For his size Grease was fast and limber. The kick hit the man solidly under his chin and Grease heard the bones crumble. The man fell to his knees and Grease jumped on his Harley and speed out of the parking lot. When he looked in his mirror he saw the bar had cleared out and the clubs Secretary was standing at the top of the steps staring at him.

Grease sped out of town. He took a couple of side streets and kept looking behind him thinking they would follow him. He hit the highway and pushed his bike to over 90. The trees along the deserted two-lane highway were a green blur in his peripheral vision he was going so fast. The sun was setting and Grease wanted to put as much distance between him and Norwalk as possible. He thought about leading the men to Happy, he also thought they were probably chasing him away from Happy, but then he thought they might just go to Happy looking for him, and if that happened he knew he needed to be there.

After a half hour of driving way too fast and with no sign of being chased Grease stopped looking behind him and started concentrating on the road ahead of him. He was concerned that Satan's Army had called someone who was south of Norwalk and that he was possibly driving into an ambush. Grease was starting to feel lightheaded from the punches he had taken so he pulled into a rest stop and drove his Harley slowly through the remote area looking for signs that someone might be there, but he was alone. He parked behind the building so that his bike was hidden from anyone driving through the parking lot and cautiously walked into the men's room.

The mirror confirmed how he felt. He had a cut that had luckily stopped bleeding above his eye and that eye was beginning to swell shut. His one cheek was puffy, scraped and was already sporting a purplish hue. He lifted his shirt and winced when he saw at the football sized black and blue mark he saw forming over his rib cage. Grease grinned into the mirror and was relieved that he still had all his teeth. Looking in the mirror reminded him of his cage fighting days. After every fight he would look at himself in a mirror to check his teeth. As Grease cleaned off the dried blood from his face he thought about the gigantic man that had obviously been hand picked to teach him a lesson for coming into Satan's Army bar. He was pissed that the other men had joined in because he knew he could have taken the big man. The roundhouse kick he had used right before climbing on his bike had felt so good. Grease couldn't remember the last time he had even attempted one.

Grease used the bathroom and then headed back to his bike. His head was pounding and occasionally a black spot swam in front of his eyes. He wanted to find a motel and sleep off the pain but he knew there wasn't one right on the highway and he did not want to drive into another town.

Two hours later he was still driving, but he knew he was in bad shape. He was nauseous and he had caught himself nodding off once. He jerked himself awake for the second time and he knew he should pull over to the side of the road before he wiped out. That's when he saw two Harleys and a truck coming towards him and they were slowing down. It was pitched black out, not even the moon was available to cast light. Grease hadn't passed a car in the last fifty miles. Was this the ambush he thought was coming?

As Grease approached the stopped vehicles he recognized the riders as Tank and Sweets. The truck was Lolly's and he saw Toby was the driver. Grease pulled to a stop. His first thought was Thank God, and his second thought was that he was in deep crap now. Tank got off his bike and Grease could see that he was angry.

"You okay?" Tank asked tersely.

"Been better." Grease tried to make light of it, but Tank didn't even crack a smile.

"Get in the truck Grease."

"I'm......"

"Get in the fucking truck." Tank told him, his deep voice stiff from rage.

Grease got off his bike, trying in vain to hold in the slight grunt he made moving his big body, and got into the truck with Toby. Tank and Sweets lifted his bike into the back on the small truck, secured it with ties, and remounted their bikes. The small caravan headed back to Happy.

Toby was smart enough not to speak to him. Grease was pissed. He didn't like being reprimanded, and he also realized that they must have figured out where he'd gone. Fucking Nancy, she was a blabbermouth. He knew that she didn't know where he had gone, but Tank would have been smart enough to piece it together if he talked to her.

When they got to Happy, Tank and Sweets pulled into the Emergency Care parking lot and Toby followed.

"Shit." Grease muttered.

Toby cut the motor and turned to him. "You could have been killed. Tank was a mess."

"I didn't want to drag the club into this." Grease then remembered that Liam had known about Shooter owning The Pen. "You didn't tell him who owned The Pen either Toby, so don't pretend to not understand why I did what I did."

Toby swore under his breath. "Your right, I knew. I just didn't want to..."

"Stir up trouble." Grease finished his sentence for him.

"Yeah, but I was going to tell him."

"So was I, when I got back."

The passenger door opened and Sweets and Tank stood side by side. Grease stepped out and grunted as his feet hit the dirt lot, jarring his ribs.

Sweets grabbed his upper arm and muttered 'horses' ass,' under his breath. Grease let him help him inside.

The Physicians Assistant put a butterfly bandage on the cut over his eye and wrapped his ribs in an ace bandage. She told him he probably had a concussion and then she turned to Tank and told him that he needed to be woken up every two hours for the remainder of the night. Tank thanked her and she left the room.

Sweets knew Tank wanted to talk to Grease alone so he left the room behind her. Tank ran his hands through his dark hair, a sure sign he was distressed.

"Why?"

"Why did I go up there?"

"Yeah, why wouldn't you tell me?"

"I didn't want the club involved."

"You are part of the club. Whatever you do involves us."

Greased tried to take a deep breath, but only managed to draw in a small one. He grimaced and stepped off the examining table.

"Tank, when Nancy told me who bought The Pen I decided to just go up to Norwalk and see if Shooter would sell it to me. I didn't tell you because I knew you'd never let me go alone, and I didn't want there to be any trouble over this."

"I get that Grease, but we're friends, we're family. I would have helped you figure out a way to see Shooter, or get word to him without you getting busted up."

Grease thought about what Tank had just said and it made him feel like a fool.

"I thought you'd give me crap. I just didn't want you getting involved. You have a wife, a little boy. I couldn't have you coming with me. It was too..."

"Dangerous." Tank finished sarcastically.

"Yeah."

"I understand you were protecting me Grease, but I'm the President of this Club. Having a family doesn't play into this. You're my brother. I know you wanted to keep me out of it, keep the club out of it, but we were in it the second Shooter became the owner. That's code man. The Pen is our turf." Tank paused. "Did you talk to him?"

"No. I gave their Secretary my card."

"So you walked into the bar, handed some guy your card, and they beat the shit out of you?"

Grease managed to give Tank a weary smile. "Something like that."

"This is not over, you know." Tank told his friend pensively.

"Shit! Tank, no. I went on my own. I just got a little beat down. Trust me you should see the other guys." Grease chuckled holding his side. "Shooter will get my message and then maybe he'll sell me The Pen, The end."

Tank shook his head. "If he doesn't want to sell it Grease, that means he's coming into our territory, and then I'm going to have to let him know we have a problem."

"I understand that, I just had to try this on my own. Let's just wait a few weeks okay?"

Tank was quiet as he thought about how to handle the situation. He didn't want trouble with Satan's Army. They were an outlaw club, mean, and unscrupulous. Even the women and children associated with his club could get hurt if his club tangled with Satan's Army. Grease was reading his thoughts.

"Tank, if he doesn't sell me the place, we better think of some way to deal with this without starting a war with them."

"Yeah, I know." Tank put his hand on Grease's shoulder and looked his friend in his eyes. "I was worried man."

"Sorry. I thought I could handle it. Actually I had it handled until they decided to use me as entertainment, you know, a little recreational brawl."

"Not like you to be marked up like this." Tank said noting his battered face.

"Yeah, I would have been fine, but the odds weren't in my favor."

"Mother fuckers, how many?"

"One big dude, a few at my back and then two others."

"You'd recognize them again?"

"You know it."

"That's good. Now let's get you home. Tess and Lolly are a mess."

"Oh shit, you told them?"

"Yeah and before you start to make plans you're sleeping at our cabin tonight so I can fucking wake you up every two hours."

"Tank I...."

"Don't even argue Grease. I'm putting you in Tommy's room with him. When he wakes up and sees his Uncle Grease in his room you get to play with him until we wake up."

"Oh for the love of....." Tank turned his back on him with a huge smirk on his face and left the room. He didn't even hear Grease finish his sentence.

5

The next two weeks passed by without any drama or word from Shooter. Grease was the recipient of a few evenings of sympathy loving from several different women, which had Tank and Sweets just shaking their heads at their friend. Grease told Sweets and Lolly, what he had confided to Tank, regarding the cabin he wanted to buy and the business he wanted to launch. Like Tank, they said they would miss him not being in Townsend during the winter, but they wished him luck. Grease could tell Lolly was concerned that he was pulling away from the club, so one evening when they were sitting by the fire; he told her it was the furthest thing from his mind. The club was his family and he needed them. That seemed to alleviate her fears.

It was the last week in June and the summer days were starting to heat up sending many of the camp members to the nearby lake to cool off during the day. Grease was trying to stay cool by sitting on his porch, under the shade provided by the roof that hung over head. Tank rode into camp and stopped at his cabin.

"What's up man?"

"Hey, I saw Nancy in town and she wants you to stop by. She heard from the owners of the cabin and they are receptive to receiving an offer."

"Really? That's great. I'm going to ride down there now and put one in."

"Yeah, come on I'll ride with you."

"I got this Tank. Go be with Tess."

"No man, I want to. Tess and Lolly took Tommy to the creek. Beside the breeze feels good."

Grease laughed. Riding on a hot day was a great way to beat the heat, if you could find roads that were tree covered. Happy was full of them. Grease grabbed his wallet from inside his cabin and jumped on his Harley.

As the two friends drove down the shaded road they heard motorcycles, a bunch of them, rumbling towards them. They couldn't see them yet, but the sound was unmistakable. Tank shot Grease a look making sure he too had heard the motors. Five motorcycles came around the bend in the road. Tank recognized the lead rider as the President of another motorcycle club, Border Bandits.

Border Bandits were a club similar to The Steel Horse Cowboys. Years ago they had been outlaw, but like the Steel Horse Cowboys they had gone legit years ago. The two clubs often rode together and went to each other's events. The Border Bandits were based in the northwest corner of Wyoming and the southwest corner of Montana, drawing members from both states. Tank and Grease slowed to a stop as the five riders neared them.

"Big Al, what's going on?" Tank addressed the clubs president. He knew this wasn't just a social visit

"Did you hear about Red?"

"Satan's Army, Red?"

"Yeah. He and four of his men were found dead in Piedras Negras, Coahuila, Mexico. They were all shot execution style."

Grease and Tank looked at each other.

"No. No we didn't know."

"We didn't think you did. We just found out because Little Richie's sister lives in Las Quintas Fronterizas, Texas and she called him when she saw the news this morning." Big Al pointed his thumb at a man sitting on a Harley to his right that had no business being called 'Little' anything.

"When did it happen?"

"I don't know all the particulars, but their bodies were found dumped along Eagles Pass. They just identified them and Little Richie's sister recognized the name and called him. It may not even make the newspapers here since they were killed so far away."

"Yeah, probably not. Shit." Tank thought back to the summer when he had met Red and earned his respect and his freedom.

"This could really screw up our club life. Red left us alone and in return we steered clear of them."

"Yeah, us too." Tank replied.

"With a change in guard Satan's Army may not play so nice anymore." The club President said, his voice was the only thing reflecting how worried he actually was. Tank pushed his hand through his hair, his one tell that he too was concerned.

"Well I just wanted you to know. You guys are closest to their territory. You know how dicey it can get when new leaders are chosen?"

"Yeah, a lot of fighting for those new titles."

"Yeah, and I don't know who was with Red, but if he was traveling, he had to have some higher ups with him."

"I met the Secretary a couple weeks ago."

The men's heads turned to Grease. Tank explained quickly.

"He ran into him, nothing crazy guys, relax."

"Well, no matter, there are going to be important patches up for grabs." Big Al stated. "Red wouldn't travel without his Road Captain or Sergeant-in Arms."

Patches were what titled members of clubs wore on their cuts to signify their role in the club. The elevated status meant more money and more privileges.

"Shit." Tank muttered washing his hand over his face. Grease was thinking about the Satan's Army Secretary he'd met in McDives. If he was going to be one of Satan's Army's new leaders they were all in trouble. The guy was a dick and Grease had recognized how much he enjoyed being in command and giving orders.

The men talked for a few more minutes about what they thought they should do. One thing they were mutually agreed upon was that no member, of either club, should ride alone. Big Al said he wanted to get back to his town and call Chapel to talk to his members. Tank said he needed to do that as well.

The men were invited to rest at the camp before heading back to Pray, Montana, but Big Al declined the offer saying he wanted to get home before it got dark. The men shook hands and Tank thanked them again for the heads up. The Boarder Bandits turned their Harley's back down the mountain road heading home.

Tank and Grease watched them for a few seconds as the reality of what Big Al had just told them sank in.

"Grease, we have to call Chapel."

"Yeah, go back to camp Tank. I'll go to Pete's and call the guys in Townsend. Rusty can send an email. You want to hold it here, right?"

"No, you aren't riding alone. We both go into town. Yeah, we're holding it here, it will be less conspicuous. I'll use Pete's computer and send the email and I'll call Gino and Rusty. Any member that can make it needs to come here. We need to make sure everyone understands that from now on no one rides alone"

"Leave some guys in Townsend Tank; don't shut down all three shops that would draw attention. Okay?"

Tank nodded. "Yeah, good idea. When we get into town you go to Hawkins while I'm at Pete's."

Grease started his bike back up. "You sure?"

Tank started his. "Yeah. Eyes wide."

Grease repeated their saying. "Eyes wide."

The two men rode down the mountain rode into the heart of the small town. Grease's jovial mood had taken a sobering turn. He couldn't believe Red Bishop was dead. Whoever took over running Satan's Army could potentially wreak havoc on motorcycle clubs like theirs. Grease wondered if Red had even known that Shooter owned The Pen. Shooter was related to Dog Flynn, the man that had kidnapped Tess last summer, and he was friends with Ditch, The Pen's previous owner. Shooter had not been implicated in the kidnapping, in fact there was no evidence that he had known about it, but it was all too coincidental.

Grease and Tank parted at the bottom of the mountain giving each other small salutes. Grease headed towards Hawkins. He wanted to put in the offer on the cabin quickly and get back to Tank. If Satan's Army wanted to cause trouble for their club the easiest way was to get rid of the club's President. If Satan's Army was making a move Tank was vulnerable right now.

There was a beat up silver car in Hawkins lot and Grease swore. He had hoped giving Nancy his bid could be brief. He got off his Harley and like before the small bell above the door tingled as he opened it. Nancy was standing in front of her desk with her hands on the shoulder of a woman whose back was to him. They both turned quickly to see who had entered.

The woman took one look at Grease and froze, and then she mumbled something to Nancy and walked into the back room. Grease watched her go and was struck with the thought that he'd seen her some place before. When he looked back to Nancy she had tears in her eyes.

He could tell she was trying to compose herself and it unnerved him. He wasn't good with emotional stuff. He'd been alone too long and when women cried he hated it.

Nancy signaled for Grease to have a seat and when they were both seated Nancy settled into her Realtors persona and that seemed to help her focus. She started talking about the cabin property and he was trying to pay attention, but he could not get the younger woman's, who had just left the room, face out of his head. He had seen her before, but where? Nancy speaking dollars and cents to him snapped his focus back to what he was doing there. "So Grease I think an offer of $65, 000 will get you the cabin. I wouldn't try to dicker with them too much."

"That seems fair. I don't want to jump through hoops either. I'm hoping for a quick closing."

"Will you need to procure a mortgage?"

"No, it will be cash."

Nancy smiled. "That's good. They'll probably like that."

Grease filled out all the paperwork that would accompany his bid and he wrote out a check for $5000.00 to be held in escrow. He handed the check to Nancy and sat back in his chair.

"So Nancy what do I…" Right in the middle of his sentence Grease remembered where he had seen the girl before. He leapt out of his chair and in two long strides was in the back room where he had seen the girl go.

Nancy also jumped up from her chair, yelling for him to stop, but he didn't.

The back room was a small homey area furnished with a couch, coffee table, ottoman, a television, two filing cabinets, and a small kitchenette complete with a table. The woman was sitting at the kitchen table and she stood when she'd heard Nancy yell. Grease approached her cautiously until they stood a yard apart. He scanned the room, looking first for another person, and then for a weapon, seeing neither he looked back to the woman.

"I remember you. You're a barmaid at McDives."

The woman paled unnerved that she had been recognized, but she promptly squared her shoulders and held Grease's menacing stare. Nancy had followed Grease into the room and had gone immediately to the woman's side.

"You need to leave." Nancy told him clearly flustered.

Grease looked to Nancy and then back to the woman. He could see that they shared similar facial features and he swore under his breath.

"Your daughter?" He asked tensely.

Nancy nodded.

"You know she's with Satan's Army? She's their property."

The woman had been eyeing Grease and then she held up her hand to stop Grease from speaking any more.

"Mom, can you leave us alone for a few minutes?"

"Sadie, I don't think that's such a good idea." Nancy said glancing at Grease nervously.

"Mom, call Liam. Tell him to come over. It's going to be okay."

Nancy left the room and Grease heard her speaking to Liam.

"You better explain yourself whore." Grease spat out. "You may be Nancy's daughter, but there is shit going down right now involving Satan's Army and I don't like that you just happen to be here in Happy."

"Sit down. Grease right?"

"I'll stand." He said scoffing at the chair she had pulled out for him.

Grease yelled into the next room never taking his eyes off of Nancy's daughter. "Nancy call Tank at Pete's General. Tell him to get over here."

Nancy poked her head nervously through the swinging door separating the two rooms.

"Sadie?"

"He's the Steel Horse Cowboy's President?"

Nancy nodded.

"Yeah, call him too."

Grease looked at the woman who had sat back down. Her speech was too polished for her to be backwoods or uneducated. If she was Nancy's daughter she probably grew up in Happy. He'd been coming here for years though and he had never seen her before. As they both waited for Liam and Tank to arrive Grease took in her appearance. She had long light brown hair with natural streaks of blond woven through it. The funny thing was that she sported a braid as long as his own, and she also held it back with a bandana, wearing it like a headband, the same way Grease wore his.

"Nice hair." he commented snidely.

"Yeah, ditto." She spat back.

The woman wasn't tall; Grease guesstimated that she was around 5'6". She had freckles on her nose and clear skin. When Grease looked into her eyes he saw that they were a soft green with light brown specks of color surrounding the dark pupil. Her lips were set in a hard line and he noticed her brow was wrinkled as if she was thinking really hard. Her relaxed position in the chair surprised him. Her arms were crossed over a chest that strained against a worn tee shirt conveying an, 'I'm in charge attitude,' that Grease actually admired. He was an intimidating man, yet she wasn't thrown by him, not even a little. Her waist was small, but her hips flared out giving her a curvy, hourglass figure.

Liam arrived first and he swore when he saw Grease looming in the kitchenette. They heard a motorcycle rumble to a stop outside and heard Tank's heavy footsteps crossing the room to join them.

"Tank, she was working in McDives. She's Satan's Army property, and she's Nancy's daughter." Grease told Tank the second he entered the room. His voice was laced with malice and Sadie cringed.

"Holy crap. Nancy you have a daughter that's with Satan's Army?"

Grease looked to Nancy who was twisting her hands nervously.

"That's how you knew who owned The Pen? That's how you knew who Shooter Flynn was, right?"

Nancy nodded and Liam quickly sat her down on the open chair. She looked like she was ready to collapse.

"Guys you need to relax." The two men turned to Liam. Liam Ross had been the Sheriff in Happy since the club had first started coming to the camp. He was one of Toby's best friends and he'd been a good friend to the club.

"Hold on a second." Liam said as he left the room. When he returned he looked to Nancy.

"I locked the front door and put up the closed sign." Liam said kneeling before the shaken realtor.

"Thanks." She mumbled.

Liam stood up and looked to Tank and Grease. "You guys better take a seat."

Grease followed Tank's lead and they both sat down on the small couch while Liam took a seat on the ottoman nearby.

"Tank and Grease this is Sadie Hawkins."

Grease recognized the play on words her name created, but he didn't crack a smile. Liam continued talking.

"She is working at McDives. She is not their property. She works for Ship It Good."

"She delivers packages?" Tank asked totally confused.

Sadie reached into her pocketbook and when Grease stood up defensively she placed her hand up as if to ward him off.

"Easy big guy, just getting my wallet."

"Relax Grease." Liam told him in a voice that indicated he was weary with the whole turn of events.

Sadie took out her wallet and opened it to show them a silver star. She passed it to Liam who passed it to Tank.

"You're an Investigator?" Tank asked still puzzled.

Sadie nodded. "I work out of Helena. In December we had a truck hi jacked. Our driver was severely beaten and the entire truck and its contents were stolen. I'm working undercover. We think Satan's Army pulled the heist and all I need is to find one item from that truck to justify a warrant."

"You're out of your frigging mind woman." Grease uttered vehemently.

"Grease, chill." Tank admonished his friend.

Tank spoke to Liam. "You've known about this?"

"Yeah, Nancy told me."

Sadie chuckled. "My mother is not the best at keeping secrets."

"I was worried Sadie. For goodness sakes you're with those barbarians."

Sadie shifted awkwardly in her seat.

"Mom come on we talked about this."

Nancy stiffened and crossed her arms defensively over her chest.

Liam gestured to Sadie with his hand. "Tank I've known Sadie here forever. She's my goddaughter. The FBI is aware of her involvement, in fact CC is her liaison."

"You're playing with fire." Tank said quietly looking at the young woman before him.

"I can take care of myself." She said with a little attitude.

Grease was staring at Sadie as he remembered the other barmaid that had been servicing one of the club members under the table. Sadie read his thoughts.

"I don't do that."

Grease was startled that she'd read his mind so accurately.

"Yeah and how do you avoid it?"

Sadie looked at her Mom and Grease caught her drift about not wanting her Mom to know any nasty details. Grease nodded letting her know he understood.

Nancy was looking between the two of them, but before she could question them Liam spoke again.

"Guys, Sadie has to stay undercover and there is a big shake up..."

"We know about Red, Liam."

"Shoot, I was going to come tell you today. How'd you find out so fast?"

"News like that travels fast through the clubs."

"Sadie do you know who else was killed with Red?"

Tank looked at her and his face conveyed how serious the problem was. Nancy groaned and placed her hands over her face. The poor woman was completely distressed.

"Yeah, Tiny his Treasurer, Bulldog, the Sergeant-at-Arms, and Kinko the Road Captain."

"Crap that's a lot of patches up for grabs." Tank said looking directly at Grease.

"That leaves Shooter Flynn, the VP in charge, and that moves the guy you saw Grease, the Secretary, into the role of Vice President."

Sadie added quickly. "You know they're brothers right?"

Tank shook his head. "No I didn't. I've met Shooter before. He's going to be trouble."

"Shooters a kitten compared to Cage." Sadie told them stoically.

"Cage?" Grease asked.

"Yeah he used to be a cage fighter. He's an animal."

The hairs on Grease's neck stood up. When Grease had fought cage fighting was just becoming popular.

Grease wondered if he'd fought him. They were probably around the same age.

Tank was looking at Grease. "You okay man?"

Grease shook off the worrying thoughts and refocused.

"Yeah, I'm good." Sadie was looking at him with an odd expression on her face and Grease looked away. His beard and mustache hid many of his facial expressions, but he still didn't want to risk anyone noticing the look of shock that probably had registered on his face just then.

"Sadie." Liam spoke to her softly. "Maybe you should step away from this. It's going to get dicey around them with Red gone."

She shook her head determinedly. "No it's perfect. Someone may slip up without Red being in control. I don't even know if Red was involved with the heist."

"Honey, please listen to Liam." Nancy begged her daughter gently.

"Mom I'm in a good spot. I've been under for a month. My cover's solid. The other women are starting to trust me."

Tank spoke to Liam. "So Toby and your deputies know about Red?"

"Told them this morning. I just found out. They've been dead for a few weeks. They were shot execution style and none of them had their cuts on. Their hands were chopped off."

Nancy groaned and Grease actually felt sorry for her.

"Sorry Nancy." Liam apologized.

"There hands were cut off making them harder to I.D. Luckily the bastards go to the dentist or we still wouldn't know who they are."

"No idea who did it?"

"No, we got nothing."

"So it could be a rival gang, a deal gone bad or insiders that wanted to remove Red?"

"Yeah, like I said, we have no idea." Liam admitted. "I will keep you posted though."

Tank stood up. "We'd appreciate that. Liam, I'm calling Chapel at camp tonight. Tell your deputies there will be a lot of bikes coming into town, but as long as they are wearing our colors they shouldn't worry."

"Okay thanks. I'll tell them."

Grease stood up and so did Liam and Sadie. Nancy remained in her chair.

Tank looked to Sadie. "Sadie, not for nothing, but coming to Happy is probably not a smart move. Satan's Army knows this is our turf and we don't like the coincidence that Red is dead and Shooter now owns The Pen."

"Yeah, I just had to see my Mom. I hadn't talked to her for a month."

Liam and Tank walked out the door deep in conversation.

Grease looked at Sadie and motioned for her to join him away from her mother.

"What? You want a blow by blow, pardon the pun." Sadie whispered thinking Grease wanted to know about her whoring herself out.

"Sheesh, you are a hard ass."

That brought a small smile to Sadie's lips and Grease felt a tiny thud in his chest seeing how cute the woman was as she acted so brazenly.

"I know you saw Missy blowing that guy. I don't do that."

"So you said."

Sadie looked angry now. "Listen, I pretended to be a down on her luck woman looking for work. First I made friends with Missy. She got me the job. I told them up front I wasn't a whore. They try shit on me all the time, but I can hold them off. Cage likes me. He thinks I'm gutsy, and the men like it when I put up a fight."

Grease's admiration for her had gone up another notch. "They're ass holes Sadie. If they want you, they'll take you."

"Yeah, but I'm careful. I steer clear of the ones I don't trust. I'm friends with their old ladies, so most of them don't bother me 'cause they know I'd rat them out."

"That's smart."

Sadie raised one eyebrow as she looked at him. "I'm sorry, did you just compliment me?"

Grease chuckled. "Hard ass."

Sadie gave him a wide grin.

"So you have an out? You know in case things get out of control?"

"Well, not that it's any of you business, but yeah, I do."

"Okay, well good luck to you."

As Grease turned to the door to leave Sadie put her hand on his forearm halting him. He looked at her small hand that strangely heated his arm and then to her thoughtful face. "I like how you fight." She whispered with a silly smirk on her lips.

Grease smiled hearing her compliment as his heart once again jigged inside his chest.

"Grease lets roll!" They heard Tank bellow from the front room.

Grease looked at the spirited young woman with a mixture of admiration and trepidation. "Stay safe tough girl." He whispered softly into her ear before leaving the room.

As they mounted their bikes Tank turned to Grease who was putting on his sunglasses. Grease noticed him looking at him. "What?"

"You okay?" Grease nodded. It always amazed him how well Tank could read people.

"Yeah, why?"

"I don't know? You had a funny look in there."

"Probably something I ate." Grease tried to make light of it.

Tank chuckled, "Okay man, if you say so." He paused again. "She's cute."

Now it was Greases turn to chuckle. "If you say so." Tank laughed as the two men headed out of the lot. As they rode, Grease couldn't get Sadie out of his mind. He pictured her in McDives and he couldn't help but visualize the other barmaid that had been servicing the biker under the table. Sadie was different than any woman he'd ever met. He liked that she wore her hair exactly like he wore his, bandana and all, and it was darn near the same length, that brought a grin to his face. He also liked how her face had lit up when she had smiled, and damn if she didn't look beautiful. He thought it was smart that she had gained access to Satan's Army through their women, and she had pluck, maybe too much for her own good. He didn't like how his gut pitched thinking about her going back to McDives.

6

When Tank and Grease got back from the Real Estate Office they gathered every adult that was in camp and told them about Red and his compatriots being executed. Tank's main concern was to keep his club members safe, so he divulged to them that Shooter Flynn was the new owner of The Pen and most likely Satan's Army new Club President. Tank could see the nervous faces on those gathered around him. They spoke in hushed, anxious voices upon hearing the news. Tank held up his hand to quiet them. He calmly explained to them that Shooter owning The Pen and Red being killed could be a coincidence, and that they shouldn't panic, but everyone needed to be cautious. He told them they were having an impromptu Chapel tonight and to prepare to host the men coming in. He concluded the small meeting by telling them that no one should go anywhere alone. He also asked that they check in with himself, Sweets, Grease, Lolly, or Tess if they were planning on leaving the camp.

The club members began arriving a few hours later. Lolly had under taken the job feeding of everyone after the meeting, and she had organized a pot- luck dinner, which meant everyone brought something to share. Tank and Sweets drove up to Toby's to tell him about Chapel and that they knew about Red. Tank told his older brother that it he needed to be vigilante too since everyone knew they were brothers. Tank noticed that Breezy looked appropriately unnerved. Tank asked them if they wanted to hang at camp until things blew over.

"We'll be fine here Tank." Toby told his younger brother as he wrapped his arm around his wife. "I'm more concerned for you."

"That's why we are having Chapel tonight, to go over details to keep everyone safe. I've already set up watches. I told everyone that no one is allowed to ride or go anywhere alone."

"That's smart. You know Red's death, Shooter owning The Pen, it could be a coincidence?" Toby interjected hopefully.

"I know, but I still think Shooter may have had a hand in my kidnapping. Maybe he was clearing the way for a take over way back then."

"I thought about that. Here's the thing though. A turf war will bring in all sorts of government heat. If Shooter was smart, he'd lay low, real low, until he gets his club under control."

"That would be the smart thing, you're right." Breezy looked up at Tank. "He's not smart is he Tank?"

Tank looked at his brother and then back to Breezy. "No, he's not that smart. He's a thug not a business man."

Breezy nodded understanding the club's anxious attitude regarding the change that Satan's Army was going through.

Toby turned to Sweets. "You watch his back good, Sweets." Toby gestured to his brother.

"I got him. No worries." Sweets clapped his hand down on Tank's large shoulder.

    That evening at Chapel, Tank explained to his club members what had happened to Red and his men in Mexico. He also told them that Shooter now owned

The Pen, and that he was also sitting pretty to fill Reds vacated position of President of Satan's Army.

He implored his members to ride and do things in groups and to be extra vigilant. The men in Townsend needed to report in to Rusty or Gino either by email or phone call once a day. There were approximately 100 men in the club, but during the summer months the number in Townsend dwindled dramatically. Many spent their weekends at camp in Happy; others headed to summer homes or vacationed at lakes and beaches. Everyone needed to be accounted for.

During the meeting they worked out a schedule so that the camp in Happy and the club businesses back in Townsend were being guarded night and day. Every male would take shifts in groups of two. Tank had Rusty emailed all the club members that couldn't come or were away to tell them what was going on.

After the meeting the men went downstairs to find Lolly had completely out done herself preparing a meal for the 60 extra men that had come to Chapel. Most of the men ate and then headed back to Townsend, or to wherever they were living right after dinner. It was better that they rode in packs. A few of the men had opted to stay over night and Tank put them up in the prefabs guest rooms and in the two vacant cabins.

It was after midnight and the bonfire had dwindled to a red-hot crackle of embers. Tank, Grease and Sweets were the last ones up as they watched the hectic activity of the day slowly wind down as everyone turned in for the night.

"If Shooter would just sell me The Pen I wouldn't be so worried." Grease admitted uneasily.

"Yeah, I don't like the crap his club is into, at least with Red we existed along side each other for years with no problem."

"Umm, man you have a short memory." Sweets busted Tank's chops.

"I know Red wasn't involved with my kidnapping."

"Yeah, but do we know if Shooter was?" Greased added.

"Don't know." Tank admitted. "We just have to be prepared. Honestly I can't see Shooter making a play for our turf. It just doesn't make sense."

The two men next to him grunted in agreement.

Two nights later a thundering rumble of motorcycles could be heard coming up the mountain. Two, one of younger members of the club came speeding down the drive on his Harley and headed to the fire pit where Tank was standing along with the others that had been enjoying the peaceful evening.

"Tank, it's Satan's Army. I counted twelve choppers but there could be more."

Tank quickly instructed the woman and children that were still awake to head for the prefab and lock themselves into the upstairs rooms. He then sent Bam, who was Two's twin, to the section of camp that housed trailers and tents, with word for them to stay put.

Sweets had run to his cabin and returned with a gun tucked into the back waistband of his pants. The men listened as the menacing thunder of motors came closer. Tank looked at the ten men that now stood beside him and knew that they were ready to defend their camp. He didn't know if Sweets was the only one with a gun, but he prayed it wouldn't come to that.

The thunderous motors could still be heard but for some reason it wasn't getting louder, then a single chopper engine could be heard coming down their drive. Grease and Sweets exchanged apprehensive looks.

The driver of the motorcycle, still arrogantly wearing his colors pulled up to the bonfire, but remained far enough from the group of men that he could easily take off if things got heated.

Tank started walking towards him with Grease following vigilantly behind him.

"State your business." Tank yelled over the choppers loud motor.

"Shooter wants to have a meet, just you and one other. He'll meet you at The Pen in twenty minutes." Then the man took off spraying gravel behind him.

Grease looked at Tank and Sweets stepped to them to hear what the man had said.

"Shooter wants to meet in twenty minutes at The Pen. He said I can bring one man with me."

"Fuck no. That ain't happening." Sweets replied adamantly.

Tank was thoughtful and the silence that hung between the three men was thick.

"I'm your second." Grease told him as matter of fact.

"No way. Tank you aren't thinking about meeting him, are you?"

"It's probably best to find out what he wants on our own turf, don't you think?"

"Tess is gonna pitch a fit." Sweets reminded him.

Tank chuckled. "Yeah, don't I know it. I have an idea though." Tank explained his plan and then he, Grease, and Sweets headed out of camp.

7

Tank slowed at the end of the drive to watch Sweets as he turned to go to Toby's. He needed time for his plan to work. He and Grease then headed down the mountain taking their time. When they got to The Pen they could see the choppers all lined up near the edge of the parking lot. There were way more than twelve. Shooter and another man sat astride their choppers in the middle of the lot, away from the others.

Tank and Greased pulled up to them, but didn't cut their engines until the other men did. Shooter turned his bike off first, and then Cage, turned his off, as he openly sneered at Grease. Grease and Tank then shut down their own Harley's.

"Glad you came." Shooter said speaking directly to Tank.

Tank remained quiet, he was smart man when it came to dealing with men like Shooter, and the less said the better.

"I'll get right to the point. We want to sell The Pen but we don't want money."

Tank knew right away he wasn't going to like what Shooter said next.

"We have a need to travel through your little town here on occasion, unchecked, if you get my drift."

Tank still didn't respond.

Shooter blew out an exasperated sigh. "You getting what I'm saying here?"

Just then the Sheriffs car and two deputy cars pulled into the lot. Liam stepped out of his car, but remained by the door.

"We just got calls from a few campers," Liam yelled to the four men as he pointed at the State Parks Entrance located across the street from The Pen. "that there was quite a bit of noise coming from over here. Tank what are you doing here?"

Shooter looked at Tank with a snarl and then focused on the Sheriff.

"Sheriff, I happened to own this fine establishment." He said waving his hand aristocratically towards the run down property. Tank almost laughed out loud when Shooter used a sophisticated accent.

"Well then I'm happy to meet you." Liam walked towards the group of four men sitting on their Harley's. Tank watched as Cage tensed and he readied himself in case all hell broke loose.

Grease had been watching Cage too, trying to recall if he'd seen him before. Cage seemed to be scrutinizing Grease as well and Grease shifted his gaze from him. If this guy had known him he sure as hell did not want to be outed.

Grease turned his attention back to Liam.

"I'm the Sheriff around here. Liam Ross. I like getting to know who owns the businesses in my town. When you open up for business, me and my men will visit you regularly, for a drink that is. You opening it back up as a bar? We could use a good bar around here."

Shooter chuckled and sent his brother Cage a sideways look to remain quiet. He then looked at Tank.

"Well we haven't quite decided that yet. We just wanted to stop by the place and see it. We haven't been here for a while." Shooters eyes never left Tank's face.

"It's getting a bit run down as you can see." Liam continued as if he was talking to just any ordinary citizen. "I actually saw the building inspector nosing around out here just last week. Don't want it to become an eyesore. In fact the Governor drove through here on his way to his summer place and I heard that he was asking about it too. He'd love a place he can stop at and feed his whole security detail. He comes through here at least once a month."

Shooter laughed out loud, finally understanding what the Sheriff was hinting at.

He held up his hand. "I get it Sheriff. Tank I'm not sure if our deal will work any more?"

Tank nodded once. Inside he was doing a fist pump. Not only had his plan of getting Liam to The Pen worked, but also Liam had embellished on the story Tank had come up with and had just told a whopper of a fib to let Shooter know that Happy was off limits to Satan's Army. There was no way Shooter would risk Club business, which were, of course, illegal, but very lucrative, just to pass through Happy now. It was well known that when the Governor traveled his security detail ran impromptu trips through those areas for security checks. The increase in security had been all over the news and had been put in place after the Governor had been shot at last year.

Grease looked at Tank and Tank knew what he was thinking so he nodded.

"I'm still interested in buying the place." Grease spoke directly to Shooter. Shooter cocked his head, turned away from the men, spit onto the gravelly lot and looked back to Grease.

"We'll see. I'll be in touch." Then Shooter started his Harley and his club members did the same causing the ground to vibrate under the onslaught of high-powered motors. Shooter gave Tank a small salute and then turned his Chopper in a wide arc and sped out of the lot with his army of men behind him. When they were far enough down the road so that the remaining men could actually speak and be heard Tank turned to Liam.

"That was brilliant Liam."

"Yeah, it was a nice touch. It was a good plan to have us show up blaming it on a camper complaining about the noise." Liam gestured towards his deputies still in their cars.

"They wouldn't want to mess with the law. I knew that. That would just bring the heat down on them." One of the deputy cars left the lot, but the other deputy car's door opened and Joe stepped out. He was not smiling when he reached the group.

"You took a big chance meeting him Tank."

Tank looked at his oldest friend and grinned. He knew he had dodged the proverbial bullet.

"Listen I had to find out what he wanted. I don't want those guys coming around here and if I didn't meet him he would have just come back or found another way to reach me."

Joe shook his head still not agreeing with Tank's decision to meet Shooter with only one guy for back up, even if that guy was Grease. "So what happened?"

"The Sheriff here couldn't have timed it better and then he adlibbed a little alluding that the Governor passed through Happy a lot. He even went so far as to tell Shooter that the Governor would love it if a restaurant was opened up here so he and his security detail could stop there."

Joe chuckled. "And he bought it?"

Liam was grinning. "It wasn't a complete lie. He does pass through here sometimes."

Tank shifted on his bike. "Liam is Highway Patrol cracking down on Satan's Army?"

"Yeah, there is a stepped up effort since that truck was hijacked."

"Sounds like it's taking a toll on them. They wanted to move through Happy without problems. Shooter basically said he'd give us The Pen if they could use the roads here."

"I'm not liking that." Liam said pensively.

Joe looked to Liam. "If Highway Patrol is making it difficult for Satan's Army to move freely on the highways, they are going to be looking for alternate routes."

"Yeah, I'll call some of the other Sheriffs in the area to alert them."

"Well guys I hate to bust this up but I have to get back to camp and get my ass handed to me by my sweet wife." The men chuckled, all thinking about small, gentle Tess yelling at her bad ass husband.

When Tank and Grease arrived back at camp the men they had left behind to secure the camp met them. Tank explained that Satan's Army was gone, for now, but he still wanted them to remain cautious. As the men left to go to back to their trailers the front door of the prefab cabin opened and the women and children that had been sequestered in the upper rooms piled out.

Grease watched Tank as he stepped away and began walking towards Tess who was holding Tommy. Tess didn't look happy, but her relief at seeing her husband was safe was obvious. When Tank reached them he took Tommy from her arms and Grease watched as Tess planted her face into his shirt.

Grease could tell she was crying. Tank rubbed her back affectionately. Yeah, he was going to get his ass handed to him, Grease thought sarcastically, all night long. He then saw Sweets folding his wife Lolly into his large chest in a similar show of affection.

For some reason Sadie's cute face came to mind. Grease headed to his cabin and an odd emotion settled over him. Seeing his best friends with their wives served as a reminder as to how alone he really was. He had the club, but he didn't have that one special person. Grease thought back and couldn't recall ever even meeting a woman that would want to spend time with outside of the bedroom. He had always thought that he had the best of both worlds. He had women when he wanted them plus he could do what he wanted when he wanted. Right now, for some strange reason, he had the feeling he was missing out on something.

8

Tank still had his club members traveling with partners, but the entire atmosphere in camp was lighter now. Tank kept a couple of men on watch, just as a precaution, at camp and at the Townsend businesses. His gut, which was rarely wrong, told him Shooter would not be back.

Grease was closing on his cabin in two days and he had been busy clearing out his place in Townsend. He had decided to buy all new furniture for his first home. He really only needed a living room and bedroom. His old furniture he donated to Goodwill. He had made a list of all the items he thought he needed and the list was getting longer every day. He'd made the mistake of letting Tess look at it and she promptly penned on a few more things that he admittedly would have never thought of like kitchen towels and garbage cans.

The day of his closing arrived and he couldn't believe that how excited he was. He hadn't felt like this since he'd been a kid at Christmas. He had spent the entire day before at the Sears in Townsend, buying everything on his list. Lolly had let him borrow her truck and he had packed it full with all new kitchen items, sheets, towels, and even a doormat. He had wanted to buy a grill but he couldn't fit it in the truck. Rooms To Go was delivering the two rooms of furniture that he had ordered that afternoon. Grease grinned thinking about how he had sat at Pete's, on his computer, choosing the furniture from the online store, and how every woman who saw what he was doing had given him their opinion. He didn't mind though and had thanked them politely.

Grease met with Nancy and the lawyer that Toby had recommended, Jenny Garrison in Jenny's office. He had the certified check ready and he was eager to finally sign the papers and get settled in the cabin.

The closing went without a hitch and Grease walked out of the office with two sets of keys to his new cabin. He stopped at Pete's General and bought some food and coffee, plus a six pack and then headed up Happy Mountain. As he turned into his new drive, which was the last driveway off the small rural road, Grease had a slight feeling of nostalgia. The clubs' camp was only a couple of miles down the road, but he still felt a little bereft. He was certainly isolated up here, but that was what he wanted anyway.

When his new cabin came into view so did the vehicles and motorcycles that lined his small grassy lawn. Grease could not hide the enormous smile that emerged upon seeing his friends waiting to welcome him to his new home. As he stepped off his bike his friends gathered around him and he saw that they had loaded Lolly's truck with all the things he had purchased the day before.

They unloaded the truck and Grease saw that the Rooms To Go truck was pulling down his drive. Perfect timing. He chuckled to himself realizing that he had just thought of it as 'his drive.' The two men from the store, with help from his friends, carried everything inside and then together they pulled off the protective wrap from the furniture. The Rooms To Go men swiftly screwed together the furniture that had to be put together then they left. While the men did that,

Sweets and Tank brought up Grease's clothes and other items that he had boxed up that were in his cabin. Lolly and Tess, with help from Gus and Tommy, organized Grease's kitchen. Breezy helped him hang new drapes and then she helped him make his bed, after Toby placed the new mattress and box spring on the assembled frame. Unbeknownst to Grease, Lolly had kindly washed his new sheets and towels. One hour later Grease stood in the middle of his living room completely awed by how spectacular his place looked. Another car pulled in and Grease watched CC, Joe, and little Josie get out of Joe's Jeep.

Now that the house was in order Tank declared that it was time for the gifts. Grease's friends burst out laughing when they saw the surprised, opened mouth expression Grease had on his face when he realized his friends had also brought him new home gifts. Tank led the group out to the stone patio and Tank and Sweets wheeled over a large gas grill that they had hidden on the side of the cabin. Tess handed him a handmade wreath for his front door and Lolly presented him with four frozen dinners, a pie, and some jam she had made. Toby and Breezy had disappeared and returned carrying two wooden Adirondack chairs, and little Gus carried a small wooden table for the patio. The previous owners had left their two chairs, so now Grease had four. CC and Joe gave him a hanging weather station and then CC showed him a rubber mat she had already put by the front door to place wet boots on during the winter months.

Grease thanked everyone. His friends were great. He was moving from the camp and away from where he spent his winters, and instead of his friends making it more difficult for him they supported him. He was a lucky man.

They enjoyed burgers and veggies cooked on the new grill and a salad Tess had made. Luckily someone had the foresight to bring paper plates so clean up was a breeze. Gus was running around the cabin showing Tommy and Josie, where he use to sleep when he and Breezy had lived in the cabin and then he led them outside and showed them the dirt pile near the patio that he had played in. The children immediately started digging in the soft brown earth dirt.

Two summers ago when Breezy and Gus had stayed in the cabin, Breezy had been in some trouble. Toby and Tank had made sure someone was always with her. Grease had taken a turn guarding Breezy and he had to smile as he remembered playing in that very dirt pile with Gus, who was only four at the time. Grease caught Toby and Breezy looking at each other intimately, obviously remembering that summer also.

One by one each couple, children in tow, left for their own homes. As the last vehicle lumbered down the drive Grease was struck with how very, very quiet it was. He opened a beer and sat out on the patio watching the fireflies and listening to the sounds of the forest and its creatures.

Two days later Grease got word that Shooter had sent a contract to Nancy Hawkins authorizing her to sell The Pen. He was asking for $350,000.00, which was a little high, but it was zoned for commercial use and Grease needed that for his business.

He was in the office signing the papers to put his offer in and he couldn't help but notice how weary

Nancy appeared. She was usually a bubbly, non-stop talker and today she was quiet and morose.

Grease put the pen down and handed Nancy the check to go into escrow account. Instead of standing up to leave he leaned back in the wooden chair and stared at Nancy.

"What?" Her voice was strained.

"Want to tell me what's got you upset?"

"It's nothing." She stood as if too dismiss him, but Grease remained seated.

"You hear from Sadie lately?"

Nancy crumbled back down in her chair and stifled a sob that she'd been holding back. "No." She managed to croak out.

"Liam hasn't given you any news?"

"No. Agent Jennings hasn't heard from her either." She said referring to CC.

Grease was quiet for a few seconds. "She's smart, your daughter, and gutsy too. I'm sure she's fine. If it gets too dicey she'll get out. CC, Agent Jennings, said if she thought something was wrong she'd go in."

Nancy was wiping the tears from her eyes. "Thank you Grease. My husband and I have been a mess. You're right, of course. I just keep thinking the worst."

"Understandable." Grease stood up. "Let me know if my offer is accepted."

Nancy nodded and gave him a small smile.

"Will do and thanks again."

Grease left the Real Estate office feeling unsettled. He was trying to be positive with Nancy, but for some reason he was worried about Sadie. Grease turned around and went back into the office.

"Nancy, give me the paperwork. I think I'll drive it up to Shooter myself."

"Oh. I don't know Grease."

"Just give it to me."

Nancy handed him the folder and Grease left. He put the folder in his leather saddle and headed to camp. He didn't want to involve Tank and the club in his business, but he knew if he took off again and went to find Shooter, Tank would kick his ass.

Grease rumbled into camp and stopped at Tank's cabin. The camp was bustling with mid summer activity. It was too early for a fire, but he saw a few men chopping wood nearby, replenishing the supply.

Tank walked out of his cabin with Tommy in his arms. The young boy was trying to bust loose from his fathers firm grip.

"Tommy quiet down I'll put you down, just don't wake up your Mom!"

When Tank reached the bottom of his steps he gently placed Tommy down and the little boy took off towards the other children playing in the grassy center of camp. Grease looked at Tank.

"Everything all right?"

Tank thumped Grease on the back. "It's all good man. Tess is pregnant. She's taking a nap." Grease smiled at his friend who had a huge grin on his face.

"Congratulations, that's great."

Tank sat down on his steps keeping a watchful eye on Tommy.

"Yeah, it is. So everything okay with you?"

Grease paused a moment thinking did he really want to ask Tank for permission to go find Shooter?

"Speak Grease I can hear your brain churning from here."

"Yeah, okay. Shooter is willing to sell The Pen. I'd like to drive the papers up to him."

"Can't they be mailed? Isn't this what a realtors for?"

"Yes to both questions."

Tank looked at Grease for a few moments.

"You're worried about Sadie?"

"Maybe. How did you know?"

"I saw how you looked at her when we were in the office. It was different than how you usually look at women."

"Yeah?"

"Yeah." Tank watched his friend closely as he spoke his next words. "Toby said CC hasn't heard from her in a couple weeks."

"Is the FBI going to go in?"

"No. Joe said it's up to Ship It Good to call them in. According to CC, if Sadie thought she was in trouble she was to call a number that is set up to look like a customer service. Sadie would say that she didn't receive a package and that was code for she was in trouble."

"That's smart."

"Yeah, so even though they haven't heard from her they aren't going to go rushing in."

Grease leaned back against the steps looking out over the camp. "Maybe she can't get to a phone?"

"Yeah, Toby was thinking that too."

"I want to go up there Tank."

Tank sighed. "It's too dangerous Grease."

"I'll go without colors and take a few guys this time."

Both men turned to see Toby's Game Warden Jeep coming into camp.

"Hey big bro is this a social visit?"

"Yeah, I guess. No, not really."

"Spill it." Tank told him with an uneasy voice.

"CC called. She's worried about Sadie Hawkins."

Grease and Tank exchanged glances.

"You plan this?" He asked Grease.

"Nope, swear."

Now it was Toby's turn to say 'what?'

Tank spoke to his brother. "We were just talking about her."

"Do you know anyone that could get close enough to just let us know if she's okay?"

Tank stood up, ran his fingers through his hair, and muttered, "Shit."

Grease stood and faced Toby. "I'm going to head up there today Toby, me and few guys. I want to drop some papers off to Shooter."

"That's perfect! I'll call CC. Let me know the second you get back. I hope she's okay."

Toby took off in his Jeep and Tank looked at Grease uneasily.

"I still don't like it man."

"We'll be careful. I do have business with him. He may not even be at the bar. I won't look for him any where else, just the bar okay?"

"Yeah, talk to Sweets first. Take only volunteers."

"Got it."

Within a half hour Grease had rounded up four other men to accompany him. He made sure none of them were family men and that they understood that he was just dropping papers off. He didn't tell them about Sadie.

Four hours later as the sun started to dip behind the mountains the four men drove into McDives lot. There were ten choppers outside and a couple trucks.

The music was blaring and Grease could hear rowdy laughter.

Grease told his guys to wait on their bikes. He didn't want anyone getting hurt. He once again walked through the door of the bar and once again he waited for his eyes to adjust to the dim lighting.

Just like before the bar became quiet.

"You got a death wish?" Grease heard Cages unmistakable gravelly voice.

"Nope, wanted to give these papers for The Pen to Shooter." Grease looked around the room looking for Sadie. "I thought he'd appreciate getting them fast."

"And why would you want to do anything for him? You want to trade colors?" The men in the bar laughed and hurled a few nasty comments at him but Grease barely heard them. He was trying to find Sadie and he was even listening for her.

"Just business. Snail mail would put me back a week. Gotta pay my bills, man."

A small commotion coming from the restroom hallway drew Grease's attention. A man stumbled into the room with his beefy arm around Sadie. Sadie was trying to stay on her feet, the man was totally shit faced and hanging on her. Her blouse had a tear in it and she had a cut on her cheek. Grease watched her as she fought off the man pawing her.

Cage noticed him watching her.

"You like my whore?"

"She looks pretty worn out to me. You got to beat your whores to service you?"

It was a bold statement, but it only produced a nasty chuckle from Cage.

"Nah, we just like to." That brought loud laughter from the men. Grease felt the hairs on the back of his neck stand up. These men were scum and Sadie did not look good.

She caught his eye, but then quickly looked away. He watched her move behind the bar.
"You gonna give that to Shooter or should I take it back and mail it?"
"Relax. I'll give it to him. He wants the sale to go through fast too."

Grease saw Sadie come out from behind the bar and hand the drunken man a beer. The man took the beer and threw it at her drenching her white tee shirt. Sadie turned to the man and kneed him in the balls. The drunk dropped to his knees with his hands clutching his privates. The room went quiet and then Cage started laughing.
"That's right Honey; I know you only want me." The other men in the bar started laughing and Sadie walked up to Cage, leaning seductively into his chest. She kept her face to the floor, her wet shirt plastered to her frame outlining her ample breasts. Grease's stomach clenched. He hoped like hell she was acting.
"You know it baby." She said saucily giving Cage a wink. Sadie turned and pretended to trip falling backwards into Grease. He felt her place something in his pocket.

Cage ripped Sadie away from him possessively and then he kissed her forehead and gave her a gentle swat on her ass. "Get to work sweetheart."
The display of affection nauseated Grease. He quickly thanked Cage for giving the papers to Shooter and this time was able to make it out of McDives with out fighting. The look of relief on the four men he had brought with him was evident when he cleared the door. They hadn't even turned off their bikes. They

rode a few blocks and then Grease pulled to the side of the road and reached into his pocket wanting to see what Sadie had put there. He found a small piece of paper and the only thing written on it was lO.

"What's that?" Ace asked.

"I don't know." Grease passed the paper around to his friends and they all had suggestions as to what it meant. Collectively they decided lO could stand for Luke Oil, the gas station on the edge of town

When they got to the Luke Oil Station at the edge of town, Grease turned into the lot and the men followed him.

Ace stopped next to him. "What's up?"

"I need to stay here. You guys head home."

"No fucking way. Tank will kill us if we come back with out you."

Grease knew that was true.

"Okay, listen. Meet me at the rest stop near Hawthorn. I'll get there as soon as I can."

"Nope. I'll wait with you." Ace turned to the other two men. "Meet us at the rest stop."

The three men didn't look too certain about their latest orders.

"Five of us will draw attention." Grease told them. "Meet us there."

The men nodded and took off.

"Want to tell me what's really going on?"

"It's a woman."

"Cripes Grease don't you get enough trim in Happy? You gotta get a woman from here?"

"This ones different." Grease said quietly thinking to himself that she really was different.

Grease had no idea if there was another Luke Oil in town but he doubted it. He didn't know whether he was supposed to look for something there or just wait. He and Ace filled their tanks and pretended to be taking a break as he looked around.

"How long are we waiting for?" Ace asked. They'd been there for a half hour, he didn't like being on Satan's Army turf.

"I don't know. You want to meet me at the rest stop?"

"I'm not leaving you man."

Grease nodded. "Thanks'."

Grease could see that the man working inside the gas station was nervous that they were hanging around. He worried that he might have a Satan's Army connection and make a call, so he told Ace to wait by the bikes and Grease headed back inside.

"Gotta hit the head before we leave."

The man behind the counter nodded towards the bathrooms. When Grease came out of the restroom he bought a water, a Gatorade and a small bag of pretzels. While he was paying for them he tried to put the attendant at ease. He knew his appearance usually had the opposite effect, but he had to try.

"Just gonna drink these down and head home."

The attendant rang him up looking a little less anxious.

Grease walked outside and opened the Gatorade; he threw the water to Ace.

A few minutes later Grease saw Sadie limping towards them, keeping hidden using the cover of the woods around the gas station.

"Get on your bike." Grease told Ace quickly tossing the Gatorade in the nearby garbage can.

Grease got on his bike and headed out of the lot, stopping only long enough for Sadie to get on the back of his bike. They rode for fifteen minutes before Grease pulled to the side.

Sadie had been holding him with one arm around his waist and she'd been burying her face in his back. He really liked that she was holding him and he loved feeling her face against his back, but she hadn't spoken or moved much and it worried him. Ace pulled up behind him.

Grease carefully got off his Harley so he could look at Sadie. She had another cut on her forehead and her tee shirt had drops of blood splattered near the v- neck line. Her knuckles were scraped and she was holding her arms protectively across her waist.

"Talk to me Sadie." Grease said softly.

"We have to get further away." She told him quietly.

"They're gonna be looking for you?"

"Yeah."

Grease sighed heavily. "You okay to ride?"

"Yeah."

Grease reached into his leather sack and pulled out a flannel and a knit cap.

"Put these on."

Sadie put them on tucking her braid inside the cap. When she was ready Grease got back on and they headed down the highway. When they reached the rest area Grease slowed down so Ace could hear him.

"Get the guys. I'm gonna keep going. You catch up."

Ace saluted him letting him know that he had heard him and then he took the small ramp to the rest area. Sadie had her one arm wrapped gently around this waist and Grease patted it and turned his head so he could speak to her.

"What happened?"

Sadie leaned up so her face was close to his. "Not now okay?"

Grease nodded. Sadie tapped him on his shoulder so he'd give her his ear again. "Thanks for coming. How did you know?"

"No one had heard from you. Your Mom's worried. So is CC"

"They broke my phone."

"Are you hurt?"

Sadie didn't answer him. Grease turned his face again. "Sadie, are you hurt?"

"Maybe a little."

"Can we keep going?"

"Don't stop Grease, please don't stop." He hated how distraught she sounded and he wished he could comfort her somehow.

Grease could hear choppers coming up behind him and he checked his mirror to make sure they were his guys. They were. Sadie gripped Grease's waist anxiously.

"They're my guys, relax."

Sadie immediately loosened her grip and Grease felt her once again bury her face in his back. He wished he had a spare helmet to give her. He never wore one and he rarely drove women on his Harley more than a couple miles so he never had the need to even buy one.

Ace pulled up next to them and gave Grease the thumbs up. Grease nodded and all five Harleys picked up their speed. During the ride back to Happy Grease would reach behind him and rub Sadie's knee or sometimes he would cover her hand that was holding his stomach with his own. Grease had always heard that riding a Harley with someone you cared about was a sensual experience. He had women on his bike before, but usually just to transport them back to his place from the bar. Riding with Sadie tucked against him Grease felt a surge of protectiveness for her. He wished he could turn around and hold her. Grease knew she was feeling their connection too because even though she was hurting he noticed that her thumb would rub against his torso.

Two hours later they were riding into Happy. It was after midnight and Grease knew Sadie had to be tired from sitting on the back of his bike for four hours. Grease pulled over and steadied the bike with his strong legs. He twisted his neck to talk to her.

"Where to?"

"I don't know." She told him honestly.

Grease sat for a few seconds while the other men waited nearby, he then waved Ace closer.

"I'm heading to my cabin. Tell Tank we're there." Ace nodded. Grease then spoke to the other riders.

"Thanks for going with me." He paused and looked at each man individually. "Just so you're clear, all we did in Norwalk was hand sales papers for The Pen to Cage, got it?"

"Who's the chick?" One of the men asked.

"She's a friend."

"We did not just ride into Satan's Army territory so you can get a piece of tail, did we?"

One of the other men laughed. "Yeah, he needs to tap new territories now." The men were chuckling at their joke and Grease felt Sadie stiffen behind him.

"Shut it guys. You never saw her. Got it?"

The men stopped laughing. Grease looked mean and they had seen him in action, but he was normally easy going. Right now they knew he was dead serious.

"If you have any questions talk to Tank." The fact that their president was privy that they had brought a woman, from a Satan's Army bar, back to Happy with them put them at ease.

Grease thanked the guys individually with knuckle bumps as each of their choppers passed by his slowly as they left for camp. When the last chopper had passed him and Sadie, Grease pulled back on to the road following the other men.

9

Grease gave a small salute to the choppers that turned down the camps drive ahead of him. Sadie pushed in closer to Grease so she could talk in his ear.
"You don't live there?"
Grease turned his head so he could reply.
"I did up until a few days ago."
"I use to go to camp there when I was little."
"I heard it use to be a children's camp. Tank owns it outright, now."
Grease turned into his drive. For some reason he was anxious as to what Sadie would think of his place. He stopped his Harley near the front steps and held his hand over his shoulder so he could help Sadie dismount. As she was swinging her leg over Grease heard her wince in pain. He saw that her lips were pressed together firmly to hold in any other groans. Grease quickly dismounted. "You're hurting." It was a statement not a question. He placed his hand gently on her lower back guiding her into his cabin.
When Sadie stepped inside she stopped and looked around.
"You bought this?"
Grease tensed next to her and Sadie realized it sounded like she didn't like the cabin. She placed her hand on his forearm. "Grease, I love it. I love how rustic it is. It's charming." She gave him a smile that lit up her entire face.
Grease let himself smile. "Yeah?"
"I really do. Will you live here all year?"
"I plan too."
"It has so much potential." She limped over to the large sliding doors that looked out over the stone patio

and the back yard, which was edged with the thick forest.

"I just moved in."

"It looks great."

"Thank you."

Grease motioned for Sadie to have a seat and then he got her a coke from the fridge and put ice in a zip lock before sitting down next to her.

"For your arm." He said handing her the bag of ice.

"Thanks." Sadie took the bag and placed it on her forearm.

"What happened?"

"After you left?"

He nodded.

"The guy I kneed decided I needed to be taught a lesson."

Grease knew he wasn't going to like what he heard next.

"He smacked me a few times." Grease swore and Sadie placed her hand on his leg to calm him.

"It's okay..."

"That is never okay!" He spat out.

"I'm fine. Do you want to hear the rest or not?" She was something else Grease thought. Most women would have been blubbering and here she was calming him down. He grunted letting her know she could continue.

"I can't fight like I know how to fight." Grease quirked an eyebrow at her. "Yes, I know how to fight. I also know how to take a hit. The douche bag grabbed my arm and swung me to the floor and when I got up he hit me a few times. Then Cage stepped in like he always does."

"Cage likes you."

"Yeah and usually he just takes what he wants, but for some reason he's been patient with me. Well sort of patient."

Grease stroked his hand over his face clearly distressed. "Sort of?"

"I had to kiss him a couple times, but nothing more. Trust me I was grossed out too. Anyway, after he thought he saved me from Peanut, the douche bag, he thought he was deserving of more than just a kiss. I had to get a little rough with him."

"Oh no you didn't."

"I smacked him over his head with a bottle that was on the bar and ran out the door. I wanted to meet you so I could tell you to tell CC that I thought I was getting close, but after I smashed Cage I thought it best that I leave."

"Ya think!"

Sadie chuckled. "I didn't know if you were going to figure out the meaning of my note."

"I really guessed. I didn't know if I was at the right place or how long to wait." Grease told her honestly.

"I know. Sorry it was so cryptic. I only had a second to scrawl the note. I was supposed to be going on a break and I always sit in my car just to get out of the bar. When I saw you come in I was thinking it was the perfect opportunity to get word to CC. On my break I was going to drive to the gas station, tell you I was okay and ask you to tell CC I didn't have a phone. Then I was hoping to drive back to the bar before anyone even knew I was gone."

"How did you get to the gas station?"

"After I snuck out the window I didn't want them to know I'd left so I ran down the street to the hardware store. I saw the owner leaving and asked for a ride. I think he was a little nervous with me looking the way that I did but he was nice and gave me a lift. I had him drop me off a block from the gas station."

"Well you are resourceful I'll give you that." Grease told her.

"You really rode back up there to give him those papers? That's pretty nuts considering what happened the last time you showed up unannounced."

"Well the papers were an excuse."

"An excuse?"

Grease looked away from Sadie almost nervously and when he looked back at her he held on to her eyes with his. "Like I said before. Toby said no one had heard from you and I just wanted to check on you."

"You came up to make sure I was okay?" Sadie's voice was soft and she put her hand on his arm. Grease looked at her hand on him feeling how warm it made his skin. Sadie's eyes locked on his and the air around them was heavy with unspoken emotion.

Before he could answer they heard a motorcycle and a car crunching the gravel on the driveway outside. It was late, too late for a social call. Grease looked out the window.

"It's Tank and Toby."

Grease opened the door before the two O'Brian brothers had a chance to knock.

"Is she okay?" Toby asked the second he saw Grease. Grease stood back from the door so they could walk inside and see Sadie for themselves.

Sadie remained seated on the couch holding the ice bag to her arm. She was feeling achy and if she stood the men would probably notice her limping. She wasn't going to be able to hide her face from them though.

"Shit." Tank murmured when he saw her.

"I'm fine, relax."

"What happened?" Toby was in Government Official mode and his face conveyed how concerned he was. The men sat down and Grease returned to his spot next to Sadie.

"I just hit a little snag tonight."

Grease made a grunting sound next to her.

"The women were starting to open up more when I was around. The men, well, the novelty of me being the new barmaid was starting to wear off. They were relaxed around me. Everything was going smoothly until Cage decided he wanted more than I was willing to give, if you get my drift?"

The men looked apprehensive and Sadie hurried with her explanation to try to alleviate their fears.

"He didn't do anything. I didn't let him." Grease snorted obnoxiously next to her and Sadie sent him a glare that silenced him quickly.

"Anyway Cage took my phone from me a couple weeks ago so I couldn't contact my safe number. It's a burner so there were no personal numbers on it. The past few days Cage has become more hands on. When Grease came today he got even more agitated. Grease do you know him?"

Grease froze. He knew there was no way Sadie knew about his past. He didn't think that he had ever crossed paths with Cage so he hoped he was in the clear with him too.

"No."

"Well it's strange. Each time you've visited the bar he's just become wired. When he gets like that he gets physical. After Grease left he slapped me around a bit because I kneed one of his men in the privates. He just had this look in his eyes. I can't explain it, but I knew I had to get out. I smashed him over the head with a bottle and ran into the bathroom and locked the door. I knew they'd take care of Cage before dealing with me. They thought I was still in the bathroom, but I had jumped out the window. I twisted my ankle, but I was able to catch a ride and meet up with Grease. I had slipped him a note, a very cryptic note, but luckily Grease figured out what I had written and he waited for me."

Grease stood up and walked to his refrigerator.

"I'll call CC to let her know you're okay. She'll probably want to see you for herself." Toby told her.

"Yeah, I know. Tell her I'll call work as soon as I can." Grease returned with two more ice packs that he handed to Sadie. "Foot and face."

Sadie smiled up at the big man taking the two bags from him and placing one on her ankle and the other against her cheek. "Thank you."

"Come to my house tomorrow. You can use my phone." Toby offered.

"Thank you. I think I need to lay low for a day or two, but then I have to go back."

"Laying low is a good idea, but going back.... Sadie, I don't know?" Tank told her.

"I left for two reasons Tank. One I needed to tell my Mom that I'm okay, but I can't tell her I'm here. She'll try to visit."

"I'll have Liam talk to her." Toby reassured her.

"That takes care of one problem. So problem number two is Cage. I'm just going to take a day or two and wait for him to cool off."

"Will he? Cool off?"

"I think so. Grease you just rile that man up for some reason."

"Will he put Grease coming to the bar and your disappearance together?"

"I don't think so. I'm hoping he'll be so happy to see me in a day or two that he'll forget all about the bottle over the head thing." Sadie said with a chuckle.

Grease couldn't believe that she was actually joking about this.

Tank read Grease's thoughts. "What if he hasn't cooled off Sadie? What if he tries to hurt you again?"

"Well like I told Grease I can fight. I just don't want to blow my cover by going all ninja on him."

"But you will if he gets rough?" Grease asked apprehensively.

"If it gets bad I will protect myself. Does that make you feel any better?"

"Yeah, I guess." Toby was looking at Tank who was smiling at Grease.

"So Toby can you ask CC if she has a place for me to stay?"

"Will do."

"Just stay here Sadie." Grease offered.

"Grease that's nice of you, but."

"No buts. My place is perfect. You can recoup and no one comes up here. You'll be safe."

Toby and Tank were staring at Grease with their mouths hanging open. The Grease they knew liked his privacy and he the only women he talked to outside of the bedroom on a regular basis were Tess and Lolly. Sadie thought about his offer and then patted his large thigh. "Okay as long as it's no trouble."

"It's not." Grease had an adorable grin hiding beneath his beard and Sadie had to hold in a laugh.
"So how will you get back to Norwalk?" Toby asked.
"I actually came up with an idea. I'll need a ride to Helena and I'll need CC to give me a fake address for my fake mother in Helena, in case they check on my story, but I'll take a bus from Helena to Norwalk. I'll tell everyone that my Mom has a bad habit of choosing boyfriends that beat on her and it was one of the reasons I'd left in the first place. I'll just tell Cage that I went home because I didn't want to fall into the same rut my Mom was in, but I'll explain to him that she had a boyfriend living with her and that he got fresh with me so I came back."
"That's a good one." Toby admitted.
"I think so too and it also lets Cage know I'm not into being knocked around."

The three men stood up and after wishing Sadie good luck they left the cabin. Grease walked them out.
Tank gave Grease a brotherly pat on his back.
"Feel better bro?" He whispered so Sadie wouldn't hear him since the door was open.
"Yeah, thanks."
"I'm going to send you up some food Grease. I know what your fridge probably looks like. I don't really want anyone else to know Sadie's here so it will be either me or Tess coming up."
"Thanks I appreciate that. Tank, can you find something for her to wear? Tess is too thin, but maybe Lolly's clothes might fit her."
"Yeah, good idea."

Tank kicked his engine on and turned back to Grease motioning for him to come closer so he could whisper something.

"Don't fall too hard Grease. She has job to do."

Grease stood back up and put his hands in his jeans pockets. He knew she had to leave. There was just something about her though that was throwing him off. He never wanted to spend time with a woman, yet he had clearly offered his home to her to stay for at least two days. Grease mouthed to Tank. "I know."

10

Grease walked back inside and shut and locked his door. Sadie was still on his couch. Her head was tilted back resting on the back of the couch and her eyes were drooping. Her eyes opened when he walked towards her.

"You need to get some sleep Sadie."

Sadie stood up but her balance was slightly off because of her sore ankle and as she teetered Grease caught her hand in his steadying her.

"Thanks." She said after she regained her balance. "Grease can I shower first?"

"Oh, yeah, sure. Sorry I should have thought of that. The showers back here. I'll get you a towel."

Grease led her down the hall towards the bathroom.

"Could I borrow a tee shirt to sleep in?"

"Sure. Here's the bathroom." Grease told her opening the door. "I'll get you a towel and shirt just a second."

Grease walked to his bedroom, which was only a few steps from the bathroom, and fished out a tee shirts from a drawer and then on the way back to the bathroom he retrieved a towel from the closet.

When he returned to the bathroom Sadie was sitting on the closed toilet seat with her looking exhausted.

Grease knelt down next to her when she didn't look up and placed his hand on her knee.

"Sadie?"

"I feel like I've been hit by a truck." She told him quietly.

"Yeah. I shouldn't have let you ride on my bike for that long."

"No that was fine. I wish I could go for a ride someday under better circumstances." Her voice was soft and Grease had to stop himself from gathering her in his arms to comfort her. She was so independent she would probably punch him.

"I think we can arrange that." Grease replied gently giving her an impish grin.

Grease left the towel and tee shirt and made up the couch with a pillow and blanket. When Sadie came out of the shower he met her in the hallway and walked her to his bedroom. "You're sleeping in here Sadie."

"Oh Grease no. You're too big for the couch."

"I'll be fine. You need to get some sleep."

Sadie was too tired to argue so she thanked him.

The next morning Sadie woke up to the smell of coffee. She slipped out of bed and made her way into the living room where she saw Grease standing in front of the stove using a spatula on something in a pan. His back was to her and she knew he did not know she was standing there. She took a second to look at him. His back was broad but it tapered nicely into his waist and hips. He had on a tee shirt, a pair of jeans and his hair was freshly washed and it was perfectly braided hanging down his back. He did not have his normal headband on. As she was watching him she noticed he was humming softly to himself and for some reason that made her smile.

Sadie walked through the living room and Grease heard her feet padding on his wood floors. He peered over his shoulder.

"Morning." He said then his attention shifted quickly back to the pan. "How do you feel?"

"So much better thank you. What are you cooking?"

"I'm trying to make bacon and eggs."

"Trying?" Sadie chuckled as she walked up next to him to look at his progress.

When she looked into the pan she cringed. He had cooked the bacon at the same time he had cooked the eggs and now the eggs were almost black and the bacon was still rubbery and drowning in grease.

"Oh dear."

"It looks pretty bad doesn't it?"

Sadie laughed and Grease stopped playing with the food in the pan and stared at her. She had a wonderful laugh and he loved that he had given her something to laugh about even if it was because of his lack of culinary skills.

"I take it you don't cook much?"

"No, not really. I try but it just isn't my thing."

"Why don't you let me do this? It will be my way of thanking you for letting me bunk here." Sadie reached across his large frame and turned off the flame.

"Yeah, well that would be nice but."

Grease pulled the garbage can out from under the sink and showed the inside of it for to Sadie. She could see remnants of eggs and bacon.

"You already threw out your first attempt?' She asked with a giggle.

"First and second. I don't have anymore eggs or bacon."

Sadie opened up a cabinet, saw bread and pulled down the loaf. She opened up another cabinet and found peanut butter.

"Okay I'm a happy woman. This is what I'll have for breakfast."

"Bread and peanut butter?" Grease looked at her like she was nuts.

"Grease I live on it."

Grease got the broadest smile on his face. The only reason Sadie even knew it was huge, since his face was so hidden under his full beard, was that she could see his white teeth showing against his dark hair.

"I love peanut butter on bread too." He told her.

"Okay breakfast will be served in a Jiff." She laughed. "Get it? A Jiff. Jiffy peanut butter."

Grease chuckled. "That was terrible."

"That was a good one and you know it!" She chortled trying to appear indignant.

They took their peanut butter sandwiches out on the patio along with mugs of coffee. Grease had made the coffee. Luckily he was good at that. As they walked to the patio Grease took a throw off the back of his couch and when Sadie was settled in the chair he put his mug and sandwich down and tucked the blanket around her. She was still wearing his tee shirt and mornings in Montana were refreshingly crisp.

Sadie's didn't speak. She was in awe that the big bad ass Grease had such a tender side to him. As he finished Sadie reached out and took his hand gently in her own.

"Thanks Grease. Thank you for everything. You really are very sweet."

Grease sat down in his chair and Sadie saw that a rosy blush had crept into the exposed parts of his cheek.

At first they ate in silence. The woods surrounding Grease's cabin was alive with the sounds of leaves rustling in the morning breeze, birds singing, and smaller animals foraging for their own breakfast. They watched as two small elk calf's emerged from the tree line and munched on the sweet grass. Sadie pointed at them and Grease nodded indicating that he too had seen them.

A few seconds later the large momma elk emerged from the woods. She stared at Grease and Sadie for a bit but she must have decided they were not a threat to her babies because she too put her head down to graze on the grass.

"I've lived here all my life." Sadie whispered to Grease "But seeing things like that still amaze me."

"Yeah, me too."

"Have you always lived in Montana?" She asked him after taking a sip of her coffee.

"No, not always." Grease repeated the cover story he had told people years ago. "I lived in a couple places before, but I settled in Montana. It suits me here."

"Where do your parents live?"

"They died a longtime ago."

"Oh. I'm sorry."

"It's okay. It really was a long time ago."

"So what do you do for a living? Oh dear, am I being too chatty?"

Grease chuckled. "I use to run the Harley Dealership in Townsend. It's a club business."

"You don't anymore?"

Grease shook his head. "I really haven't shared this with too many people yet, but I want to open up my own place of business here in Happy."

"That's cool. Doing what?"

"I like to design and revamp motorcycles, specifically Harley's. I've been doing some on the side for a year now and I really love it. I love working with the metals and creating new designs. I'm trying to buy The Pen and put my shop in the back barn on the property and convert the front building, where the bar was into a retail store for all things motorcycle."

Sadie heard the enthusiasm reflected in his voice and she smiled.

"That sounds great. I guess you just have to wait on the sale of The Pen right?"

"Yeah. I've been drawing up plans and trolling the internet for supplies for the past six months."

"I'm happy for you Grease. You seem like you have it all."

Grease smiled at her but inside he was thinking, 'Do I have it all?'

They spent the next hour talking about themselves. Grease spoke candidly about his life in the club. Sadie told him about growing up in Happy and how she had gone to college for criminal justice and then had taken the Public Service exam hoping to become a Highway Patrolman but she had shown an affinity for solving problems so she was fast tracked through the system. She told Grease how she served with the State agency for a few years and then was recruited by Ship It Good.

"I couldn't pass up the money they were offering me. I know that sounds awful but that's why I took the job initially."

"And now? Are you happy that you took the job?"

"Yes, I love what I do. My assignment is always changing. I help map routes for the trucks, handle security for the warehouse, and track down lost cargo. I'd never gone undercover like this before."

"Do you like being undercover?"

"Honestly I don't think I'll do it again. It's a little scary."

They discovered they had some things in common like their taste in music, their love of being outdoors, they both loved football, and their favorite meal was a cheeseburger."

"As you can see by my size that I love to eat." Sadie told him with a nervous chuckle.

Grease wasn't sure how to respond to what she just said. He didn't want to say anything that would make her uncomfortable. He decided reacting honestly was best, so he did.

"Sadie, you have a great a body." he said giving her a sexy wink.

Sadie colored. "Thanks, but I know I'm heavy."

"Woman who the hell told you that?"

"Grease come on. My hips and butt are ginormous. My breasts are too big. I..."

Grease cut her off.

"Sadie stop. I'm telling you I think you're friggin perfect. I love that you aren't skin and bones. You are." Grease struggled to find the right word. "Voluptuous. Yes, that's it, voluptuous."

Sadie burst out laughing and Grease loved the smile she had plastered on her face.

"Like Jessica Rabbit, from the movie Roger Rabbit?" She asked giggling.

"Yeah, like her!" Grease chuckled thinking about Sadie stuffing herself into a slinky dress. That was so not Sadie.

Sadie was all smiles and Grease's heart swelled with how good he was feeling. He couldn't ever remember opening up to female like he had with Sadie. He was so comfortable with her and she was laughing and swapping stories with him as if they were two old friends.

When they heard a car coming down Grease's drive Sadie looked at Grease nervously. Grease hated the apprehensive look that had replaced the carefree smile on her face. Grease stood up and Sadie jumped up next to him. She kept the blanket wrapped around her. They walked around to the front of the cabin, Grease kept her protectively behind his large frame and he chuckled when she kept trying to push in front of him. Sadie glared at him and instead of him being put off he gave her a smile that melted her insides.

When they reached the front of Grease's cabin they saw Lolly's truck come to a screeching stop in front of his cabin.

"They have Sweets Grease! You took a Satan's Army whore and they took my Sweets. What the hell is the matter with you bringing one of their whore's here?"

"Lolly slow down. What's going on?"

Lolly was glaring at Sadie and Grease felt badly for her, but he couldn't break her cover.

"Sweets and I were coming out of Pete's when two guys sucker punched him and threw him in a van. They told me not to involve any cops or Tank or they would send him back to me in pieces. Lolly was crying now. "In piece's Grease!"

"What did they say?"

"They said for me to find you and tell you to bring them the girl to the rest stop between here and Norwalk."

Grease and Sadie said "Shit." simultaneously.

"You go get my Sweets back right now Grease. Do you hear me right now!"

Grease turned to Sadie who was still in his tee shirt. She looked as mad as he was.

"Let's go Grease. I have to go back anyways. Might as well get Sweets back."

"How the frig did they know?" Grease muttered.

"Waldo at the gas station probably saw me get on your bike. He is not Satan's Army but it would not take much for him to talk."

"Okay go inside and get dressed."

Sadie ran back inside.

"How could you Grease?" Lolly was till irate.

"It's not what it seems Lolly. Listen you need to do me a favor."

Lolly cut him off. "I don't need to do anything for you!"

"You do and you will." Grease said in a voice so steely that Lolly froze. She had known Grease forever and he had never talked to her like that before.

Lolly did not look happy but she nodded. "Go get Tank. Tell him what you told me."

"But."

"Shut it Lolly I know you're worried, but we don't have a lot of time just do what I'm asking."

Again Lolly nodded a little unnerved by this side of Grease she had never seen before.

"Tell Tank to meet me at the end of the drive with a burner phone. Tell him I need a driver, a fast driver, to take Sadie to Norwalk using the back roads. I'll be right down."

Lolly got back in her truck and sped off.

Sadie reappeared in her tattered beer stained clothes from yesterday. She did not look unhinged, she looked pissed.

"I'm sorry Grease."

"I'm sorry she went off on you. I didn't want to break your cover."

"I appreciate that."

"I'm going to have someone drive you back to Norwalk using the back roads. Hopefully you will be back there before Cage gets back. You can use your original cover. I'll make sure Toby tells CC to make sure it's set up. Tank and I will get Sweets back."

"That's a good idea. I'll just tell Cage you drove me to the bus station in Gary. I'll tell him I knew he would figure out where I'd gone and I was trying to cover my tracks."

"Yeah, that should work. I'm a little nervous for you to go back to them Sadie."

"Don't worry. I really can fight. If it's a fair one anyways."

They drove quickly down the mountain. Tank was waiting at the end of the drive along with Meeks, one of the club members. Meeks was in a Camero and it was loud.

"Sadie this is Meeks. He races cars. He'll get you back fast."

Sadie got off of Grease's bike and he felt her give his shoulder a gentle squeeze as she dismounted. As she got into the car Grease couldn't take his eyes off her. He felt like he was being torn apart from the inside. Sadie was watching him and he felt like she wanted to say something to him but she remained quiet. He straddle walked his bike closer to Meeks car so he was right next to her. "Stay safe Sadie."

"I will. Be careful with Cage. He's not a nice guy."

Tank handed Grease the burner phone without question. Grease handed it to Sadie. "It's a burner phone. Hopefully he won't take it from you."

"Thanks. I owe you."

Grease looked to Meeks. "Get her back to Norwalk. Avoid the main roads, but you have to book it. She has to be there when Cage gets back."

"I got this Grease. You guys be careful."

Meeks tore off down the mountain and the ache in Grease's chest had him absentmindedly rubbing the center of his chest.

"What's the plan Grease?" Tank asked.

"We're going to get Sweets back. We are driving up to the rest stop and we just pretend that we don't know anything about Sadie except that I dropped her at the bus station in Gary."

"Lolly said she wasn't suppose to tell me or they'd cut Sweets."

"Yeah well they'll have to get over that won't they?"

"So we're just driving up?"

"You got a better idea Prez? Grease asked seriously.

"No. Let's ride."

After two hours on the road they steered into a roadside rest stop. They slowed their pace and looked around cautiously. A beat up white van was parked in front of the one small building. The door was open and Tank and Grease could see that Sweets was sitting in the open door. He looked like he had a split lip but besides that he appeared to be all right. Grease breathed a sigh of relief upon seeing his friend. He'd been worried that Cage would get nasty with Sweets. Grease and Tank drove towards the van that was surrounded by five bikes and six Satan's Army members. They parked their bikes and stood next to them.

"Where's my girl?" Cage yelled.

"If you're talking about the whore I dropped at the bus station in Gary I couldn't tell you."

"She got on your bike. I know she did."

"Yeah, she wanted a ride. I thought I could get a free blow out of it but the bitch wouldn't give it up."

Cage smiled. "Yeah, she's tight that one." Grease could tell he had bought his story.

"You came into my town and took one of my men ass hole." Tank was a bad ass and he was in total control right now. Grease knew they were going to brawl.

"Sweets you okay?" Tank yelled over to his friend.

"Dandy." Sweets said sarcastically.

Sweets stood up and started walking towards them and one of the men clocked him from behind. That's when all hell broke loose. Grease and Tank tore into the cluster of six men and fist flew. One of Satan's Army was wearing brass knuckles and Grease took a shot to his chin that had him seeing stars he felt his chin rip open and the blood begin to pour down his neck. He roundhouse kicked one of the men in front of him and then overhand punched the man closest to him. Both men went down.

Tank had dropped one of the men he was tangled up with but two others were on him. Grease took on one of them by delivering an axe kick along with a jab to the mans face. He looked to Sweets who was brawling with Cage and saw Cage use a sweep kick putting Sweets on his back. Grease ran towards them and rammed his body into Cage before he could deliver a devastating blow to Sweets who was stunned on the ground.

The two men stared at each other both breathing heavily.

"I remember you, now." Cage said to Grease through clenched teeth. "Romeo."

"I don't know what the hell you're talking about." Grease tried to throw a punch but Cage blocked it. Cage spun and was about to deliver a kick but Grease saw that it was coming and blocked it with his own leg. Sweets had rolled away from the two of them and Tank must have finished off his two men because they stood away from Cage and Grease listening and watching.

Cage made another attempt to kick him and then punch him but Grease blocked both with ease.

"Yeah, it's you. Romeo. We were supposed to fight next."

Grease looked at Cage uneasily as he tried to remember his fight schedule so many years ago.

Cage sneered at him. "Until you turned States Evidence, that was supposed to be my big break, going up against the famous Romeo, and you had to go and be a fucking hero." Cage's face was red with rage. Grease could see Tank and Sweets looking at him with confused expressions on their faces and the Satan's Army men that had been down were now standing next to Sweets and Tank watching the action. Grease knew he needed to shut Cage up.

"I don't know any Romeo." Grease countered again. Then Grease realized that he was going to have to prove that he wasn't the well known cage fighter Romeo, by letting Cage knock him out. Romeo had never been knocked out before. Hell, he'd never even been knocked down before. Grease had to do something obvious. Something a professional fighter would never do. Shit! This was gonna hurt he thought. He saw Cage start to wind up for another two hit combination and Grease stepped into it, a true no - no in the fight world. A real fighter would never step into a combo punch so Grease did just that. Cage hit him in the cheek with his fist and then countered with a follow up kick to Grease's chin and Grease went down hard. He heard Tank yell his name and he heard Cage laughing before he blacked out.

Cage was standing over Grease laughing hysterically and Tank and Sweets were momentarily stunned as they saw their best friend, the best fighter they knew, laying unconscious on the pavement. To their horror they watched as Cage whipped out a switch blade from his pocket. Sweets was still feeling the effects of being laid out by one of Cage's kicks, but Tank started running towards Cage.
"Noooo!" Tank screamed as he saw Cage lean over Grease. His gut rolled; sicken with the awareness that he would not reach them in time. His friend was about to be stabbed.
Cage grabbed Grease's braid and at the base of Greases skull he sliced off the long braid.
Cage stood up holding the braid in his hand and Tank halted abruptly since the knife was now pointed at him.
"Relax Prez." Cage said sarcastically. "I just wanted a little trophy to bring back to my club."
"You son of bitch. This is all because of some whore you couldn't control. This isn't over. You came into my town. You took one of my men." Tank hissed at him. Cage chuckled and then directed Tank's attention to one of his men that was holding a gun that was pointed at him.

"It's over for now Tank. As for the woman, she rode out of town behind Grease here. It was only natural that I would assume she was with him. Now you just stay right there while we leave."

His five men had all seen Cage take down Grease and they jogged to their Secretary congratulating him with high fives before they all took off out of the rest stop. Tank reached Grease who was still out and fell to his knees. The hit he'd seen Grease take was vicious and he feared Grease might be hurt badly. Sweets joined him.

Grease was bleeding from the cut he'd taken during the brawl and his chin was split open from the kick he had taken.

"Should we call and ambulance?"

"Is there a pay phone inside?"

"I don't know. If there is, call Toby and get Liam on the radio. Tell him to get here ASAP!"

Sweets stood up and ran for the building.

When he returned a few minutes later Grease was still out and Tank had his head resting on a leather jacket he'd taken out of his motorcycle saddle.

"He's coming. Liam's coming too. They are in Liam's car using the lights they'll be here in an hour. Liam didn't want to call the Sheriff here. He said he's by the book and would probably haul us to jail for fighting."

"Good I'm glad they'll be here fast. I felt his jaw I don't think it's broken but he's still bleeding. What a hit he took. I was afraid to move him but he moaned once and I saw him move his neck so I figured it was alright."

"Shit! He better be all right."

"Did you hear what Cage was calling him? Romeo?"

"Yeah, and what about turning States Evidence?"

Tank was quiet for a second and Sweets knew he wanted to say something. "Spill it Tank."

"He stepped into that punch. Grease is a good fighter. He'd never step into a punch like that."

"Yeah that was strange."

"Well I'm thinking our boy Grease here wanted to shut Cage up."

"Because what Cage was saying was true?"

"I don't know. He better be all right though. God he went down so hard. We'll ask him about it later."

Grease groaned and then turned on his side and puked. Tank helped him as best he could and Sweets ran into the rest stop and grabbed wet paper towels.

When Grease finished puking he returned to his back. Tank could see that his eyes were still not completely focused and that the one pupil was completely dilated.

"We're here man." Tank told his best friend quietly. Grease closed his eyes again and when Sweets returned he pressed the wet towels to Greases mouth and then to his head. Grease opened his eyes again.

"Grease we need to move you from the middle of this parking lot in case people come in. Do you think you can stand with our help?"

Grease grunted and Tank saw him trying to sit up by himself.

"Whoa, go slow. We're gonna help you."

Tank and Sweets lifted Grease up and held him up. His legs were not holding him so they stood there for a few seconds so Grease could get his legs back.

Slowly they helped Grease to behind the building where there was a picnic table. They got Grease up on the table even though Grease tried to sit on the bench.

"Listen Grease; just lay on the damn table okay?"

Grease was hurting too bad to argue. His brain was

still fuzzy, his head was pounding his jaw was on fire, and he thought he was going to throw up again. He lay on the table and tried not to move, moving hurt.

About a half hour later they heard Liam's Sheriff car careening into the parking lot. Sweets jogged around to the front of the building to meet them. Tank watched as Sweets came back and behind him Liam was pulling his car around the corner trying not to hit the trees and building as he went off road with his car.

Toby jumped out of the car and took one look at Grease and swore. The neck of Grease was swathed in blood and his lip was swollen along with his cheek. "Shit! What the hell happened?"

Liam had retrieved his med kit from the trunk of his car and was tending to Grease so Tank decided it was a good time to explain everything. Sweets did not know about Sadie being at Grease's, only the men that had gone with Grease to retrieve her knew she was there, along with Toby, Liam and himself.

"Sadie was up at Grease's house recovering from a beating."

"Wait! Wait! Who's Sadie?" Sweets interrupted.

"Sadie is a woman working undercover for Ship It Now. She's working to recover items they believed Satan's Army took in a truck hi jacking. Sadie is Nancy Hawkins' daughter. Grease went up with a few men yesterday because no one had heard from her. She took a beating from Cage and managed to get to Grease. Grease brought her to Happy. She was only going to be with him for a day or two then she was going back. She had a good cover worked out."

"Wow. You didn't say anything." Sweets said quietly.

"He wasn't allowed to." Toby told him rescuing Tank from his friend's scrutiny.

"Cage kidnapped Sweets thinking Grease had his woman."

"His woman is Sadie?" Sweets asked.

"Cage likes her, so yeah."

"So what happened here?" Liam asked.

"We rode up here to get Sweets back. When Cage and his crew took Sweets they told Lolly..."

"Oh God Lolly must be going nuts!" Sweets was clearly distressed thinking of his wife.

"I'll call one of my deputies to go up and tell her that you're okay."

"Oh thanks. Yeah that would be great. Thanks."

"So what happened?"

"Well before Grease and I took off we sent Sadie back to Norwalk, using the back roads. Meeks drove her so I know she's getting back ahead of him. It's important that she's there before Cage so that Cage thinks she wasn't with Grease."

"Okay that was smart." Toby told his brother.

Tank grinned at the compliment. "This is all Grease's plan. So when we got here we told Cage that Sadie wasn't with Grease, that she had taken a bus out of Gary yesterday. Then all hell broke loose."

"So there were six of them and three of you?"

"Yeah."

"You're lucky you weren't shot Tank!" Toby admonished his younger brother.

"Can we just get Grease to a hospital please? I've never seen him go down before and he's puking so I know his head was rattled good."

Grease was awake now and had been listening to the conversation as he tried to keep from throwing up. His head getting rattled was a frigging understatement.

"No hospital." He managed to bite out.

The men stopped talking and looked at Grease who was attempting to sit up. Sweets grabbed him and helped him so that he was sitting on the table with his feet resting on the bench below. Grease's hand was supporting the side of his face.

"Grease you probably need to have your head scanned." Liam told him seriously.

"Man, you have to go. I'll stay with you." Tank offered.

Grease was quiet for a few seconds. "I'll go, but no one is staying with me. Tank you need to get home to Tess. She's going to be a mess knowing where you were, and Lolly needs to see Sweets. She was scared to death." Grease was talking slowly and Tank could tell his friend was hurting.

Tank took control of the situation. Grease was correct, Tess and Lolly needed to see that they were all right and Tank knew Grease didn't want to inconvenience any of them.

"Sweets can ride Grease's Harley back and Toby you can ride with me. Liam will you take him to Helena?"

"Yeah. This way I can get him admitted without a lot of questions."

"Thanks Liam. You're a good friend." Tank told the Sheriff.

The men helped maneuver Grease into the back of Liam's car. Grease had wanted to sit up front but Liam told him he couldn't because it was a Government car. Tank retrieved Grease's leather saddle off his Harley and threw it in the car. Tank knew it had Grease's ID in it, along with some money and other things.

After Liam sped out of the lot with his lights going Sweets turned to Tank.

"How long do you think before he realizes his braid is gone?"

11

Liam parked and walked Grease in the front door of
the emergency room at General. Grease still felt like
hell but his thoughts were not as jumbled as they had
been. He asked Liam what time it was wondering if
Sadie had made it back in time. He prayed she'd be
safe. Something wasn't right. He felt air hitting his
neck and as he walked he realized why. He reached
behind his head and felt the void where his braid used
to hang.

"That mother fucker." Grease swore.

Liam looked at him and then he too saw that Grease's
braid was gone.

"Looks like Cage took a trophy."

"Son of a bitch." Grease was still a little unsteady so
Liam grasped the big man around the waist and Grease
draped his arm around Liam's shoulders.

When they got inside Grease sat down in front of a
nurse that was behind a partition. Liam stood behind
him in case he was needed. Grease was asked to fill
out paperwork and Liam flashed his badge and said
this was official and the nurse could get all the
information she needed from Grease later. Grease
handed the nurse his license and Medical Card and
after she copied down the information she handed the
cards back to Grease and motioned for someone in the
back of her, who Liam and Grease couldn't see.

An orderly came out from behind a door with a
wheelchair and Liam and the man helped Grease to
settle into the chair.

"Liam you don't need to stay. I know they have to run
tests. It's going to take some time. I appreciate the
ride."

"Yeah, it might be a while. You sure you'll be okay?"

"Yeah, I've been alone most of my life. I promise, I got this." Liam couldn't help but think how sad Grease sounded. He was lucky. He'd been married to his Bethy for thirty years.

"Take care Grease."

"Thanks again Liam." Grease was rolled through the swinging doors of the Emergency Room.

Liam ducked his head so he could talk through the glass partition. "If there are any questions regarding that young man they are to come to me." Liam handed the nurse his card.

12

The first thing the doctors told one of the nurses to do was shave his beard. He had a feeling that was going to happen. Hell! What a day. He had to say good bye to Sadie much earlier than he wanted to, he had to step into a punch that he knew would take him down, his beard was about to be shaved off, and his hair had been chopped off! A small part of him wondered what he looked like under all the hair on his face. The nurse first cut off his long beard and then she used an electric razor to get the curly growth down to stubble. The she brought out a razor and shave cream and carefully cleared his face of any hair. The poor nurse apologized the entire time and Grease felt sorry for her. When she finished he felt air touching parts of his skin that hadn't seen the sun in ages. Next the doctor sutured the cut under his jaw. The cut on his lip had stopped bleeding on its own and the doctor applied some hospital grade crazy glue to it.

When the doctor was satisfied he left the cubicle and he was wheeled to a regular patients room where they divested him of his clothes and made him put on a gown. He balked at first so the matronly nurse brought him a pair of scrub bottoms so he would be more comfortable. When he was in hospital attire he climbed into his bed exhausted.

Another nurse carrying a clip board came in and asked him questions that Grease knew were from the forms that he hadn't filled out at the front desk. By the time she had finished with the questions his head was pounding and he wished everyone would just let him sleep. He was getting ready to lose it when the questions stopped and the nurse left. Grease settled back on the bed and just as Grease shut his eyes an orderly came in to transport him to get his CAT scan.

Two hours later Grease was lying on his bed, in his room when the doctor came in and told him that he had a grade 2 concussion, but luckily there was no bleeding. The doctor told Grease he was going to be spending at least one night there, which Grease had figured on since he was all ready in a room.
After the doctor left Grease got out of bed and went to the bathroom. He wanted to see what he looked like with shorter hair and cleanly shaven. When he looked into the mirror the only thing he recognized was his eyes. Out of habit he ran his tongue over his teeth, once again relieved that they were still intact. His face was swollen on one side and he had an abrasion on his cheek. He tried to visualize what he would look like without the swelling, but he couldn't. He now looked at his hair. The sides were long, almost to his shoulders and hanging limply down the side of his face. He had hardly anything in the back. Cage had really done a number on him by cutting off his braid. He was so ugly!

"Mr. Prentiss?" Grease turned and saw a nursing assistant standing just outside of the bathroom door holding a stack of magazines. Grease colored; embarrassed that he'd been caught looking at him self.
"Are you okay?" The young lady asked him.
"Uh, yeah. I was thinking of taking a shower." Grease told her.
"Oh, you can't do that today. Maybe tomorrow. Please get back into bed. If you have to use the bathroom call me and I'll help you."

Grease looked at the slip of a woman and smiled. There was no way she could help him if he fell.

"Hey! I'm stronger than I look buster." She said laughing, reading his thoughts. "Now get back into bed."

Grease chuckled and let the little woman help him back to bed. When she got him settled, she stood back from the bed and shuffled through the magazines she was holding. Grease had a feeling she wanted to say something to him.

"If you have something to say, just say it." He knew he sounded terse.

"Oh gee, ok, I'm sorry. It's just, well I noticed you touching your hair. I can tell it was cut off. My sisters are all stylists."

"Yeah, I hadn't planned on it being chopped off." Grease wasn't mad at the young nurse. He was pissed that the whole thing had even happened.

"Well if you want. After you shower tomorrow, I can shape it for you. You know, even it out a little?"

"That's very nice of you. It looks like hell doesn't it?"

"It, well, yeah, it looks a little ragged."

"Okay, then. Yes after my shower tomorrow I would be much obliged if you would cut my hair."

The nurse was giggling and Grease recognized that she was now flirting with him. Well he must not be that ugly he thought. She left the room and returned with ice packs for his face. She gently placed one under his jaw and the other on his cheek. Then she patted his arm.

"Have a good night Mr. Prentiss I'll see you tomorrow."

Grease had a fairly decent night in the hospital. They had given him some meds for the incessant headache that was making him ill, so thank goodness his head wasn't pounding any more. The nurses had been replenishing his ice packs throughout the night and at one point in the evening one of the nurses said his swelling had really gone down. He had to be woken every couple of hours because of the concussion, but in between the wake ups he was able to get some sleep.

The next morning he still felt a little achy and he attributed that to falling on the pavement after being knocked out. His headache was not as bad as it had been yesterday, and he was excited that he'd get to go home today. After breakfast he asked if he could shower and a nurse walked besides him as he made his way to the shower located down the corridor. She showed him the cord to pull if he needed help. She then applied a large plastic adhesive over his jaw to seal the stitches from getting wet.

Grease took his time washing up and noticed a few black and blue marks on his shoulder and legs. He was aware at how easy it was to wash his now shortened hair. When he got out of the shower he dried himself off and rubbed the steam off the mirror to look at his face. His swelling had all but disappeared and except for the abrasion and the stitches he looked pretty normal. He kept staring at his face, looking at it from all different angles. He hadn't seen the skin on his face in years.

Grease put on a new gown and new scrub pants and headed back to his room where he brushed his teeth and used the plastic razor to shave, being careful of his stitches and the abrasion. He couldn't stop staring at his face. He looked older than the last time he'd been hair free, but he didn't think he looked bad. He'd forgotten that he had dimples when he smiled. When he finished his head was starting to hurt a little and he knew it was because he had exerted himself the doctor said that would happen. Grease climbed back into bed and closed his eyes.

He must have dozed off because a gentle touch on his arm alerted him that someone was in the room with him.

"Mr. Prentiss. I'm sorry to wake you." The nursing assistant stood next to his bed holding a spray bottle, scissors, and a towel. "I'm only working until noon today and I have my break now if you would like me to do your hair."

Grease smiled and saw that her name tag read Maureen.

"Thanks yeah, I would." Grease got out of the bed and settled on a wooden guest chair.

Maureen placed the towel over his shoulders and used the spray bottle to dampen his hair.

"I like cutting hair when it's wet. I hope you don't mind?"

"Nope that's fine."

"So how short?" She asked him seriously.

"I don't know." He told her honestly. "How about you just do what you think would look best, just not so short that you can see my scalp." Grease joked with her.

Maureen laughed and then set to work. Twenty minutes later she used her fingers to comb through his hair. Grease could see she was smiling.

"Am I done?"

"Yes. You have nice hair. You have a natural wave so it will curl up a little on top and on the sides."

Grease stood up and walked to the bathroom. What he saw in the mirror made him smile.

"Wow, you did a great job thank you."

"I'm glad you like it."

Grease walked over to his motorcycle bag that was on the chair near the bed and took out a twenty.

"Here." He said handing it to her.

"Oh no, I couldn't possibly take that."

"Please take it. You have no idea how much I appreciate not having to walk out of here today looking the way I did. "

Maureen took the bill and placed into her pocket.

"Okay, thank you. Well I have to get back to work. It was nice meeting you."

"You too and thanks."

After Maureen left the room Grease got back in bed and turned the television on. He was watching one of the shows that he liked where guys remade cars when he saw Tank walk into his room.

Tank looked at him and turned to walk out.

"Tank!"

Tank turned back towards the bed and stared at Grease before getting a huge smile on his face.

"You didn't recognize me?" Grease chuckled.

Tank shook his head not able to take his eyes off his friend.

"You have no idea how different you look." Tank told his friend with a small laugh.

"Yeah, it's pretty weird huh?"

"Not weird, just different."

Grease got out of bed and sat across from Tank in a chair. He ran his hand through his hair and got a goofy smile on his face, which made Tank laugh out loud.

"It's going to take some getting use to I bet."

"No beard, no long hair, do I look, you know whimpy?"

Tank burst out laughing.

"Grease I can absolutely promise you that you do not look whimpy at all. You look good bro, promise."

"Thanks."

They noticed someone coming into the room and Grease stood when he saw that it was Sadie. She did not even hesitate. His best friend for years hadn't recognized him, yet a girl he'd only seen a few times knew it was him the second she had seen him. Sadie walked right to Grease and buried her face in his chest as she wrapped her arms around him.

Grease rubbed her back affectionately. She wasn't crying but Grease felt the tension drain from her as he held her to him.

Sadie pulled back out of his arms.

"I was so worried." She told him softly. "Cage came back and nailed your braid up in the bar. Then he got shit faced as he told and retold how he took you down."

"Yeah, it wasn't pretty." Grease admitted.

"I called CC. She told me what happened. I have to work in a couple hours, but I had to see you." Sadie then remembered Tank was in the room and she looked from Tank to Grease uneasily. She had no idea how Grease felt about her and here she was telling the bad ass motorcycle guy in front of the clubs president that she had to see him. God, she was a drama queen she chastised herself.

Tank was watching the exchange quietly and then he excused himself telling Grease he'd be right back after he tracked down the doctor to give Grease his discharge papers.

Sadie took the seat that Tank vacated still a little worried that she had over stepped their friendship.

"I'm sorry I didn't mean to go all cuddly on you. I was just so relieved to see you were okay. CC didn't know the extent of your injuries."

"First of all you can go all cuddly on me anytime you want." Grease told her mischievously making Sadie grin like a silly teenager. "Secondly, I have a concussion, that's all. Tell me what happened? I take it Meeks got you back in time?"

"Yeah, wow, can that man drive. It was a perfect plan. When Cage got back to McDives I was already there waiting on tables. Cage was on a major testosterone high so he wasn't as mad as I thought he'd be. I told him the story about my mom having dead beat abusive men and I swear, I think he actually felt sorry for me."

"I'm glad he didn't hurt you. I thought about you all night."

"Awww, you better watch it tough guy or I'll start to think you're getting soft."

Grease chuckled. "Still a tough ass."

"So the new look?" Sadie said reaching out to touch his face.

"Is it bad?" Grease asked her honestly.

"You're kidding right?"

Grease cocked his head at her not understand why she had said that.

"Grease you're handsome."

Grease laughed out loud. "Sadie, come on."

"You are. Wait until all your women see you." She said softly.

Tank chose that moment to enter the room again.

"Grease we can go. The doctor signed your papers. I have the prescription for pain medicine and the instructions for home care.

"Thanks." Grease said standing up.

Sadie stood up with him and Grease looked to his friend. "Tank can you give me one minute?"

"Sure. I'll be in the hall."

Grease placed his hand on Sadie's cheek and she leaned into his touch.

"I'm so worried about you girl." The emotion in the room was palatable.

"I'll be all right Grease. I will."

"So you say, but it doesn't make it any easier knowing you're going back there."

Sadie placed a hand on Grease's large chest and leaned forward. Grease took the next step and touched his lips gently to hers. It was a short kiss but it meant everything to Grease.

"Stay safe Sadie."

"I will. Take care, tough guy." Then Sadie walked out of the room, taking Grease's heart with her.

Tank reappeared and reached into a brown sack he had brought with him.

"Here's a clean shirt. Now get dressed man. Everyone is waiting for us back at camp and I can't wait for them to see you."

"Sheesh Tank lets not make a big deal about my new look okay."

Tank laughed out right. Grease had no idea how handsome he was Tank thought.

After leaving the hospital they stopped into a Helena Pharmacy to fill Grease's prescription and then they headed home. Tank wanted Grease to stay at camp while he recovered, but Grease was adamant that he was staying at his cabin.

"Well we're stopping at camp first Grease. Lolly's upset that she yelled at you and from what I understand you were pretty rough on her too."

"Yeah, I was, but she was going crazy calling Sadie a whore and I was worried about Sweets too."

"I know and she knows that too."

"The plan worked Tank. Cage bought her spiel and he did not even give her a hard time. He was too busy bragging about how he took me down." Grease said somewhat disgusted.

"I'm glad Grease." Tank hesitated for a second. "I actually wanted to talk to you about that."

Grease shifted uneasily in his seat. He had a feeling he knew what was coming.

"Grease I've seen you fight in a ton of times. I know how good you are. You stepped into that combination."

Grease remained silent.

"Come on bro, talk to me. Why did you let him knock you out and what was all that shit about Romeo?"

Grease did not answer him right away. He was actually deciding what to tell Tank. If his identity got out he'd have to be relocated and he really didn't want to leave Happy. On the other hand who better to confide in than Tank?

"Tank what I tell you stays between us. Not even Sweets can know, okay?

"I'm not liking how this is sounding."

"Yeah, well I guarantee you're gonna like it even less in a few minutes."

"Shit."

"Yeah, shit." Grease echoed.

Grease began telling Tank his story and he carefully watched Tank for any reaction. When Grease finished telling Tank everything they were almost at camp.

"You've kept that all to yourself all this time?" Tank asked him.

"Had to."

"You're a friggin college graduate with an Engineering degree?"

"Yup, never used it, unfortunately."

"Are you still in contact with the US Marshall's?"

"When I first got to Townsend it was daily, then weekly, and now once a month my guy checks on me."

"Are you going to tell him about Cage?"

Grease thought about that for a second. "I don't think so. I'm hoping that stepping into that combination that he threw will make him rethink who he thinks I am."

"Who he knows who you are, Grease. He knew."

"Yeah, but Romeo had never been knocked to the canvas. He would never have walked into such a telegraphed punch. Romeo was good Tank."

Tank chuckled. "Grease is good too my friend. I bet when you fought that gorilla at McDives, he saw some similarities between you and Romeo."

"Yeah, that's what I think too. I don't want to relocate Tank. I like my life, my friends."

"Now I know why you can do everything so well, like when you put in my sliding door, and rewired the electrical panel at O'Brian Choppers, and how you can create those awesome choppers. You're a smart man Grease. I always knew there was something more to you than 'Grease-boy'." Tank said with a chuckle remembering when his dad had given Grease that name so many years ago.

Grease chuckled too. "I'm happy though. I got good friends. I like the outdoors. Montana is beautiful Tank. I can't imagine living anywhere else. I love working with my hands. My life is good."

"And now there's Sadie." Tank interjected shooting Grease a sideways glance.

"Yeah, Sadie. I like her."

Tank laughed so loud that it startled Grease momentarily.

"Ya think?" Tank added sarcastically with a grin.

"So you'll keep what I told you a secret right?"

Tank had stopped the truck in front of Sweets cabin since the truck belonged to Lolly, and he turned to Grease. "I'll be telling Tess, Grease. I'll never keep anything from her, but your secret is safe with us."

"Okay, I get that. Thanks and thanks for coming to get me."

The passenger side door opened and Sweets and Lolly practically pulled him from the truck. When he was standing in front of them they froze and Tank once again started laughing. Grease glared at him.

"Sorry man but that is not gonna get old."

"Your face, your hair?" Lolly stammered.

"Yeah, well I was due for a change." Grease retorted good naturedly.

"Grease you're so handsome." Tess told him honestly.

Tank looked at his wife and was not happy that she had called Grease handsome, which prompted Grease to laugh out loud at Tank's frown.

Lolly couldn't stop hugging him and she got all teary eyed when she apologized for how wild she had been.

Grease told her all was forgiven and she then told him she'd made him dinners for a week. Grease was getting ready to ask Lolly for a ride up the mountain to his cabin when Bettina came running towards the small group. When she reached them she froze and then she looked at Grease from head to toe before launching herself at him. She was blubbering into his shirt and Grease felt badly that she was upset, but he didn't want to hug her or even hold her. It didn't feel right.

"Grease what's the matter?" Bettina whined. "Oh my God, you have amnesia right?' Tank, he has amnesia?" Tank shook his head and Bettina looked back at Grease. "You know who I am?"

"Yes, Bettina I know who you are." Grease said slightly exasperated.

Bettina took a step away from him and put her hands on her hips. "So what's the deal then? Aren't I good enough to hug you in front of your friends?" She asked him indignantly.

Grease looked around at his friends who were uncomfortable with Bettina's little out burst. He sighed wearily and took Bettina by the arm and led her away from the group.

"What the hell Grease?" Bettina pulled out of his grasp to face him.

"I'm sorry Bettina. It's just that I've met someone that I like and I'm not comfortable hugging someone else. I know that sounds lame but it's the truth."

"Who Grease? I won't tell her that we fool around."

"We're friends you and me. Let's not wreck that."

"Friends with benefits?" Bettina tried one last time pushing her front up against his chest.

Grease chuckled and stepped back from her.

"Ha, nope just friends."

"Well when you tire of her you know where my trailer is." Bettina said to him totally miffed before walking away.

Grease walked back to his friends and Sweets got into the drivers seat of the truck while Lolly brought out the dinners she made. Tess brought out some cookies for him as well and after a few quick good byes and another thanks to Tank for picking him up at the hospital Sweets drove him to his cabin.

14

Three weeks had passed since Grease had last seen Sadie. His headaches had subsided and except for the unfamiliar melancholy emotion that he felt when he thought about Sadie he felt good. Joe stopped by twice to let him know that he had checked in with CC, and she had asked that Joe let him know that Sadie was okay. It made Grease feel good knowing that she cared enough about him to keep him posted.

He couldn't stop thinking about her. The nights were the worst because he knew she was working in the bar and near Cage. The thought that he might be touching her was tearing him apart.

The good news was that Shooter had faxed the papers back to Hawkins Realtors and Grease was now the proud owner of the property. He threw himself into remaking The Pen into his dream business. It was the only thing keeping him sane. Grease would put in sixteen hours a day, sometimes more, mostly so that when his head hit the pillow at night he was so exhausted that he would fall asleep before the images of Sadie working at the bar filled his head.

Grease had hired a couple of men from the club that wanted to make some extra money to help him remodel the bar area in The Pen into retail space. He had also decided to put in a small luncheonette.

He had drawn out plans that converted the main area of the bar to display all the motorcycle accessories he was selling. He had connected with a few reputable wholesale sales people and after he placed money into those accounts that he could draw upon, he was able to order the items that he wanted to sell.

He installed a big picture window in a corner of the old bar, and had tables put in for the little luncheonette that was separated with a wall from the retail space. The old bars kitchen was still in pretty good shape and his menu was simple; hamburgers, hot dogs, sandwiches, chips, french fries, pop, and milk shakes. He purchased three picnic tables and placed them out in front of The Pen where customers could enjoy the food that they had bought.

The back barn was where Grease would remake the motorcycles. It was being outfitted with two lifts, and tools that Grease had pre-ordered and were already lining the walls. The front of the barn had two huge sliding doors that Grease would open on really nice days. Customers could watch Grease working if they wanted and he hoped that may also bring in business. After much debate with all his friends chiming in, Grease decided to keep The Pen as the name of his retail store and sandwich bar. The back barn he would call Grease'd Hogs. Tank surprised him by asking if he would like to purchase some Harleys from the Townsend dealership to sell in addition to his rebuild business. Grease thought that was a great idea, but he didn't want to step on the clubs business. Grease agreed only if Tank and the club, would agree to co-own that part of the business with him. They decided to build a small area to the left of the barn and attach it to the main structure. This is where the Harleys would be displayed. People could walk into the barn through a side door and watch what Grease was doing behind the safety of a plexi-glass window on the right or turn left to go into the small dealership area. The dealership area was also fixed with a large barn like sliding door so the Harley's were very visible to anyone passing by. It was large enough to hold six bikes and Tank and the club would manage the sales and sales persons for that area.

The sun had set and all the workers had gone home for the night. Grease was in the back barn installing a vice when he heard a car pull up. The barn sliding doors were open and when Grease looked up he saw Joe stepping out of his Deputies car.

"Hey Joe." Grease greeted him, wiping his hands off on the rag that he had in his back pocket.

"This place looks great Grease. When do you think you can open?"

"I'm hoping in two weeks. I want to get the August riders. I know business will be slow in the winter for the retail store and sandwich shop, but if I get the word out, I'm hoping to keep the money coming in with remakes."

"Well it looks great."

"Thanks."

"The reason I'm stopping by is CC heard from Sadie today and she asked that we tell you that she was going to be at her Mom's tomorrow. Satan's Army is going to a rally in North Dakota. I think Williston she said. Anyway she is going to be here tomorrow and CC said that she was kind of weird about it, but she said to tell you."

"Weird?"

"Yeah, CC said she wasn't sure if you would even want to see her, but in case you did she would be in town around noon tomorrow."

"Thanks Joe. I appreciate you telling me."

Joe left and Grease had two feelings pummel him simultaneously. The first was a giddy feeling that he was going to see Sadie tomorrow and the second was of apprehension. Why would she think he wouldn't want to see her? Didn't that short kiss they had shared in the hospital tell her how he was feeling? Grease finished bolting the vice onto the wooden work table and locked up the barn. He smiled the entire ride up to his cabin.

15

When Grease got back to his cabin he spent some time straightening up just in case Sadie wanted to come up and visit. He had made a few changes since she'd been there last. He had put a television above the fireplace, but he hadn't used it at all since he was working on his place. He had also installed a sky light in his bedroom. He lay in bed looking up through the large plated window at the stars that still amazed him and wondered what Sadie was doing at that moment and if she would let him take her out on a date. It was after midnight when Grease finally drifted off to sleep.

Grease got up early the next morning and put in a few hours at The Pen. The shelving had arrived and Grease had to show the guys where to bolt them into the walls. By the time he had finished it was already 11:30. Grease hopped on his Harley and dashed home to shower and change.

When he reached Hawkins' he saw Sadie's beat up little car sitting in the lot and his heart thudded hard inside his chest. He couldn't wait to see her, and the unnerving thought that what he was feeling towards her may, very possibly, not be reciprocated. The unpleasant thought weighed heavily on him.

Grease walked into Hawkins' and smiled when the bell jingled above him. Nancy came out from the back room all smiles and greeted him warmly.

"Hi Grease, is everything all right? I see you working on the property everyday. It's the talk of the town." She told him animatedly.

"Hi, Nancy yes, everything is going well."

Nancy waited, thinking he was there on business.

When Grease realized this and he wasn't sure what to

do. Maybe Sadie was embarrassed that they were friends and didn't want her Mom to know? But then why tell him that she was going to be there?

"I was hoping to say hi to..."

Sadie emerged from the back room. She had on a sundress and cowboy boots. Her hair was pulled back into the long braid and she wore the bandana like the first time he had met her. She looked gorgeous and it took the air out of his lungs

"Sadie." He finished softly staring at her.

Sadie stopped just outside the door staring at Grease. She got a huge smile on her face.

"Hey tough guy." She said softly.

Nancy was looking back and forth between the two of them and then started grinning. She politely excused herself going into the back room. Sadie walked towards Grease.

When she was right in front of him she placed her hands on the sides of his face looking him over.

"Well you healed well." She said giving him a sweet grin.

Grease smiled at her and bracketed her cheeks in his hands moving her head side to side. "And you don't seem to be sporting any more bruises." He replied.

Sadie had let her hand fall away from his face, but it had found its way to his large arm. Grease's thumbs rubbed her cheeks gently and he leaned in giving her a tender kiss.

"I've missed you." He told her nervously.

"I've missed you too." She admitted. Grease felt all the weighty apprehension he'd been carrying around lift from his shoulders. She missed him!

He leaned in again and this time kissed her passionately.

When he pulled away her eyes were full of emotion and she touched her puffy just kissed lips with her finger tips.

"How long can you stay?" He asked almost afraid of what she would say.

"Four days. Then I have to be back."

"Would you have dinner with me tonight?"

"I would love that. It will give me time to catch up with my parents."

"Where can I come get you?"

"My parents place is near Pete's place on the lake. Have you ever been there?"

"Yeah, which house is it?"

"It's the one right after Pete's."

"Okay I'll pick you up at seven. Would you like to eat at Happy Endings?"

"Oh, I love that place. I sometimes dream of their cheeseburgers and fries, but."

"But what?" Grease asked apprehensively.

"I don't think I should be out in public. CC told me to lay low. You never know who I might run into."

"I get that. No worries I'll figure something out."

They were still holding each other and neither wanted to let go, but Grease knew he had a major errand to run so he gave her peck on the cheek. He turned to leave and then turned back.

"What's your favorite color Sadie?"

"Blue. What's yours?"

"Blue." He said with a grin.

Then he left the office.

Grease got on his bike and drove into Helena. Just outside of town was a car dealership. They sold all different makes and models of Chevy's and GMC's.

Grease pulled into the lot and walked up to the first sales person he saw.

"I want a Colorado, one that I can put my Harley up into the bed and strap it down." Grease told him. The young sales person smiled sensing that his customer had already knew exactly what he wanted.

"Okay, I have a couple on the lot. 2014 or 2015?"

"2015."

"Black, silver, or red?"

"Black."

"Okay, Let's go for a test drive."

"Nope just want the truck. I'll pay cash, but I want to drive away in it, in under an hour."

"Well okay. Let me get my manager." The sales man jogged towards one of the cubicles in the show room.

Grease drove his new black Colorado off the lot with his Harley safely secured in the bed. The truck was smooth riding. Four door and an extend bed that was already sprayed with the rubberized protective liner. The interior was tan leather and the seats were even heated. He knew he'd like that feature come winter. His next stop was a shop called Phantoms that installed tailgate lifts. Grease had already researched them and he was hoping this place sold Tommy Gates. Tommy Gates is hydraulic tailgates that lower to the ground and then lift back up placing your cargo even with the truck bed. It was a perfect business solution for him. He would be able to load his truck, when he was by himself, without lifting. It was a no brainer to have one of these installed. It would be how he would lift the Harley's he rebuilt into the truck to deliver them.

Phantom's had the package he wanted and when Grease asked if he could have it installed today the owner told him he could, but it would take a couple hours. Grease looked at the time and decided to run errands instead of waiting in the shop. He still had plenty of time to pick up Sadie.

Grease killed the next two hours by finding a full service barber shop where he got his hair trimmed and an old fashioned straight edge shave. Next he went to a department store where he bought a new pair of jeans, a belt and a new navy blue tee shirt. A tall thin lady tried to spray him with cologne and Grease politely declined, but then he decided to go check out the cologne section himself. He hadn't been into a store like this in forever. He'd led a very simple life and his clothing selection proved this. He purchased a small bottle of Dolce and Gabbana for men. He liked that it wasn't over powering. He didn't think he'd ever even worn cologne before. In college he just washed with Irish Spring soap and that was good enough for him. The last stop he made was to a florist where he purchased a beautiful bouquet of flowers that had every blue flower the store had mixed with some white small ones to complete the beautiful arrangement. Grease headed back to Phantom's where the owner showed Grease how to use the lift system and explained the weight limitations. It was such a cool feature on his truck that he couldn't stop smiling. Grease thanked the owner after paying him and handed him one of his 'Grease'd Hogs' cards.

"Hey I've heard of you. You did a custom chopper for my cousin who lives in Butte. He owns one of these businesses too. He used the chopper you built him to demonstrate how the tail gate lift works."

"Oh yeah. He was one of my first customers. Henry Phantom."

"Yeah, I'm Brett Phantom. It's nice to meet you."

The two men shook hands.

"Will you do one for my shop here?"

"Sure we'll need to talk specifics."

"Ok I have to buy a bike first."

"I can help you with that too." Grease said with a chuckle.

"Wow, I'm really glad you came in today." Brett said enthusiastically.

Grease explained how his shop in Happy would be opening in two weeks and that he should come down. He could choose a bike from the Harley's he'd have on site and then they would discus customizing it.

Brett said he would be down in two weeks and Grease headed back to Happy.

What a great day. He saw Sadie and he was seeing her again in about an hour. He'd bought a new truck and had the lift gate installed. He had also, probably made a sale for Tank and for himself. Their first joint sales for Grease'd Hogs.

Grease had just enough time to check on the shop, lock it up and change for his date.

Grease drove into Sadie's parent's driveway precisely at seven. He got out of the truck and saw Sadie heading down the stone steps towards him. He could see both her parents looking out from behind a pulled back curtain in the living room and he thought to himself. Yeah, I'd be curious too, if someone like myself were taking out my daughter.

Grease met her on the walkway. "I would have met your parents you know?"

"I know and thanks. I just didn't want to waste our time together chatting with the units."

"The units?"

"Parental units." She said laughing. "What's this?" She said waving at the shiny new truck.

"I need it for the winter months so I decided to buy it today so you wouldn't have to ride on my Harley."

"But I like your Harley." Sadie pouted.

Grease chuckled. "And I am very happy to hear that because I'll never stop riding it, but my little tough gal, tonight I'd like for you to sit next to me so we can talk easier."

Sadie gave him a huge smile and Grease placed his hand at the small of her back leading her to his truck. It was easy to get into even though it was a big truck. The running boards were silver and wide with rubber material right where the feet step. Grease assisted Sadie up into his truck and jogged around to the other side.

When he got inside the truck he picked up the bouquet of flowers that was on the front seat and handed them to her.

"Grease they are beautiful. Thank you."

"Blue." He said.

Sadie started laughing. "Yes, blue, very thoughtful. Thank you."

As they drove Grease told Sadie how he bought the truck and had the tail gate lift installed. He was smiling so broadly when he explained how he thought he'd also made a sale. Sadie loved how enthusiastic he was about his new business venture.

"Will you take me to your shop while I'm home?"

"Sure. It's coming together nicely. The store inventory and cash register is arriving tomorrow. I'm looking to hire someone for the store and the luncheonette. You interested?" He added teasing her.

"Oh no, but thank you. I think I'll stick with fettering out the bad guys and playing with my guns."

"I had to try." He chuckled.

Sadie turned to him in her seat. "Does it bother you Grease? What I do?"

Grease turned into Happy Endings parking lot and pulled to the back of the lot. He backed into in a spot that was slightly obscured with a huge bolder on one side and trees on the other.

Sadie noticed where they were.

"Um Grease I..."

Grease held up his hand and cut her off.

"We aren't going in. I'm going in, ordering our food and we're going to eat on my tailgate, like a picnic. Is that all right?"

"Yes, that's great. Smart man!"

"About your job Sadie." Grease had taken his seatbelt off and was facing her as much as he could from behind the steering wheel.

"I'm not going to lie to you. Your job us dangerous and I'm concerned for your safety. I know you love it though, and I'd never tell you not to do something you love." Grease's vice got real low and he placed his thumb pad on her lips. "But woman, I do worry about you."

Sadie unhooked her seatbelt and slid next to him. She curled her feet up underneath her body and angled herself so she was facing him.

"You are a very sweet man, Grease Prentiss. A very sweet, bad ass tough guy." Then she rose up so she could reach his lips with hers and kissed him tenderly. It took all of a second for Grease to wrap her possessively in his thick arms. He slipped his tongue into her warm mouth and stroked hers until they were seductively moving together. Sadie whimpered the kiss was so hot and Grease felt his jeans tighten over his groin. This woman set him on fire.

Grease pulled away and grinned at Sadie's annoyed face.

"Darlin, I could kiss you into next week, but I promised you dinner."

"Oh yeah, dinner." Sadie said trying to reign in her libido.

"So what do you want to eat? Should I go get a menu?"

"No, that's not necessary. I want the Happy Ending Cheeseburger, medium rare. French fries and a diet soda, cause I know you can't sneak me out a beer."

"Okay I'll order then come back out."

Eating their dinners in Grease's new truck turned out to be more perfect than they could have guessed. Their conversation turned into a question and answer session that had both of them grinning as they got to know each other on a more personal level. They liked the same kind of music, rock but did not exclude some 50's, 60's and blues. Their food choices were similar. Grease had ordered exactly what Sadie had except he had a coke. They knew they both liked peanut butter, pancakes, fried catfish, and any dessert.

Grease took their garbage to an outside trash can and then got back inside his truck.

"So do I have to have you home at a certain time?" He asked half jokingly.

"Not really. My Mom won't fall asleep until I'm in though so I don't want to be too late."

Grease smiled at her because he thought it was cute that she was twenty seven years old and she had a curfew. There was a ten year age gap between them but Grease didn't feel it. He hoped she didn't either.

"What? Too old fashioned for you?"

"Actually no. I like that you care about your parents."

"Oh, thanks. So what's next?"

"Well as much as I'd like to take you back to my place I have an idea."

"Okay you're the boss."

Grease laughed out loud. "Ha, I wish!"

Sadie knew he was referring to her being an in-charge type of person so she laughed too.

Grease ran back inside the bar and came out with a six pack of beer and then they headed out of Happy Endings parking lot.

Twenty minutes later Grease pulled off of the main road and followed a small dirt road up a windy mountain pass. The moon was full and the light cast shadows on the road making it seem magical. Finally he pulled off the road and drove over a grassy hill then backed in so the bed of the truck was facing a bluff looking over the town of Happy.

They got out of the cab, Grease grabbed the beers, and then he lowered the tailgate so they could sit on it.

"Wow I never knew this was here." Sadie exclaimed delighted that they could see Happy, a million stars, and the mountain range.

"Tank and I found it a couple years ago. I don't know who owns the property. We've come up here a couple times on our bikes. I love how you can see everything, yet it is so far removed."

"It's gorgeous. This was a great idea."

Grease opened the beers and they sat enjoying their drinks and the view. Neither spoke for a while and Grease actually liked that Sadie didn't feel the need to fill every silent void with senseless chatter.

Sadie finished her beer before Grease did and that made him chuckle.

"What? So I like beer. Sue me."

"Honey you can drink as fast or as slow as you like." Grease said with a husky sexy voice. "As long as you're with me and I get to watch you."

"Well darn, here you go being all sweet again." Sadie said giving him a soft knuckle to the arm.

"So Grease I actually wanted to ask you something."

"Shoot."

"I over heard a couple of the guys talking about when you and Cage mixed it and they, of course, didn't say this in front of Cage, but they thought you stepped into his punch. On purpose."

Sadie let her comment hang. She had seen Grease fight the first time he was in McDives. It shocked her that Cage had beaten him.

Grease shifted uncomfortably. "Nah, those guys don't know what their talking about."

"See, now that right there really makes me think they are right."

"What? Why?"

"Cause any other man would love to have some excuse for losing, but not you. You want to share why that is?"

Grease sighed. "Maybe someday Sadie, but not now okay?"

Sadie got up onto her knees and straddled Grease's lap. Her arms were draped over his wide shoulders and his hands held her hips gently.

"I like that." She said quietly before nipping her lower lip with her teeth.

Grease ran his hands up her sides and back down again.

"Yeah, and why's that woman?"

"Cause you said someday." Then Sadie gave Grease a kiss that told Grease all he needed to know before he took control.

The kiss was hot and warm and consuming. Grease's cock responded immediately and he lifted Sadie so he could adjust himself. When he lowered her she was perfectly aligned so that her female lips were resting on his length. She was wearing a skirt and a tiny thong so she felt every delicious inch of him.

Grease could feel her female heat through his jeans and as they continued to kiss he moved his hands to her rear and encouraged her to move on him. Sadie groaned and lifted her lips from his to pull in a much needed breath.

Grease took advantage of her exposed neck and sucked on her creamy skin. Sadie was rolling her hips and had laid her head into his chest as the sensations created by her sensitive bits massaging erotically against his filled out denim worked her into a frenzy.

"I got you Sadie. Let go baby."

"Oh God Grease." She panted as she continued to move on him.

Grease reached underneath her and ripped her thong from her. "I hope you weren't fond of those." He said gritting his teeth. Grease knew he needed to pleasure her soon or he was going to cum like a randy teen in his jeans.

Her bare mons rubbing against his denim encased length was too much and Sadie trembled as an orgasm rolled through her.

"Grease, I'm coming." She moaned into his tee shirt. Grease pressed upwards to increase the pressure and he felt her wetness soak into his jeans. He held her tightly as she floated back to earth.

Sadie leaned back and grasped Grease by the back of his neck and pulled him down for another emotional kiss.

"Thank you." She whispered.

"My pleasure."

"Actually tough guy, it was all my pleasure."

Grease grinned.

"Now you." She said shifting off of him cupping his thickness.

Grease gently took her hand in his and kissed her palm.

"No, not now. Tonight was all about you."

"Are you sure?"

"Yeah, baby. I'm good."

Grease wasn't really good. His cock was so hard that it ached. He'd been friends with benefits with his hand for the last month and he knew tonight he'd have to fist himself at least once if he wanted to get any sleep.

Grease pulled Sadie back with him so he was leaning against the back of his cab and she rested between his legs. They watched the stars blanketing the beautiful Montana summer sky and the moon as it crossed the sky above them.

Sadie had fallen asleep in his warm arms and Grease rested his cheek against her head. She was like a drug, a really good drug. He was so content with her in his arms. He loved talking to her. She was funny, smart, and sexy as sin. When he wasn't with her he was thinking about her. He was concerned that what he was feeling for her was more that what she felt for him. It was killing him that she was going to have to return to Norwalk.

Sadie stirred in his arms so he gently shook her awake. "Sadie, time to go. Your Momma's waiting up remember?"

Sadie opened her eyes drowsily and gave him a smile that had his heart pounding. "Oh, geez, I can't believe I dozed off like that. Sheesh, what a lousy date I am."

"You were great date. I enjoy spending time with you."

"I like being with you too."

"So when do you have to leave again?"

"Well I have a couple more days before the guys come back. I have to go to Helena one day for a quick debriefing."

"How is the investigation coming?"

"I really am making headway. I heard from one of the women that Cage has a chair in his house that he just got and it fits the description of one of the big ticket items from Brookstone that was on the truck. If I could see the chair I'd know for sure. I also over heard the guys talking to Cage about a test run. I think they were discussing what they are doing in South Dakota this weekend, but I'm not sure. Here's the thing. I don't think Shooter and Cage are that close. Shooter didn't go this weekend and he was annoyed that Cage was so insistent about the attending this rally. Sturgis is coming up and Shooter wants everyone to go to that and show a united front. Cage just does his own thing.

Whenever they are together they argue. Shooter was really loyal to Red and is taking the Presidency of the club seriously. From the limited time I've seen him he has actually been a good guy. He doesn't come to McDives that often, that's Cage's hang out. When he does he has been friendly and actually nice to me. I heard Shooter has been busy taking care of Red's wife and kids. Cage is the one I'm worried about. He has his own little group of followers and they are always meeting in secret."

"I worry about you Sadie."

"I know. I really think I'm close to closing this case though."

"Well I sure will be happy when you're done with it." Sadie leaned back and kissed him on his chin.

"So Grease, one; I'd like to see your business, and two, I'd love to go for a ride on your Harley."

"Done! How about tomorrow? I'll pick you up at 2, show you my shop and then we'll go for a ride."

"Perfect."

They rode back to Sadie's parents' house each lost in their own thoughts. Again the fact that Sadie wasn't a chatterbox appealed to him on a personal level since he wasn't a big talker either. As they started down the drive Sadie put her hand on his arm and asked that he pull over, which he did. He was concerned something was wrong. Maybe she'd been quiet because she was rethinking their date. He really sucked at this whole dating thing.

Sadie unclipped her seatbelt and slid next to him then she turned so her back was to the windshield and she was facing him.

"I'd really like to give you a good kiss good night without worrying that my Mom or Dad will be watching us out of the window. Is that all right?" Grease answered her by snatching her to him and melting his mouth to hers.

When they pulled apart Grease was once again granite hard and Sadie had a dreamy look on her sweet face.

"I could kiss you forever woman." Grease told her huskily.

Sadie didn't answer right away and once again Grease thought perhaps he had over stepped a first date protocol. He couldn't remember the last time he'd even been on a date. His M.O. was that he would pick someone up, or usually they picked him up at a bar, or party, they would have sex, then say good bye.

"Grease."

Oh boy, here it comes thought Grease.

"Would you like to have a sleep over with me?"

Grease started laughing. "Like when we were ten?"

"Yeah, only we would hopefully be doing adult stuff."

Grease chuckled. "What about Mom and Dad?"

"Well I was thinking I could tell her I had to go back to Helena, but stay with you instead. Am I being too forward?"

"First of all, not too forward. I like it when people speak their mind. Secondly, hell yeah to the sleep over." He grabbed her again and kissed her hard.

At precisely 2:00PM the next day Grease pulled down Sadie's parents drive. She had a backpack hanging from one shoulder, her hair was braided, and she wore a red bandana across her forehead. She had sunglasses, aviators, just like his and that made Grease smile. She had on long sleeve tee shirt advertising a bar in

Helena, tucked and belted into blue jeans that had rips in both knees.

Grease handed Sadie a helmet that he had borrowed for her.

"Hi." He said over the loud oversized muffler on his Harley.

"Hi." Sadie answered with a grin. She then gave Grease a peck on his cheek before climbing on behind him and putting on the helmet. When she was settled she grasped his athletic hips and Grease took off.

He drove into Happy and to The Pen. He had spent the morning there and was pleased with how much they had accomplished. He was excited to show his place to Sadie. He gave Sadie the tour and she admitted she was surprised at how much he had changed the place in such a short amount of time.

"Well I want it opened by the last week in July and I have to find reliable workers by the time we leave for Sturgis."

"You go to that?"

"Usually every year. Last year I didn't because of all the stuff going on with Tess and Tank. A few of our club members went though. This year the Border Bandits want to do a joint ride to and from. Tank wants us all to go to show solidarity."

"I heard it gets crazy there."

"Yeah, it can be nuts."

"Tank was supposed to tell Tess last night he was going. She is not going to be happy."

"Why can't she go?" Sadie asked indignantly.

"Relax Tiger." Grease chuckled. "She could, but she's pregnant. It's not a place for a pregnant woman."

"Oh. That's nice."

"Yeah, Tanks on cloud nine. He told me he never thought he'd find someone to settle down with, much less have kids."

Grease finished touring Sadie through the back workshop. She asked what the specific pieces of equipment she saw were for and Grease took his time and explained it to her. Sadie realized how patient he was being and her heart did a dance inside her chest. This man was not at all how he had seemed when she first met him. He was way smarter than he let on.

They walked back to his bike after Grease talked to Chucky, the man who had been his right hand man the last few weeks, about what still needed to be finished. Satisfied that everything would run smoothly while he took the afternoon off he and Sadie rode out of The Pen's lot.

Grease treated Sadie to glorious ride. He made sure he took her on all his favorite routes. Sadie would lean into him when she wanted to tell him something and Grease relished the contact of her up against his back. They drove up a steep incline on a dirt road and Grease pulled off and rode down a dirt road no bigger than a path. When they emerged from the thick woods it was into a clearing where the Elkhorn Mountain Range stood majestically in front of them.

Grease turned the bike off and he heard Sadie murmur 'beautiful.'

He offered her his hand so she could stretch her legs and while he was dismounting she took off her helmet.

"Grease, I grew up here and never knew this was here."

"Nice right?"

"Nice doesn't quite do this view justice." She chuckled.

They stood for a few minutes and then Grease got back on his Harley. Sadie walked back to the bike, but instead of getting behind him she got on in front of him, facing him. She had a mischievous grin on her face as she gently dropped her helmet onto the grass and placed her hands on Grease's shoulders. She lifted her thighs so they rested on top of Greases and pressed up close to his chest lifting her mouth to him.

Grease placed his hands on her rear and urged her closer before settling his mouth over hers. Sadie wrapped her legs around his hips and then she kissed him with such passion that they groaned simultaneously causing them both to separate and laugh.

Grease rested his forehead on hers. "Woman, what you do to me." He whispered.

"Ditto tough guy." Her voice was thick like she'd just chugged syrup surprising even her.

Sadie could feel his thickness through her jeans and she wiggled provocatively giving Grease a sexy smile. "Sweet heart, there is no way I can ride with a hard on and for some reason when I'm with you I'm always hard.

"Oh Grease." Sadie said with a mock southern accent. "You say the sweetest things."

Grease softly swatted her ass and lifted her from the front of him.

"Let's take this home." He said giving her a swift kiss.

Sadie swung off and remounted behind him. She put on the helmet and then Grease felt her lift the back of his tee shirt, kiss him on his back and place her hands underneath it and around him so they were just above his hip bones. Her hand felt so small warming his bare skin.

"You're not going to make this ride back to my place any easier are you?"

His answer was her settling her finger under his belt and into his jeans.

His cock stiffened inside his jeans as he thought how close her fingertips actually were to touching him. "Damn." He hissed to himself as his cock hardened further, and then he started his bike and headed home.

By the time Grease pulled down his drive he was so hard that he hoped he could get off his Harley. Sadie had kept up a tortuous sexy assault on him the entire ride. She had kissed his back, rubbed his skin with her thumb, and pressed her full chest against his back. He could feel her pebble hard nipples through his tee shirt. 'Well at least she's as turned on as I am.' Grease thought to himself.

He stopped his bike, helped Sadie off and gingerly got off himself. Then he picked Sadie up, threw her over his shoulder, helmet on and all. Sadie shrieked and started laughing. As he walked towards his front door Sadie managed to drop her helmet on the grass and then she wrangled free of her backpack letting that plop to the ground just outside the front door.

Grease kicked the door closed behind him and then he let Sadie slide down the front of his body letting her feel how she had affected him. When her face was even with his, her feet still a foot from the floor, he held her there so he could see her face. Sadie was smiling at him and she wrapped her legs around his hips and clasped her arms around his shoulders. Her crotch was aligned perfectly with his steel shaft and he grasped her rear and pressed her against the heat in his jeans.

Grease repeated himself. "Woman, what you do to me." He murmured softly.

"Ditto, tough guy." She murmured back.

"Bedroom?" He asked. He wanted to make sure they were on the same page where this was headed.

"Bedroom." She affirmed.

Grease held her to him as he walked them down the short hallway and into his room. He knelt on his bed still holding Sadie to him and knee walked them so they were in the center of his mattress. Then he slowly leaned over, using only one arm to hold her to him while leaving the other around her. Sadie knew he was strong, but it wasn't until just then that she realized how very strong he actually was. She wasn't a slight girl and he was holding her up effortlessly.

Grease gently eased her down onto the bed and then placed his hands on the mattress, bracketing her shoulders, holding his body away from her.

"Grease?"

Grease smiled at her and gently ran his index finger across her jaw line, down her soft neck, and down the center of her chest. Sadie's heart was pounding inside her chest and she wondered if he could feel it.

"You are so pretty Sadie." He whispered.

Sadie cocked her head to one side. "I think you may need glasses." She joked.

Grease lowered himself, but kept his weight off of her with his forearms.

"Why do you think that? Don't you know how beautiful you are?'

"Grease, I know what I look like."

"Maybe you're the one that needs glasses." He said kissing her gently. The kiss started out slow and sweet and became hot and consuming. Sadie's body was on fire. Her nipples were protruding uncomfortably rubbing inside her lacy bra. Her female lips were wet and she could feel her own heat. Grease was running his large hands up and down her sides and then he stopped at the sides of her breasts only to sweep his thumbs across and under her roundness.

Grease lifted from her and gazed into her eyes. "Last chance Sadie. Do you want this to happen?"

Sadie placed her hands on his cheeks and locked onto his eyes. "I want this. I want you."

That's all Grease need to hear. He smiled down at her and then sat back on his heels pulling her to a sitting position with him. Sadie laughed at his exuberant smile.

"We are wearing way too many clothes and I have been dreaming of seeing you naked."

Sadie colored. No one really wanted to see her naked. "Sadie, stop." Grease realized what she was thinking. "You have a great body." He said softly running his fingertip over her collar bone down to one distended nipple that sparked with his touch.

She reached for his tee shirt and started to push it upwards. Grease grabbed the hem of his shirt and pulled it over his head throwing it on the floor. Sadie ogled his thick chest. Grease was a big man. He wasn't chiseled and grooved, but he had muscles, thick slabs of rippling, 'do not mess with me', massive muscles. His skin stretched and bulged showing each muscle group as they worked with each of his movements that accompanied his tossing his shirt off.

Grease reached towards her and pulled her tee shirt from her belted jeans. He did this slowly. For some reason he wanted to take his time with her, make sure she was okay with everything they were doing. It was their first time and Grease wanted it to be special, memorable.

Sadie got up on her knees and pulled her own tee shirt over her head throwing it on top of Grease's on the floor. Their eyes were locked on each other and Sadie shivered with anticipation. She loved that Grease wasn't staring at her chest, he was looking her in the eyes and she knew it was because he was making sure she was all right. Sadie reached behind her back and unhooked her bra. Grease took the straps on her shoulders and slowly lowered them still looking in her eyes. Then he pulled the confining lacy article from her body and tossed it.

Sadie heard him suck in a breath when he looked at her breasts.

"Jessuuuss, you are gorgeous." He whispered.

He lowered his head and used his tongue to trace around her dark nipples. He heard her moan softly and he loved that he had barely touched her. Grease cupped one of her large breasts in his hand using his thumb to sweep across her nipple as he latched onto the other nipple and swirled the hard, distended flesh with his tongue. That prompted an even headier moan form Sadie.

Her head was back pushing her chest out towards him and Grease knew he had never seen a more erotic sight. Her braided hair was back off her glowing face, her back was slightly bowed, her slim neck was exposed and her luscious breasts were full and inviting. Her areolas were the color of a pale pink roses, lighter on the outside circumference that touched her plumb firm breasts and darkening in the same soft shade of rose as it stretched inward to her tight nipples.

Sadie reached for her own belt and unhitched it. Then she unsnapped the top rivet on her jeans and unzipped the zipper. The denim material slipped down her abdomen and sat low enough that Grease could see her pale blue underwear peeking out. He gently eased Sadie back onto the mattress and reached behind him to divest her of her boots and socks, and then he splayed his fingers over her soft belly and very slowly eased her jeans down over her hips. He moved his body to one side of her so he could take them off, and now Sadie was left with nothing on but her pale blue thong undies that had a small bow centered on the top. She had chosen her under garments with care hoping Grease would be doing just as he was doing now, taking them off of her.

Sadie reached up, hoping to take off Grease's jeans but he gently moved her hand away.

"Let me look at you first." He murmured. His eyes roved her full figure, but she didn't feel embarrassed. He was appreciating her, all of her.

Grease ran his fingers around her breasts moving them lightly across her sensitive nipples and then trailing them down to where she really wanted him to touch her. She knew she was wet and her clit was so engorged she bet he could probably see its outline protruding from her satiny thong cover.

Grease bent his head and kissed her clit over her underwear. Holy smokes she was going to cum and she wasn't even naked. Her whimpers slammed into Grease's chest like a sledge hammer. He wanted to own this woman. Make her body sing. He wanted to hear his name on her lips as she bucked underneath his mouth as he pleasured her boneless.

"Grease." She pleaded softly.

Grease stood up and took off his boots, socks, jeans, and finally his boxers. Sadie watched his firm body as it flexed. He was an Adonis and when he stood and she saw his ridged flesh standing tall against his abdomen she gasped. Grease stilled unsure of her reaction.

She then smiled at him coyly. "You are proportionate, aren't you tough guy."

Grease stretched out next to her on the bed run his hand up and down her body, massaging her breasts and trailing each pass downwards closer to her female lips. Sadie sat up quickly and took off her own underwear causing Grease to chuckle.

"I was going to do that." He whispered.

Sadie pulled Grease on top of her and felt his broad shaft settle against her slick lips. She pushed into him and felt the hum begin in her stomach. Grease obliged her with a few strokes that see sawed his length against her sensitive clit and Sadie moaned at the contact.

Grease began kissing her softly first on her mouth as his hands lit a fire as he massaged her chest, sides and hips. He slowly eased his way down her curvy form, nibbling and sucking her into a hot mess. When he reached her bare mons he kissed her tenderly on her fleshy lips while his large hands found perched on her thighs holding her limbs apart.

Grease settled his large body down on the bed in a comfortable position so he could take his time. He was dying to taste her. Her lips glistened and he could smell her sweet arousal. He glanced up at Sadie who had her hands on his head while her own head was bent back on the pillow exposing her neck. His tongue licked up and down both sides of her lips and Sadie's body tightened as she pressed her pelvis upwards seeking more contact.

Grease pulled away and Sadie swore softly in frustration.

"Baby put your hands above your head and hold that headboard for me."

"What? No. Grease I want to touch you."

"You will, I promise but I want to take my time loving you and you need to give me some control here."

Sadie had moved so she was propped up on her elbows so she could see him better.

"Is this, you know a Fifty Shades kind of thing?" She asked skeptically.

Grease chuckled. "No this is a Grease kind of thing. You need to give me control and with your hands on my head you will be trying to direct me."

"Well, yeah, duh."

Grease chuckled again.

"I'm going to make this memorable for you and for me. Trust me."

Sadie was smiling. She had no idea how memorable this was going to be.

"Okay Grease. I trust you."

"That's my tough gal." Grease bent down and gave her clit a quick swipe of his tongue causing Sadie to shiver.

"Now put your hands on the headboard and let me love you proper."

Sadie lay back on the bed and grasped the wrought iron, ornate frame with her hands.

Grease placed his strong forearms on top of her splayed thighs holding them firmly in place. He then opened her nether lips with his fingers and feasted on her silky slit. Sadie moaned and he felt her body try to move but he held her tightly in place. His mouth worked up and down her female lips licking and sucking her wetness. He knew she'd taste like heaven. He readjusted his fingers so only one hand held her open. His other hand he rubbed through her folds gathering her juices on his fingers. When he felt her opening he slowly and gently worked his large middle finger inside her.

He pulled his finger back and pushed it back in. She was really tight. He added another finger and heard her gasp. He peered up at her and saw that her eyes were closed and her lips were drawn tight. He pulled his finger out of her tight sheath.

"Baby, you okay?"

She didn't answer immediately and Grease was worried that she was strictly traditional when it came to sex. Vanilla. He hoped not.

"I'm good I promise. Please don't stop. I want this." Her voice was thick and Grease thought she sounded sexy.

He kissed her just above her mons before lowering to her sweetness again.

Grease tongued her into a frenzy and used his fingers to rim her vaginal hole. He had decided to bring her pleasure with just his mouth first. His lips and tongue were blissfully torturing her. He had been skillfully avoiding her clit, but her whimpering was too much and he wanted to hear her cum. He licked his way to her engorged nub and ran his tongue over the small piece of goodness before latching on to it and sucking hard.

Sadie erupted calling his name out over and over. Her body had bowed and he had to really hold her so she wouldn't twist away from his mouth. Grease gently grazed her sensitive clit with his teeth and he felt another orgasm ripple through her. She was drenched. Her core was coated and he knew it was now time for him to introduce his thick, rock hard cock into her tightness.

Grease kissed his way up her still trembling body settling between her thighs. He took her hands that were white from holding the bed frame of the rails and placed them on his shoulders.

"You ready for me darlin?" He asked sweetly.

Sadie's eyes were so round and filled with emotion. She pulled him down to kiss him and tasted herself on his lips. It was salty and sweet and she devoured his mouth with her own causing Grease to groan. Grease see sawed through her wet lips and then positioned his broad head at her entrance. Sadie lifted her legs to wrap around his hips urging him inside her.

"Grease now, please now."

He didn't need another invitation and pressed inside of her. Her wetness aided her to take him and he pulled slightly out of her only to push back in. He was trying to open her to his width. He knew some women had trouble taking his width.

"No. Grease, now. I want all of you now."

His hands were on her cheeks as he looked into her eyes and he smiled before kissing her and lifting back up.

"I'm big. I don't want to hurt you."

"Let me adjust to you when you're inside." She whispered grounding against his length.

Grease kissed the tip of her nose and held her eyes with his. Then he drove into her fitted tunnel. He felt the barrier as he tore through it, but he was surging quickly and couldn't stop. Her lips were pressed together and he swore as he saw her trying to keep the pained expression off her face.

He pulled completely out of her and rolled off of her as panic settled in his chest. She was a damn virgin. How the hell could she be a virgin?

"What the hell. Sadie?"

"I'm good. I'm good. Please come back."

"No. Shit you should have told me. Crap." Grease was sitting on the edge of the bed and saw the blood on the tip of his shaft.

"Fuck me." he murmured as he ran his hand over his face.

"Are you mad at me?" She whispered touching his back.

"Sadie you should have told me."

"I was afraid you wouldn't want to be with me." Grease turned towards her. Her face screamed vulnerable and he hated that he had hurt her.

"I don't do virgins Sadie." Grease told her with distain in his tone.

"Well guess what tough guy. You just did." Sadie retorted acidly as she rolled out of the other side of the bed reaching for her clothes.

"Fuck." Grease stood and walked to where she stood with her clothes wadded in her hands.

He took the clothes from her hands and she looked up at him. She knew he was going to be a little thrown, but not mad. Grease let the clothes tumble back to the ground and pulled Sadie to him. Sadie went into his warm embrace somewhat hesitantly. He held her to him and Sadie realized he was the one that needed the hug. She ran her hands over his wide back and began kissing his chest. His semi erect cock stirred against her belly.

Sadie pulled back. "I wanted you to be my first Grease." She explained softly.

Grease hesitated before answering.

"How have you not?"

He didn't even finish his question as Sadie cut in.

"Oh, trust me; I came close to losing it a couple times. My boyfriend in collage was a Christian and wanted to wait until he was married. Then when I got into Law Enforcement I was dating a guy and all ready to do the deed until I discovered the men in our unit had a bet to see who could get me into bed first. After that I had a heart to heart with Liam. He's my Godfather, did you know that?"

Grease shook his head.

"Well Liam warned me about fooling around or getting into relationships with men on the job. I've learned there are no secrets, and the rumor mill will cross over into different law enforcement sectors. I had a girl friend that got drunk, slept with a Deputy, and next weekend the State Troopers were teasing her about it. I've done other stuff Grease. It's just the main deed that eluded me. Once I thought about just picking up some random man and just doing it, just to get it over with, but then I decided to wait. I'd waited this long, I decided to do it with someone I care about."

"I hurt you Sadie. I never want to hurt you. You should have told me."

"I thought about telling you." She told him honestly as she ran her hands over his firm chest. "I was afraid you wouldn't want me."

"How can you doubt that I would want you? I just would have done things differently."

"Grease, for goodness sakes! I came twice! I know I was wet, really wet." It was a little unsettling to be so frank with him, but she knew it was important for Grease to understand.

"Is that why you told me to bring it? That you would adjust later?"

"Please don't be mad at me."

"You know I would never hurt you, don't you?"

"I know. I wanted to be with you Grease. I wanted you to be my first."

Grease sat her back down on the bed and then maneuvered them so they were lying down and facing each other so they could talk.

"I'm honored that you wanted me to be your first, but it's really important to me that you're honest with me, about everything."

"I'm sorry. I guess it was pretty underhanded."

"Ya think?" Grease scoffed. Sadie was starting to get pissed again. "Maybe I should have taken Cage up on his many offers? Would that have made you happier?" She started to roll away from him again.

Grease grabbed her shoulder and roughly hauled her back towards him. "I can't believe you fucking said that to me." He was irate and Sadie knew she'd gone too far.

Grease blew out and exasperated breath as did Sadie. Sadie could tell he was trying to reign in his emotions so she let him gather himself before speaking.

"I wanted you Grease. I've been waiting my whole life for someone special enough. Someone I trusted, someone I cared about. I'm twenty seven years old. Think about it. I've waited for someone for that long, and that person is you." She ran her fingers over his lips tenderly hoping he would soften. "I shouldn't have said that about Cage. I can't even stomach him touching me."

Grease cupped her chin looking into her soft eyes.

"I don't want anyone else touching you Sadie. It would wreck me."

"So I'm special to you too?" She asked quietly.

Grease leaned in and kissed her tenderly. His body responded to her softness. Her nipples tightened with her arousal and he pulled her closer to feel the hard points against his chest.

"You have no idea how special." He murmured into her ear, which had her squirming.

"Grease please make love to me." She whispered against his cheek. He pulled back and stroked her cheek with his thumb while looking into her eyes.

He kissed her again, this time with more passion and Sadie rubbed against his chest. He was hard again and he wanted her. The mere thought of Cage getting to be her first time set his blood boiling. He knew, in that instance he was going to love her so well that she'd be wrecked for any other guy. He had had sex with many women and he had always pleasured them, but this time he was going to love the woman in his arms so she would always remember him.

Grease held the back of her neck tenderly while the other hand roved her creamy skin. He took his of time idolizing her full breasts, dipping his head to suck the hard buds into diamond hard points. By the time he reached her mons she was a quivering mess. He spread her bent legs wider to accommodate his wide torso. Grease ran his fingers through her pink folds spreading her moisture around her sensitive pearly bud, which he then strummed rhythmically until she was bucking unabashedly into his hand. He worked his fingers into her sheath and felt her channel welcome him into her body. Sliding in another finger her channel gloved them tightly. Grease's cock was so hard he could hammer nails. Her slit wept knowing that he would soon be replacing his fingers in her creamy heat. Grease thumbed her clit and thumbed it using enough pressure to send her flying.

"Greaseeee." She whimpered as her hips convulsed and her channel tightened around his fingers. Grease moved so his big body was over hers and she opened her legs and cradling his hips with her thighs.

His smooth large dome was poised at her entrance and he could feel her heat on his satiny flesh.

His hands bracketed her cheeks as he held his weight off of her with his forearms.

"If it's too much you need to tell me, okay?"

Sadie nodded. "I want this Grease. You've already done the hard part. Make love to me."

Grease watched the myriad of expressions crossing her face as he sunk into her. He slowly stretched her by pushing in an inch, and then pulling back out. In, out, repeat. Her molten sheath engulfed his primed manhood and his greedy cock wanted to surge into that heaven, but this time was all about Sadie. He loved how she was gripping his shaft from within, trying to prevent his retreat. Grease sucked a tight nipple into his mouth causing Sadie to moan as more juices coated her velvety tunnel.

Grease released her nipple to nuzzle her neck. He knew he shouldn't leave a mark but he couldn't help suckling the soft skin on her neck. His cock was almost completely inside her lovely body, and he had to grit his teeth to stop himself from quicken the slow pace he had set. He wanted her boneless, mindless, and begging.

Finally, fully seated, his wide base rubbed against her clit and he heard her moan as her sensitive bit dragged on his skin. He pulled almost completely out, causing Sadie to whimper, but then he quickly pushed back inside of her, burying himself to her hilt.

"Oh God." Sadie moaned against his throat. Grease withdrew again and this time when he pushed back in he changed the angle of his thrust knowing his thick rim would drag over her g spot. Sadie groaned and clutched his shoulders. He felt her trembling; her core was rippling around his buried cock. He increased his pace making sure that each pass inside her creaming channel slid across her textured sweet spot, and that his wide base dragged across her engorged clit.

Sadie was moving with him now and making small mewling sounds that were sexy and needy. He knew the original pain that had accompanied their first joining was gone now. Her body was quivering, her distended nipples dragged across his chest and her hips met each one of his thrusts with ones of her own.

Grease felt his balls start to draw up, flagging him that he was going to cum. He reached between their dancing bodies as he continued thrusting into her and strummed her quivering clit. Sadie's fruition was instantaneous. She detonated underneath him. Waves of pleasure rolled through her as she moaned his name in a husky voice. Grease rocked into her again before allowing himself to spill. He pressed into her and his backside and balls tightened as he felt the heat rushing through his cock.

It was at that moment that he realized that he wasn't wearing a condom. He grabbed the base of his pulsing shaft quickly pulling out of her warmth. He pressed his length against her wet lips and his pearly white semen shot over her abdomen.

Grease grunted and the sound was a mixture of pleasure and pain. He see- sawed through her lips as his cum continued to burst from his slick dome. His thickness lay across Sadie's still sensitive clit and she reached between their bodies placing her small hand on top of his pulsing shaft and pressed it against her needy clit. Another orgasm, smaller than the last, but still bone melting rolled through Sadie.

Their breathing was heavy, as if they had just run a race. Sadie could feel his heart pounding against her chest and she wondered if he could feel hers. Grease held his weight off of her, but it was a chore. He felt like his insides had been cleansed and set free. He leaned down and kissed her eyes, nose and then her mouth before carefully rolling off of her.

He lay on his back as his breathing returned to normal and watched Sadie waiting for a reaction from her. Her eyes were closed and she had a tiny smile playing on her lips. She rolled towards him and perched her chin on his chest. Her hand lay on his bicep. It felt so right, so natural. Her eyes twinkled and his heart thumped in his chest.

"So tough guy, was it good for you?"

Grease chuckled. "I think that's my line, lady."

"Well since I actually have no prior experience I thought perhaps I should ask you."

Grease fingered a lock of hair that had pulled from her braid. "Darlin, best ever."

Sadie snuggled against his chest happily.

"So when can we do it again?"

Grease laughed out loud and kissed the top of her head. He then remembered that he hadn't worn a condom.

"I didn't wear a condom. I've never gone ungloved before. I'm sorry about that."

His voice had turned serious and had Sadie looking up at him.

"I'm on the pill Grease. Obviously not because of sexual activity, but because my job dictates that I be regular."

"That's good, but a condom also protects..."

Sadie cut him off with an, "Ohhhhhhh, right. Yeah, well I just got a clean bill of health two months ago."

"I was clean my last check up too." He hesitated. "And except for tonight, I have always worn a condom."

A snippet of sadness seeped into Sadie's as she thought about Grease being with other women. Her body tensed and she rolled from him uneasily.

"Hey." Grease rolled towards her placing his hand on her far hip drawing her into his frame. "I am sorry." He thought she was upset about not wearing the condom.

"No, we're good. I promise."

"So why the sad face?" He said trailing his finger across her lips.

Sadie sighed deeply and ran her fingers through his hair. "I'm going to be honest here, okay?"

"Always be honest with me." He said seriously and suddenly concerned.

"It actually bothered me that you're with other women. Like hit me in my gut, made me nauseous, bothered me."

Grease smiled down at the angel in his arms. "Sadie, I'm no saint. I've had my share of women, but I haven't been with anyone for weeks."

"Weeks?"

"Yeah, weeks."

"You, um, are usually with women a lot then?"

"I don't know what you think a lot is, like I said I'm no saint, but not lately I haven't been with anyone. When I came home from the hospital, I even told a woman, that I'd been with before, that I didn't want her to hug me because I liked someone else and it didn't feel right."

A small smile spread across Sadie's pink lips and she leaned up and kissed his mouth.

"I like you too, Grease." She said back to her normal jovial persona.

Grease leaned over her and kissed her tenderly. His lips were warm and soft against hers and she felt his tongue slip inside to stroke her own. It was a meaningful kiss, full of honest emotion. Grease ended the kiss and leaned up cupping her chin in his strong fingers.

"Sadie, right now, since we are being honest, I have to confess, if I ever saw you with another guy it would destroy me. The thought of you going back to Cage, well, it's not a good feeling."

"I wouldn't want to see you with anyone either Grease. I'm just not in a good place right now to make any demands of you. I have to finish this case."

"I know and it's killing me. When are you going to Helena?"

"I need to leave the day after tomorrow."
"Will you stay with me until then?"
"Yes, I'd like that." Sadie snuggled against him.

16

They didn't sleep much that night. When they weren't making love they were talking. Grease had unbraided her long beautiful hair and ran his fingers through her silky tresses as they spoke. During the sexual down time Grease found her intelligence to be refreshing. She was easy to be with and her fun personality bubbled out as she described growing up in Happy. While they talked Grease realized he was post-coitus cuddling and he couldn't remember ever doing that or even wanting to.

Sadie couldn't stop touching him either. She loved having Grease inside of her. Sex with him was better than she had ever imagined. He was huge and she felt so connected to him when they were making love. She learned that his eyes betrayed his emotions and she was beginning to be able to read him just by looking at them. He never failed to pleasure her, and treated her to positions that she'd only read about in her romance novels. He took her on the edge of the bed while he was on his knees suckling her nipples. Once he lifted her thighs over his shoulders and hammered into her driving her wild, and the last time, she had ridden him while he sent her into a cataclysmic climax that had her gushing as he fingered her clit.

Exhausted and deliciously sated Sadie fell against his broad chest. They were sticky from cum, sweat, and her juices.

"Tough guy, what are you doing to me?" She whispered into his neck.

He began to soften inside her and he rolled her to the side while holding the condom on his relaxing length. He disposed of the condom and then plucked Sadie off the bed holding her in his arms and walked her to the bathroom.

"Hey." She mumbled I was comfortable mister. Grease chuckled.

"Woman we need to shower."

"Together?"

"Yup, a quick rinse off." They walked to the bathroom hand in hand.

"Don't get frisky on me I didn't bring a condom with me." He told her with a silly smirk.

Sadie laughed and allowed for her strong man to lead her into the tiled stall. Grease turned the shower head towards the wall and turned the water on. When it was warm enough he moved the head so the stream splashed against their bodies.

Grease soaped his hands and massaged her curvy form with the suds before rinsing her off. Sadie wished he would continue rubbing her since he had succeeded in torquing her up again. He had magic hands that man! Sadie soaped up her hands and ran them over his solid body. She captured his cock with both her hands and felt it fill with desire. She couldn't take her eyes off of the magnificent sight as it swelled in her soapy hands.

"Sadie." Grease murmured thickly.

"You are so beautiful Grease." Sadie told him as she knelt and kissed his satiny smooth head.

"Baby." Grease looked down at the woman that had stolen his heart as she grasped his solid shaft between her hands. She rotated her hands in opposite directions working them up and down his steely length and then she began licking his broad head. Grease widen his stance so he wouldn't fall over. A few women had tried to satisfy him orally, but his width prevented them from being noteworthy. Sadie however was blowing his mind. Her lubricated hands were sliding up and down his cock with ease and her mouth was working him hungrily. She licked and sucked and moaned around his head. She teased the sensitive skin under the edge of his dome with the tip of her tongue, and just when he thought it couldn't get any better she took one hand off of his heated shaft and gently rolled his balls in her soft palms. Grease groaned and shot his seed. Sadie sucked his head into her mouth and captured the spurting essence as she continued to massage his pulsing cock.

Grease had to hold the walls of the shower so he wouldn't collapse. His woman had just given him two first times in one night. He had been her first and she had given him a very memorable blow job.

Grease sunk to his knees and pulled Sadie to him. He held her against him and Sadie felt his heart pounding against hers.

He composed himself enough to speak. "That was spectacular Sadie. Thank you."

Sadie smiled up at him as the water splashed over their bodies running down their faces and shiny bodies.

"I've never had that done to me where I came before." Sadie pulled back to look into his eyes. "So I gave you a first time?"

Grease wiped the sluicing water from her face. "Yeah, we're having good first times here tonight aren't we?" He whispered to her before settling his lips over hers and kissing her passionately.

"I like having firsts with you." She replied softly.

After the shower they made peanut butter sandwiches, shared a glass of milk and fell back into bed. Sadie turned on her side and Grease pulled her body against him so her back was to his front. His one arm she used as a pillow while his other arm wrapped around her. His hand was splayed against her stomach holding her possessively to him. Sadie felt so safe right then, so cared for. She knew that this was that special feeling her girl friends had talked about, that she had read about. Had she met her happy ending?

When Sadie awoke she knew immediately that Grease wasn't in bed with her. She sat up and listened hoping to hear him in the bathroom or kitchen, but it was quiet. Then she saw the note on the pillow.

Sadie

Gone to town to check on the shop. I'll be back shortly.

Grease

Sadie smiled at the simple note and lay back on the bed. The sheets around her smelled like Grease and sex. She pulled the top sheet up to her nose and inhaled the musky scent remembering the magical night they had shared. Sadie drifted back to sleep wishing his arms were still wrapped around her.

She was awakened as gentle kisses tickled her forehead and moved down her face, and then her neck.

"Mmmmmm." Sadie ran her hand through his hair. "You're back."

Her nipples were visible against the white sheets and Grease continued to trail his giving lips lower over her responding body.

He suckled a path that had her squirming with anticipation.

"Missed you." was all he said before he pulled down the sheet that was acting as a barrier.

Grease ran his tongue around her dark nipples leaving them wet and achy before sliding lower. Sadie opened her thighs so he could settle between them. He kissed her belly button and rained light kisses to the juncture of her thigh.

"Thought about doing this the whole time I was gone." He said huskily. His hands held her legs open and his fingers swept through her already slick lips gently parting them. Grease thrust his tongue into her channel causing Sadie to buck against his mouth. He then flat tongue licked her until he reached her yearning clitoris.

Grease latched on to the pearly button and ravished it with his tongue. Sadie moaned and felt the sizzle of an orgasm begin in her sensitive nub as Grease vigorously French kissed it. Sadie exploded calling out his name as her body became ridged from the electric release bursting through her body. Her eye lids fluttered and her back began to bow off the mattress, even her toes curled as the potent orgasm gripped her soul.

Grease loved how she responded to his touch and he realized she was pulling on his shoulders.

"Grease I want you in me, now. I need you." Her voice was low and sounded so sexy. Grease kissed his way up his body and he felt Sadie wrap her legs around him trying to line his erect cock up with her warm channel. She reached between them and guided him to her opening and when he sank into her they groaned in unison.

Sadie had her fingers wrapped in his short strands of hair and she used her grip on him to pull him down so she could kiss him. Grease placed his forearms under her shoulders and while he kissed her sweet mouth he drove into her, claiming her as his own. Once again Grease had her teetering on the edge of a climax and when he knew he couldn't hold off much longer he separated their bodies slightly so he could reach between them. Sadie captured his hand with her own and guided his hand with hers to her needy bud, where together they rubbed her into an epic orgasm that had her crying out. Her core gripped his cock tightly as she shook uncontrollably beneath him. It was such an erotic act that Grease's own unbridled orgasm sped through him while Sadie was still trembling. His cock pulsed into her rippling vagina as he came harder than he ever had before.

Their bodies were lightly misted from sexual exertion and they lay quietly not wanting to break the special aurora that was surrounding them. Grease moved off of Sadie, his large cock sliding out of her warmth. Sadie turned to him wrapping her arm over his chest and lifting her leg to rest over his hip.

"I like having sex with you." She murmured drowsily into his chest.

"I like sex with you too." He kissed the top of her head. "I didn't put a condom on and I didn't pull out Sadie."

"I like it better that way. I'm not worried Grease. You shouldn't be either, okay?"

"Yeah, I should have wrapped, but woman you make me lose my mind."

Sadie snuggled closer. "I like that." She said kissing his chest.

Grease stroked her warm back. He really did lose his mind around her. He had always been in control and it worried him that the woman that finally makes him want to be exclusive was unable to give him that.

"Sadie?" His voice hinted at his anxiety and Sadie perched up on her elbow so she could see his eyes.

"You okay, tough guy?" She said stroking his cheek.

"Is this just sex? You and me?"

Sadie scrunched her brow unsure what had prompted his question. She knew that for her what she and Grease were enjoying was far from just sex; even if he was the first man she'd ever had it with.

"It's not just sex Grease. It's really good sex." She tried to joke. His expression did not change and Sadie sighed worried that this impeding discussion was going to change how he treated her.

"Oh, you're serious?" She said tapping his sweet lips with her index finger. "Okay, you want honesty, here goes. I like everything about you Grease. I've been attracted to you since I saw you kick that Satan's Army brute in McDives. You do something for me that I've never felt before. Is this just sex? I've only had sex with you, but I can honestly say it's more that just physical when I'm with you. I feel a connection. Is that weird? I like talking to you. You make me laugh. I feel safe with you." She paused sliding her palm to his cheek again. Grease was gently twirling a strand of her hair around his fingers. He looked so serious that Sadie felt trepidation build within her as the silence stretched between them.

"Sadie. You make me want things I've never even considered before." His fingers left her hair and he reached for her face sliding his large hand to palm her cheek. "I love having sex with you, but you're right we have a connection and it's not weird. It's a little unnerving but it's not weird. "

"Unnerving? That doesn't sound good."
"If you were living here and I knew I could see you every day and we could build on this I'd feel better."
"Oh."
"I don't even know when I'll see you again. That's unnerving. I think about you all the time. It's not just sex for Sadie. It's more. That's unnerving. I'm worried about you going back to Cage. My heart hurts when I think of him touching you. That's unnerving." Grease smiled at her sadly.
"I have to go back. You know that."
"I do."
"What do you want Grease? Do you want me to leave? You're scaring me."
Grease shifted and gently pushed Sadie onto her back. He rolled on top of her careful to keep his weight off of her. He bracketed her face with his hands and looked into her beautiful green eyes.
"I'm scaring me." He admitted softly. "I do not want you to leave. I'm trying to tell you that I care for you Sadie, and what I feel is not going away just because you do. Do you get that?"
Sadie feathered her hands through his hair and smiled at him. He was so handsome and laying his heart out to her only endeared him to her more. "I get it. I have a job to do Grease, but it's just that, a job. What I do around Cage is a means to an end. I'm going to miss you too, a lot."
Grease leaned down and gave Sadie a kiss that set off a herd of butterfly's into her stomach.
"Wow." She said breathlessly. "That was a very memorable kiss."
Grease was smiling again and Sadie ruffled his hair playfully.

"So what's on the agenda to day, Tough Guy?"
"I want to take you for a swim in the creek outback and then Tank said they are roasting a pig at camp tonight. Would you like to go?"
"Sure, sounds fun." Grease rolled off of her and helped her out of bed.

17

They spent the afternoon splashing in the creek behind Grease's cabin and then napped on the grassy ledge before heading back to shower for the pig roast.

As Grease assisted her on to the back of his Harley Sadie confessed to him that she was nervous about meeting his friends.

"Well you've met Tank and Lolly."

"Yeah, Lolly was not a happy camper if I remember correctly." Grease chuckled at her memory.

"She's the best Sadie. She was really upset, and well, she thought you were just a piece of tail."

"Ha, a piece of tail, that's awful."

"You'll love Tess. She is sweet and kind and wait until you see how she has Tank wrapped around her finger."

"Yeah, just meeting him I can't see anyone ever getting the upper hand on that man."

"Well Tess does. Sweets is Lolly's husband. He's one of my best friends, along with Tank. I'm not sure who else will be there. Someone of the guys that rode with me to get you might show."

"What about girls?"

"Girls?"

"Like the women you have slept with, girls."

"Um, yeah there may be a couple of old hook ups there." Grease was thinking about Bettina and Gretchen. Bettina especially would think nothing of letting Sadie know she'd been with him. Gretchen wasn't vocal, but if Bettina put her up to something she'd go along with it.

"Ugh, I'm already jealous, shit!"

"You have nothing to be jealous of Sadie. You know how I feel about you. When I was with them it was sex, just sex."

"Not helping!" She whined as he took off towards camp. When they got to the beginning of the camps drive Sadie tapped Grease on the shoulder and told him to stop.

He pulled to the side and held the Harley up with his strong legs as he turned to see what she wanted.

"Grease I don't think I should go."

"Because of the other women?"

"No, no. I have to keep a low profile remember? What if I see someone from Satan's Army while I'm with you?"

"Sadie, The Steel Horse Cowboys don't run with them. We avoid them if possible."

"Yeah, but your paths do cross sometimes, right?"

"On occasion. You said they are going to Sturgis and so are we." Grease then realized what Sadie was trying to tell him.

"Sadie you aren't going to Sturgis with them are you?"

"I, um, I'm not sure. Cage hinted that he was bringing me."

"Shit."

"It could be where I finally get my proof Grease."

"Sadie are you riding behind him?"

Sadie knew that riding behind a motorcycle club member was a big deal. It showed ownership.

"I think so."

Grease cut his engine.

"You know I'll be there right?"

"Yes."

"Shit."

"Can we talk about this back at your place please?"

"Yeah, okay. Stay here for a minute I need to tell Tank we aren't coming." Grease helped Sadie off the bike and tore down the drive. Sadie was leaning against a tree when she heard a motorcycle coming from the other direction. A large black and blue Harley pulled up beside her and a really handsome man with dark brown hair. The large man stopped next to her and took off his aviators and Sadie saw the greenest eyes she'd ever seen. They were mesmerizing and she realized she was staring at him.

The man was smiling at her and he had an adorable dimpled grin that Sadie knew would put most girls into a gushing mess.

"Hey pretty thing. You lost?" His voice was deep and gravelly and sexy as sin.

"No, I'm waiting for someone." she said cautiously. She heard a motorcycle coming from down the drive and watched as Grease rode towards them. He was so big on his Harley. His short hair whipped in the wind and she could see his handsome face had a small smile on it. He pulled up and took his sunglasses off.

"Dak, man good to see you." Grease said slapping the other rider on the shoulder.

"Grease, Holy cow. You were hiding that handsome mug under all that hair. Who knew? Shit we will really scored with the babes now." He said laughing. Grease saw Sadie frown and felt badly that Dak was bringing up what he knew already bothered Sadie.

"Look what I found out here." Dak said motioning to Sadie. "This pig roast just got way more interesting." He said chuckling.

Grease extended his hand to Sadie who took it right away and mounted up behind him.

Dak was staring at them opened mouth and Grease laughed.

"Catching flies, my man." Grease teased him.

"She's with you?"

"She is."

"Lucky bastard. See what losing all that hair did for your love life?"

Grease laughed out loud.

"Dak this is Sadie. Sadie this is Dak. He's one of my best friends. He owns a gun shop and shooting range outside of Townsend."

They shook hands.

"You aren't coming to the roast?" Dak asked still looking at Sadie.

"No, not today."

"So much for the pig roast being interesting." Dak grimaced.

"Dak are you going to Sturgis?"

"Of course! Can't wait. I heard Tess wants to go." Grease laughed. "Yeah, that's not happening."

"You're going right?"

"Yup, my shop will be up and running and Tank wants us riding strong. We're riding with the Border Bandits."

"I heard. Should be wild. Bought a new box!" Dak said with a laugh as he began to roll away towards camp.

Sadie leaned up so Grease could hear her. "A box?" Grease turned slightly so she could hear him. "A box of condoms. He'll probably use the whole box, too."

"Oh." She paused for a second before continuing. "Grease can you drop me at the real estate office?" Grease turned back towards her. "You want to see your Mom?"

"No, my Mom and dad are away. I left my car behind their shop. I want to get it."

Grease nodded and took off. He could tell something was bothering Sadie. She was still holding him gently as they rode, but it wasn't as intimate as usual. He dropped Sadie off and pulled her to him after she dismounted.

"I'll meet you at my cabin?" he asked.

"Yes, I'll follow you up."

He kissed her again and he could tell just by her hesitant kiss that something was up. He wasn't sure if Dak had maybe said something to upset her but he sure as hell was going to find out.

When they got back to Grease's cabin Grease hopped off his bike and opened her car door for her. When she got out of the car he closed the door and then backed her up against the car. Corralling her between his large body and the car frame.

"What's the matter Sadie?"

Sadie had her hands on his chest and she was looking down. She was upset, but she didn't think Grease would pick up on it. She smiled up at his and pressed her soft body against his firm chest.

"Nothings the matter."

Grease held her chin gently with his fingers. "Darlin, honesty remember?"

Sadie signed. "I'd rather not say."

"Talk to me Sadie."

"Crap." She paused. "Okay, are you taking a box too?"

Grease didn't answer right away and the tightness that Sadie felt wrapped around her heart ached.

Grease leaned down and placed a small kiss on her lips. "No baby, no box for me unless you're riding with me that is."

Sadie fell into his arms and held him tightly. "You know I can't."

"Come on we have to talk about this."

He led Sadie to the back of his cabin and he sat on a chair pulling Sadie down on his lap.

"Sturgis is the biggest, nastiest, wildest, bike rally Sadie. I'm sure you've heard of it."

"I've been doing a little research."

"Honey, it gets wild."

"I know."

"If you ride with Cage he is going to be expecting to be with you physically. I don't know how you can hold him off without getting hurt or blowing your cover."

"I realize it's going to be dicey Grease."

"Sadie if I see you with him, especially if he's got his hands on you... I just don't know. It's asking a lot."

"Too much?"

Grease was quiet. "I've never had a reason to ever be jealous about a woman before. I don't know. Just thinking about you riding behind him bothers me."

Sadie feathered her fingers through his hair.

"It doesn't have to be difficult, Grease. This, you and me, I'm not expecting anything from you."

"What are you saying?"

"I'm saying I can't offer you more than what we have now. Not until this case is over."

"You want to be with other men? With Cage?"

"No, I'm not planning on being with anyone romantically. You've set the bar pretty high for who ever comes along next. As much as it kills me to say this." Sadie sighed sadly. "I understand if you are with other women."

"You want me to be with other women?"

"It will kill me, Grease. I see red just thinking about it, but I have to play up to Cage, and that means riding behind him to Sturgis and who knows what else. I can't ask you to wait for me."

"Maybe you'll wrap up your case before Sturgis? It's a few weeks away."

"Possibly."

"I have to go to Sturgis Sadie. I have to keep Tank safe. That's my job in the club."

"Will you bring a girl with you Grease?"

"No I never do."

"You pick up girls there?"

"You want to really know the answer to that?"

She nodded and he saw she was biting her lower lip.

"Normally I'd need a box too."

"Ugh."

"You've set the bar pretty high too Sadie. I know we aren't in a relationship, you know exclusive, but right now I don't want to be with another woman. I want you."

Sadie turned in his arms and straddled his athletic hips. "Ditto tough guy." She placed her lips close to his and with tip of her tongue traced his lips. He could feel her warm breath he slipped his own tongue out to meet hers causing them both to groan. Just then they heard a vehicle coming down Grease's drive. Sadie pulled back looking questioningly at Grease.

"It's probably Lolly and Sweets. Lolly said she was going to bring us dinner."

"I didn't think she'd ever even want to see me again?"

"She was upset. She wants to apologize."

Sadie and Grease walked around to the front and sure enough Lolly and Sweets exited Lolly's truck and Sweets was carrying an enormous bag.

"Hey." Grease greeted them.

"We have dinner!" Sweets announced proudly holding up the bag.

"Come on in."

Sweets and Grease headed for the door and as Sadie started to follow Lolly gently grabbed her elbow to hold her back.

"Sadie, I wanted to apologize for calling you all those nasty names."

"It's fine Lolly. I can't imagine how upset you were."

"I was pretty out of my mind, but I am sorry."

"Apology accepted and for the record I am so sorry Sweets was taken. I know it was because of me. I didn't mean to cause any trouble."

"I know you didn't."

The women began walking towards the door.

"Sadie, one more thing."

Sadie stopped walking Lolly sounded so serious.

"Grease is like a brother to me. I know you're special to him. "Please don't hurt him."

"I won't Lolly. I care about him, a lot. We were just talking about this. I have to finish up my undercover work with Satan's Army, and I'll be going to Sturgis."

"With them?"

"Yeah."

"Honey, Sturgis is wild."

"I know Grease and I have been discussing this. The thing is I'll be riding with Cage."

"Oh no, you can't."

"I have too."

"Sadie that's a big deal."

"I know, trust me, I know."

"If Grease sees you with him, even if he knows you're just acting it will kill him."

"He said that."

"Oh I do not have a good feeling about this Sadie. You need to rethink this. Unless you don't care about Grease, because watching someone you care about riding with and being with another man, well that's just hurtful."

"Lolly I know. This sucks, but I can't not go, and Grease has to go. Maybe we won't even run into each other."

"Yeah, maybe." Lolly didn't sound too optimistic though.

The two couples enjoyed the dinner that Lolly had brought up in Tupperware containers, leaving the leftovers with Grease. After they cleaned their dishes they went outside to Grease's patio. Grease once again pulled Sadie on to his lap and Sweets did the same with Lolly.

The stars were out blanketing the sky with their twinkling luminescence. It was gorgeous and they sat back enjoying how beautiful it was. Sadie loved how Grease was rubbing her arms and she melted into him leaning her head against his strong shoulder. Grease looked down at her a small smile played over his face. He then kissed her forehead tenderly and leaned his cheek against her head.

The mosquitoes began to alight and Lolly stood up declaring she was tired and getting bit. Sweets stood up next to her and gave her behind a gentle swat. "My woman hates bugs." He said laughing. "We'll see ourselves out."

Grease extended his hand to Sweets and then to Lolly. "Thanks for bringing us dinner."

"Yes, thank you." Sadie echoed.

"No problem, enjoy. Sadie I hope we see you again." Sweets said.

"Uh, yeah but not in Sturgis." Lolly said honestly.

Lolly!" Sweets admonished her thinking she was being rude.

"No, she's right Sweets. She'll explain it to you." Sadie said sadly.

"Well shit, that doesn't sound good." He said as they left.

"You told Lolly?" Grease asked her when they were alone.

"Yes, it just came out after she asked me not to hurt you."

"She said that?"

"Yeah, she says you're like her brother."

"Yeah, we're close. I spend all my Holidays with them."

"Well she's worried about you seeing me in Sturgis."

"Yeah, I am too."

"I'm sorry Grease. I really am."

"I know Honey. I'm just going to hope you get lucky and wrap it up before. Then I want you to ride with me."

"I'd love to go with you. I'm not sure about the wild stuff. I'd probably have to beat the women off you with a stick."

"Nah, they'd see how I would be looking at you and they'd know they didn't stand a chance."

Sadie kissed his chin.

"I'm going to miss you Grease."

"Ditto baby."

Grease carried Sadie inside and they made love so sweetly that Sadie shattered when she climaxed. She felt her heart slam into her chest and she knew she was in love for the first time in her life. They made love three more times that night before falling asleep wrapped around each other.

When the sun filtered through the blinds Sadie groaned knowing she had to get on the road. Grease read her thoughts.

"I know you have to leave, but I really wish you didn't have too."

Sadie kissed his chest. "I wish I didn't have to go either, but the faster I go the faster I can try to find the cargo and then I can leave Norwalk."

"I'm going be worried. Will you send word through CC again?"

"Of course. You will be so busy getting your place up and running, you won't have time to think about me."

Grease rolled Sadie to her back settling on top of her. "You are so wrong Sadie." He said quietly before kissing her gently. Sadie wrapped her legs around his hips and his erect cock pressed into her wet heat. He loved that she was ready for him. Her walls clutched his shaft and he made love to her with a purpose. She was moaning his name as he rocked into her and only when he felt her unravel did he allow himself to come. Grease rolled off of Sadie and she hated the emptiness that accompanied his cock leaving her. They were both breathing heavily.

"Sadie."

"Ummm?"

"I really care for you. This isn't it for you and me. Don't let this be all we have."

"I care for you too. I'm going to miss you, miss us. I'm not going to fall for anyone Grease. I need you to know that what ever happens in Sturgis you have to know it will mean nothing. It's a means to an end. Please understand that."

"Honey my head understands it but my heart is really having a hard time with it."

Sadie leaned up and kissed him tenderly.

"Will it help if I told you that I'm falling in love with you?"

"Are you Sadie?"

"I'm falling so hard Grease that I'm afraid I'm going to crash and burn. It's like I'm in a hot air balloon and I'm on top of the world, loving you, loving us, loving how right this feels, and I'm so afraid. I'm afraid of losing it. I don't think I'll ever care about anyone like I care about you, and that's scary."

"Baby we'll get through this. We have too. I'm falling for you too you know."

"Really?"

"Yeah and I'm afraid too, but I'll fight for us Sadie. I'll fight for you."

Sadie pulled Grease to her and they clung to each other knowing it would be the last time for a while. An hour later Sadie pulled down his drive heading to Helena before heading back to Norwalk. Grease felt a sense of loss so profound that it reminded him of when he lost his parents and grandfather. Sadie was watching him in her rearview mirror as he became smaller and smaller. The tears came immediately and she cried knowing the sad, empty feeling that was spreading through her would remain there until they could be together again.

18

The next weeks were heaven and hell. The days were great. Grease opened the retail store and luncheonette. He had hired four women from town to operate the luncheonette, and a man from the club, along with his wife, to run the retail store. It was a perfect set up. The man, Ed, was 55, and had been working in Townsend for the town until he'd been forced to retire just that summer. He really had not wanted to stop working, and he had been thinking of moving to Happy year round. His wife had worked as a manger in Townsend's Sears store so she knew all about sales. Grease rented them the top floor of the store for a very reasonable rate in return for them managing the store and luncheonette. This included opening up every morning and locking up each night. Something Grease had been concerned about.

Polly, Ed, Grease and the four women had spent one afternoon training to use the special cash registers that Grease had installed, which tracked the merchandise sold, so reordering was easy. Grease also spent an afternoon with his accountant learning how to use QuickBooks, which would keep his books in order. The four women who were running the luncheonette, Minnie, Bitsie, Peach, and Ivy, loved Grease's simple menu, but after the first week they had asked to add a few items like grilled cheese and chicken nuggets. They made their own schedule and Polly implemented a way to track what foods they sold by assigning each food a number. When the women rang up the customers on the luncheonettes register, they would input the food number attached and the price would automatically come up. This also helped them track what foods sold the most and it made reordering easier.

Tourists and club members were coming into the store and they were selling any where from $250 to $600 a day. The luncheonette was proving to be a hidden gem and campers from the nearby campground and passing tourists kept the place busy.

Grease opened Grease'd Hogs the next week. Tank had his retail space stocked with a few bikes and tourists would wander back, look over the bikes and watch Grease working.

His first job he took on was revamping Ed's Harley. It was a simple job, but Grease loved staying busy and the people that came back to watch him work were fascinated. Grease also liked how he was so busy that he was not constantly thinking about Sadie. He thought about her all the time, but at least when he was working he was distracted.

Like last time Joe would stop by every couple of days and tell him that Sadie had checked in with CC and she was fine. Those the nights he was able to get some sleep. He missed her something fierce and physically ached sometimes when he lay awake at night thinking about her.

One night after Grease had just arrived home from work he heard two cars coming down his driveway. He stood on his porch and watched Liam's car pulling down his drive followed by a car he didn't recognize. His heart was in his throat thinking they were coming to tell him that something had happened to Sadie. Liam parked next to his truck and the other car pulled next to Liam's. Grease held tight to the porch rail, his stomach was rolling and he had to remind himself to breath.

Grease watched Liam get out of his car and then to Grease's surprise the US Marshall that worked with him stepped out of the other car. Maybe this wasn't about Sadie at all, and then a whole new set of fears pummeled him. Grease stepped off the deck and headed towards the men.

"Liam. Kirk. Everything all right?" he asked shaking their hands.

"Can we sit down and talk Thad."

Liam gave Grease a sideways look upon hearing his WitSec given name.

"Sure come on in."

The three men sat down around Grease's table and Kirk got right to business.

"Thad, Aguilar died in prison a week ago. We were worried that his death was going to stir up a new hunt for you, but truth is, the opposite had happened."

"What? You're kidding?"

"No, when Aguilar died there was a scramble to take over the family and Aguilar's son was killed. A new family is running things now and word on the street is that if you were ever to turn up, they'd welcome you with open arms. You made the take over possible by testifying."

"I don't know what to say?"

"You already opted to keep your WitSec name and social when your ten years were up, so it be best if you kept keep those now anyways. I just wanted to give you the good news."

"So no more hiding my past?"

"No you can tell who ever, whatever. You can even tell them about Romeo."

Grease smiled. "It's been so long that I have had to lie about my past."

"Romeo?" Liam asked.

"It's his story to tell." Kirk said standing up to take his leave.

Grease walked both men out and before Liam left he told Grease he really wanted to hear about Romeo, which made Grease chuckle.

"Some time Liam. I promise, okay?"

The two men drove away and the first thing Grease thought of was that he wished he could share the news with Sadie. He had so much he wanted to tell her.

When the men left Grease got on his Harley and drove down to camp. He had a few beers with Tank, Tess, Sweets and Lolly. After they spoke about Sturgis and some of the particulars Grease swung the conversation towards his surprise. He then told them the story about Romeo, testifying and WitSec. He saw the shock register on his friends faces. Tank already knew, but he pretended that he was hearing it all for the first time.

Tess was the first to recover and she threw her arms around him congratulating him. Grease said he wanted to keep it quiet until he could tell Sadie and they all agreed she needed to hear this from him.

Their intimate group began to grow and soon they moved to the bonfire and the conversation turned to Sturgis once again.

They were leaving soon and meeting up with the Bandits at a rest stop so they could ride into town together. Tank told the group that he heard that there were easily forty men and women from their club that had told him they were going and the Border Bandits had around thirty.

Bettina was sitting next to Grease and she was telling Gretchen who was sitting next to her about a bar called Poppy's that held shot drinking contests and that it involved men using the women to hold the shot glasses on their bodies, and it could get wild. Gretchen was smiling and she looked to Grease.

"Do you go in the contest, Grease?"

"I have, but I don't think I will this year."

A few of the men sitting near him began telling Gretchen about the raunchiness that accompanied the contest and he saw her eyes watching him shyly. He knew if he just held out his hand to her that she'd go with him, right then, and right there. His thoughts drifted to Sadie and he wondered what she was doing at that very moment. Was she touching Cage? Letting him kiss her? His stomach tightened at the thought, and he stood up from the log saying good night to his friends.

As he left the group he saw that Gretchen was following him with her big blue eyes. The woman was gorgeous. Her blond hair was long and shiny, and he remembered how her pretty pink lips had roved his body freely that one night. She definitely had one of the hottest, tightest bodies he'd ever pleasured. She had been a cheerleader in high school and even though that had been a good six years ago, she was still was still flexible. Her petite frame and large breasts could have graced any centerfold. She watched him leaving the bonfire and a sad smile crossed her face. Grease saw that many of the single men were watching her, hoping. He'd learned that she didn't sleep around like some of the other women did, and he heard that she had been turning the other men down every night.

Still she wasn't his Sadie. Grease left camp knowing he was going to have to relieve the pressure building in his groin before falling asleep that night. He thought back to the night he'd spent with Bettina and Gretchen, but it was the fervent memories of him with Sadie that had him rocking a hard on as he drove home.

It was the morning they were leaving for Sturgis. His shop was doing better than he ever thought possible and he had a job lined up for a complete overhaul when he returned. Ed and Polly were running The Pen and over seeing the luncheonette, which continued to do a booming business. The women had now added pies, which they supplied, to the menu.

Grease had not heard from CC regarding Sadie in over a week and the thought of her making her way to South Dakota on the back of Cage's Harley clawed at his sanity.

The trip to Sturgis, South Dakota was about seven and a half hours away. They had made reservations at a camp ground to break up the trip coming and going. The men rode their Harley's and their line in the road precession was in direct correlation to their rank in the club. Women drove trucks, some hauling campers, or rode with their men. Lolly had her truck and was hauling a Silver Bullet that she, Sweets, and Tank would share.

Grease had his tent, bedding and clothes thrown into the back of her truck along with Dak's. Dak and he had always slept in tents not far from each other or from where Tank slept. Grease was always cognizant of having Tank's back. This year Tank had opted to sleep in the trailer with Lolly and Sweets so Grease knew he and Dak would be pitching their tents somewhere not too far from the camper.

The two clubs had reservations at a farm just outside of Sturgis that opened up as a campground just for that week. The owner hauled in port-o- potties and portable showers and there were always a few activities going on either right in the freshly mowed fields or nearby in the back woods.

The Steel Horse Cowboys and the Border Bandits pulled into Sturgis and were met with cheers from other clubs. Every club was greeted this way. The two clubs made their way through town seeing that it had already gotten wild. Cops had a few men sitting on the curb with their hands held behind their back with zip ties. One bar had a brawl from inside spilling out on the street as the bouncers and police ran towards it.

The clubs drove through town and then drove down the drive leading to the farm turned campground. As they drove towards the farmhouse where they would be directed to their area Grease caught sight of a group of Harley's speeding down a side road and sitting on the back of one of the Harley's was woman with a braid hanging down her back, tied back with a bandana. Grease knew the second he saw her that it was Sadie. Dak must have noticed her too because he shook his head no. Letting Grease know not to go near her.

The night before he and Dak drank way too much and Grease had told him how he felt about Sadie, and that she was undercover. He knew he wasn't supposed to say anything, 'loose lips sink ships' and all, but he was drunk and it just spilled out.

The first night in the campgrounds Grease called a meeting and reminded everyone to be safe and to use the buddy system. Sturgis was attended by motorcycle clubs and motorcycle enthusiasts across the nation. The police force bulked up just for that week, calling in retired State Troopers, and their jails were always full.

Grease knew he would not be getting crazy like he had in the years past. His heart wasn't really in it, and one night when he was talking to Tank, he found out his friend was feeling the same way he was. Tank told him that he already missed Tess and Tommy. Crazy stuff happens at Sturgis and Grease knew he was going to stick close to Tank on the trip. There was no way he ever wanted to have to tell Tess that something had happened to her man.

The two clubs had areas near each other and as soon as the trailers were parked and the tents were set they hit town. Grease was glued to Tank, as was Sweets and Lolly, so they were a foursome. Everywhere they went he watched for Sadie. Part of him wanted to see her, just so he could know that she was all right, and the other part prayed he wouldn't see her because he knew that seeing her with Cage would kill him.

Two days into the rally and he saw her again on the main drag, on the back of Cages bike. Grease was standing at a corner with Tank as Satan's Army past them. She was wearing a pair of jean shorts, motorcycle boots, a halter top, and her hair was braided and held back with a bandana. She had on mirrored aviators, just like his. He knew she saw him as they watched each other. She wasn't smiling and he noticed how her hands rested on her thighs and not on Cage, and he thanked God for small favors. The bikes stopped for a red light and Cage held up his Harley with his strong legs.

Grease was staring at Sadie, he couldn't tear his eyes from her and Tank watched as the man riding next to Cage knocked Cage on the shoulder and pointed at Grease.

Cage looked behind him at Sadie just as Sadie had pulled her braid to her front and stroked it. Grease knew she was letting him know that she was thinking of him. It had been a running joke about her hair style being like his, before it had been chopped off.

Tank elbowed Grease and Grease tore his eyes from Sadie only to see Cage grimace. The light changed and Cage reached behind him and yanked Sadie's hand from her braid and firmly placed it around his waist. He then sneered at Grease and took off in a thunderous peal out, laughing at Grease's enraged expression.

"Man, you have to cool it." Tank admonished him.

"I know. I know. I can't stand seeing her with him."

"I hear you bro. If that were Tess I know I'd lose it too, but you know she's just acting. It's all for her job. You have to get that through your head."

Grease ran his fingers through his hair swearing under his breath. Tank was right. If Cage thought there was something between them he could hurt her. It could jeopardize not only her, but also her case, her job. He had to pretend she meant nothing to him if he saw them again.

The next evening Tank, Grease, Lolly, Sweets, Dak, Bettina, Gretchen, and a good twenty other Steel Horse Cowboy's entered Poppy's for the shots contests. Poppy's was a small, old time bar, but for the week of Sturgis they opened their back door, erected a large tent, and put up a stage in the middle of the tent. The bar which would normally hold thirty people and that would be a squeeze now could accommodate a couple hundred. On a nice day, like it was, the tent flaps were opened to allow for even more patrons. Picnic tables were situated around the outside, port-o-potties were in each corner of the cordoned off area, and a large outside bar poured only beer from kegs and shots. Because it was outside the clubs were allowed to wear their colors. Tonight they also wore their colors because of the shot contest.

Poppy's had a cover charge for the evening and burley bouncers collected the money at the front door. The bar patrons would then walked through the small bar and down a hallway until they got to the back door where they were ushered into the large tented area. This was usually a fun night as it pitted club against club, as they vied for the coveted Best Shooter Award.

As the Steel Horse Cowboys emerged from the hall into the tented area Grease knew immediately that Sadie was there. He followed his friends to a small area near one of the open picnic tables and scanned the crowd.

Tank nudged him and Grease followed his eyes to where he saw Satan's Army. Sadie had her back to him as she spoke with the girl that Grease recognized as Missy. Sadie's fine globed ass was peering out from underneath denim shorts that were far too revealing for Grease's comfort. She had on a light blue tube top, her biker boots, and as usual her hair was fixed in the braid with her bandana.

"Maybe we should leave." Tank whispered to him. Grease shook his head no. "I can do this."

"I don't know Grease." Tank was tense and Grease knew if he had to leave, that Tank would go with him. Lolly had also seen Sadie and she looked up first to her husband Sweets and then to Grease. She had a bad feeling about this. Sadie turned to accept a beer from Cage and that's when she saw Grease. She momentarily faltered and the beer sloshed over her hand. Cage turned to see what had caught her attention and when he saw Grease, Sadie could tell Cage was pissed. She tried to placate him by giving him a kiss and even though she knew Grease would see that fake endearment she had to do something to calm Cage down.

Cage pulled her to him and nuzzled her neck and Grease saw red. His hands flexed into a fist and Dak and Tank bracketed him to hold him in place. If there was a fight it would not be pretty. They'd destroy the tent and probably land in jail.

Sadie pulled out of Cages embrace and Lolly saw her heading for the port-o-potty line. She looked up at Sweets who nodded at her and she took off after Sadie. Lolly was right behind Sadie in line and because Cage knew who Lolly was from the day he had taken Sweets, the two women knew they could not appear as if they were talking.

"Lolly." Sadie said her voice was tight with anxiety. "You have to get Grease out of here."

"He won't leave. He say's he can handle this."

"I'm so close to ending this Lolly. He can't lose it. Cage is already suspicious."

"Honey, that man loves you. This has got to be destroying him."

"Lolly trust me. I love him too. This means nothing to me. I'm only acting. It's my cover. What ever is happening I think is going down tonight. Cage found my phone though so I hope CC has been good about tailing his guys. She is here somewhere."

"CC is here?"

"Yeah. I can't explain it now, but this was no ordinary heist."

"I guess not. Sadie can't you walk away now?"

"No, I want to see the truck for myself. That way I can testify in court. It's here somewhere and I know it's being guarded."

"Well can't you at least leave the bar?"

Sadie hesitated and looked to the ground as the two women moved closer to the port-o- potty as the line moved.

"Cage and I are in the contest Lolly."

"Holy crap! That's so uncool Sadie."

"I have to do it. I have to make it look like I'm, drunk and that I'm into Cage. Cage won't leave me if I'm drunk, he's real possessive, and hopefully he'll take me with him when the deal goes down tonight."

"But the contest?"

"I know. I know. Tell Grease it means nothing. Please. I wish he would just leave. It's hard enough to fake that I have feelings for Cage, but when Grease is here it's freaking impossible."

The line moved forward and Sadie reached for the door handle. "Please Lolly tell Grease it means nothing." Sadie then shut the door.

When she reemerged Lolly wasn't in line anymore and when she looked to where the Steel Horse Cowboys were she saw that Lolly was talking to Grease. Sadie saw that her man did not look happy. As she worked her way through the crowd she covertly watched Grease and his friends. She saw Tank and Sweets, neither of them looked happy either. Dak was there, too. He was laughing with a tall dark haired woman. An absolutely gorgeous platinum blond stood between Dak and Grease. Sadie could see that she swayed with the craziness under the tent and she was standing really close to Grease. The woman was breathtakingly beautiful and Sadie felt a rock form in her stomach. The woman was clearly into Grease. She looked up at him with her large eyes and stood near him brushing her shoulder against his thick arm.

Lolly said he loved her, but maybe this was too much for him? Maybe she was literally pushing him into another woman's arms? The thought sickened her.

As Sadie reached Satan's Army's area a bell sounded, signaling the beginning of the Shooter's contest.

The roar from the crowd was deafening as men and women yelled and pounded the tables and stage. Every club present was expected to enter the contest. A woman dressed in jeans and cowboy boots with help from two other bouncers scanned the crowd counted out the appropriate number of shot glasses needed. There were twelve in all. A bottle of Jack stood next to the glasses.

Sadie was nervous as to what Cage would have her do. She was by no means an exhibitionist and even though she had on fewer clothes than she normally would wear, she was at least, still covering her private parts, unlike some of the other woman.

The first couple on stage was from the Border Bandits. The man dumped the shot glass on his woman and lapped off the liquid, his tongue sliding low into the woman's cleavage. The crowd was clapping and encouraging him to go lower. The next couple was from a club Sadie didn't recognize and the man placed the full shot glass on the woman's back very close to her rear and got behind her doggie style pressing his denim clad pelvis into her, much to the delight of the spectators, before lowering his mouth to drink the shot. Sadie realized that the shots had to be drunk without the male using his hands and that worried her. Two other couples went and then it was Sadie's turn. Cage held her hand as they walked up on the stage. She kept her eyes firmly glued to Cage. There was no way she could look at Grease. A bouncer handed Cage the filled shot glass. Cage put the shot glass on the ground and deftly lowered her tube top just enough that her nipples were barely covered. Sadie was shaking. Grease watched as his nemesis fingers played seductively over her bared skin. He couldn't breathe as rage ran through his veins like liquid fire.

Cage placed the shot glass between her breasts; only the rim of the glass was visible. He then placed her hands behind her back, which thrust her plump breasts out. Her nipples were protruding provocatively from behind the elastic top. They were very close to spilling out the top of her altered top. Grease shifted uneasily looking away from them momentarily and he saw everyman in the place was riveted, hoping her top would fold down further, baring her lovely breasts to them. Sadie pulled her hands from her back and Grease watched as she attempted to pull her top up, but Cage captured her hands again placing them behind her. He smiled at her and then wiggled his finger at her gesturing no-no, which the crowd loved. He then leaned in and gave her a tender kiss on her lips. Something she was not expecting. It momentarily dazed her and Tank had to place a hand on Grease's forearm to hold him back.

Cage knelt down in front of Sadie and gently grasped the sides of her tube top, his thumbs resting on her creamy exposed skin, essentially pushing her round breasts together to firmly hold the shot glass in place. He then pulled her forward so she was bent at the waist and the brown liquid poured from her cleavage into his mouth. The crowd screamed their approval and when Cage finished drinking, he stood quickly and took the shot glass from her breasts using his mouth, which the crowd also loved.

Cage helped Sadie from the stage. Her legs were barely working. He was all smiles as they wound their way back to the Satan's Army area. His men thumped him on his back and praised him. Even the women were complimenting him.

Sadie accepted a beer from Missy and chugged the entire contents down, which Cage saw making him laugh. He knew he had just rattled her big time. Cage leaned in and whispered, "We will be so good together, Sadie." Sadie still hadn't looked towards Grease, she was actually afraid too. Cage had kissed her and touched her breasts; she knew he was not going to be happy.

Another couple was being called to the stage and when Sadie heard they were representing the Steel Horse Cowboys Motorcycle Club she looked up.

Grease was leading the beautiful platinum blond onto the stage. Sadie saw Lolly looking at her and Lolly simply shrugged her shoulders. She obviously hadn't known he was going to do this.

The blond was gazing at Grease with eyes that spoke volumes. The woman adored him. Grease had his hands on her slim shoulders and was speaking into her ear. The woman was nodding at him, a sexy smile turning her perfectly shaped desirable lips upward. After he finished speaking with her he gave her a quick kiss. Sadie thought 'touché Grease', as her heart thudded inside her chest.

The woman, who had been introduced as Gretchen, wore the skimpiest pair of denim shorts that Sadie had ever seen. The thing was that the damn woman looked hot in them. Her body was fabulous. Her small ass peeked out from underneath the tiny fringed hem and every man in the place was gawking at her. She had on a tight white shirt that was laced up the front with leather ties, her round breasts straining against the thin material. Gretchen's areoles were clearly visible and her dark nipples were evident as the hard points strained against the shirt. The men in Poppy's were going crazy and the couple hadn't even done anything yet.

Grease took the shot glass that was handed to him and placed it on the floor. He then slowly unzipped the front of Gretchen's shorts. The crowd could see that she wore a lacy thong. The men were screaming and Sadie could see some were so turned on that they sported bulges in their jeans. Grease picked up the glass and situated it inside Gretchen's unzip shorts, under the front band of her teeny tiny thong, just above her mons. Sadie, along with every other person in the place knew that the base of the shot glass was probably pressing between her female lips.

Then Grease squatted in front of her, his face was even with the shot glass then wowed both the men and women in the crowd. He tapped Gretchen's thighs so she spread her legs and then he placed his hands on the inside of her thighs, as if he going to bench press, putting them where her legs met her pelvis. He then lifted the petite beauty off the stage and into the air. His large hands were splayed wide on the inside of her thighs, his finger tips disappearing under her shorts and Sadie felt her heart ripping. The tented area was rocking. The men banged their fists against the tables and stage cheering loudly, and even the women were perceptibly aroused witnessing Grease's display of strength. His thick neck sporting a visible vein, which was the only indication, that he was lifting a weight. He was so strong and the women were cheering just as loudly as the men.

Gretchen smiled down at Grease, her hands were laced through his hair, and then she arched her back thrusting her perfect breasts out as she gracefully spread her toned legs in an acrobatic split. The crowd erupted at the erotic sight. Gretchen holding her legs apart displayed the carefully placed shot glass. Her small body was toned and supple, a man's dream. Gretchen's slim body arched backwards erotically as if she was having sex. Grease held her up easily, his massive arms bulged with definition and Sadie heard the women gasp with admiration.

Grease lifted Gretchen even higher, moving his hands to her round ass, which was now totally visible, with only a small denim strip hiding her ass crack. Sadie's stomach lurched as she watched as his mouth, the one that had kissed her and loved her, closed over the rim of the shot glass. Grease tilted Gretchen's pelvis upward and Sadie could see that he was drinking the contents of the small glass. Then he did something that no one expected. Grease stuck his tongue into the shot glass and moved the tiny tumbler lower into Gretchen's thong. You couldn't see the glass any more, and everyone, absolutely everyone knew where it was and what it was touching.

Sadie sickened as she watched the woman throw her head back and even though no one could have heard her over the ruckus the onlookers were making, Sadie and everyone else saw that she was moaning with pleasure. Grease then placed his face into her crotch and plucked the glass from her female lips with his mouth before lowering her to the floor.

The woman was smiling up at Grease and Sadie saw that she was so aroused that Sadie wouldn't have been surprised if he had made her cum. Once again he bent down and gave her a quick kiss. The crowd had exploded into cheers and clapping as Grease led Gretchen off the stage.

Sadie had tears running unchecked down her face. She couldn't have stopped them if she'd tried. Her chest ached as if her heart had physically been ripped apart and the sense of loss she felt was overwhelming.

Her legs buckled and as she stumbled backwards Cage caught her and held her against his front. At first he thought she was seeking his attention, and that pleased him immensely, but when he saw her tears he knew what he'd suspected all along. There was something going on between his woman and Grease. If they had been someplace private he would have shown her how mad he was. The more discerning question was why was she pretending to like him, if she really liked Grease. Cage tossed around a few scenarios and the bottom line was none were very good, for him or for her.

The only comforting thought was that Grease must not care about Sadie, not after that sensual display on stage. Sadie was cute and curvy and Cage liked that she didn't take any shit, but the woman that Grease had trembling on stage was a stunner. He was going to have to figure out what was up with this bitch.

Gretchen was still gripping his hand as Grease pushed through the crowd. By the time they reached their friends, Grease hated himself. He knew what he had done would bother Sadie, but he had originally justified going on stage hoping to make it appear to Cage that he didn't care for Sadie. Unfortunately, he recognized that he was out of his mind with jealousy and that had played into his scene with Gretchen. How mean was it that he wanted to hurt Sadie, like she had hurt him? How could she have let Cage touch her so intimately? His grand scheme to help Sadie had totally blown up in his face.

When he reached his friends Tank was looking at him with his lips set in a tight line. Grease knew that face, he was mad. Sweets had his arms crossed over his chest, and Lolly physically slugged him in the arm. The rest of the group was pounding his back, praising him. When the congratulations ended Tank leaned into him.

"Are you happy now?"

Grease didn't answer.

Lolly tried to slug him again bit Sweets caught her arm. "You suck Grease." She hissed.

Grease knew Sadie might not be happy with him, but she was a tough woman and she was smart. All she cared about was her damn case. She would see through his charade, but his friends acting like this, this he didn't get.

Sweets nodded towards Sadie and that's when he realized he had really crossed the line. His tough girl had tears cascading down her sweet face and she looked like she was about to vomit. It was at this moment that Cage saw her tears too, and Grease watched him as he physically dragged Sadie out of the tented area.

Gretchen was still holding his hand and Dak was looking at him with a friendly smile on his face. Grease released Gretchen's hand and murmured a thank you to her for going on stage with him. She didn't move far from him, but Grease didn't even notice. He was feeling physically ill himself. What had he done?

"Hell of a show bro." Dak slapped his friends broad back.

Grease shook his head. "I just fucked up big time, Dak."

"Looking at Gretchen's face up there, I don't think so."

"I don't care about Gretchen, man. It's Sadie I screwed up with. I made her cry."

Dak saw that Gretchen had heard Grease and her lower lip began to tremble as her eyes misted over.

Dak swore and put his arm around her.

"You are batting 1000 ass hole." He said steering Gretchen away from him.

"Fuck me." Grease swore out loud. He turned and the first thing he saw was the gray wooden siding planks of the little bar. Grease punched it with all his might and the wood splintered around his fist. The crowd was busy cheering for another couple on stage so most didn't even notice his temper tantrum, but a few of the bouncers did.

"Fuck." groaned Tank. The bouncers came charging over and Tank reached into his chained wallet grabbing out every bit of cash he had. Sweets had already grabbed Grease by the arm and was pushing him out of the tent area ahead of him. Tank handed the wad of cash to the first bouncer to reach him and it must have been enough, because they stopped heading for Grease.

Outside the bar Grease was a mess. Lolly was still pissed at him and Sweets hadn't said a word yet.

"What the hell Grease?" Tank swore.

Grease was shaking out his bloody fist.

"Screw you Tank I was pissed! So what I hit the fucking wall. I'll pay you back!" Grease had never spoken to Tank like that and Sweets and Lolly took a step away in case Tank retaliated.

Tank blew out an exasperated breath and laid his large hand on his best friends shoulder.

"Grease, I meant why would you be so demonstrative on stage knowing Sadie was watching?"

"It wasn't for Sadie, well it was, but I did it to show Cage that Sadie wasn't my girl. We know he thought she was with me in Happy that one time. He thinks I took her to the bus station in the next town so he knows we know each other. He has seen me looking at her and her looking at me. I was afraid he'd hurt her if he figured things out."

"Yeah, well I think he has definitely figured it out now, and you don't have to worry about him hurting her; I guarantee you hurt her a whole lot worse than anything he could ever do to her." Tank was pissed.

"Shit."

Sweets finally spoke up. "What you did on stage Grease was not just a show for Cage. I know you were pissed that Cage had been on stage with Sadie. I can't imagine how you felt seeing him touch her like that. I think you were getting back at her a little."

Grease ran his hands through his hair. "I'm so fucked. I was out of my mind. Honestly, I thought about going up there and just doing a low key shot, you know, something that would throw Cage off, but you're right. After I saw him with Sadie I was jealous and so pissed. I wanted to hurt her like she'd hurt me."

"Mission accomplished you idiot." Lolly chastised him.

The four friends got on their Harley's and headed back to camp. It was still early, by Sturgis standards, and the streets were crowded with partiers, making their ride to camp a slow one. Back at camp there weren't too many people around. Lolly and Sweets went into the camper leaving Grease and Tank outside. Tank built a small fire in a little rock enclosure and then he set up two folding chairs. Grease just stood there. His mind was racing and he couldn't get the image of Sadie crying off of his mind. Tank handed Grease a beer and told him to sit.

The two friends sat quietly for a while. Every once in a while they could hear laughter wafted over from another camp site. Tank knew that his best friend was upset and there was nothing he could say to help him. He just needed to be there for him.

Finally Grease broke the silence. "Tank I know you need me here, but I can't stay."

Tank grunted softly. "Yeah, I know."

It was silent again until Tank spoke.

"I actually have been thinking of leaving a little earlier than planned."

Grease looked at his friend and Tank continued. "I miss Tess and Tommy. This rally is wild and crazy, and we have had great times here, but it's not the same."

Grease nodded, he knew exactly what Tank was saying. A Harley pulled into their circle and Grease watched as Dak helped Gretchen off the back of his bike. Grease knew he needed to apologize to her so he got up and headed towards Dak's tent where they were standing in front of the tent flap.

"Gretchen, can I have a minute?"

"Anything you have to say Grease you can say in front of Dak." Her authoritative tone surprised Grease and he fumbled for a second.

"I'm sorry if I hurt your feelings tonight. Thank you for being my partner, but I should have never gone on stage. I thought I was helping someone, someone I care about, and instead I really hurt her and I know I hurt you too."

"Yeah, she did not look happy." Gretchen said softly. Grease looked at her with an open mouth.

"You know about Sadie?"

"Anyone with two eyes knows you are into her Grease." her voice was laced with attitude and it made him feel even worse.

"Yeah, well, I'm sorry that I hurt your feelings." Gretchen placed her hand on his forearm. "I would have done it anyway Grease, even though I knew you liked her. I wish you had just been honest with me. I thought you liked me." She paused and looked away from him from and then looked from Dak to him, as if contemplating about what she was going to say next.

"It was exciting being on that stage with everyone watching us. I miss being in the spotlight."

Grease looked at her and waited for her to explain, however it was Dak that filled him in.

"Gretchen use to star in porn movies Grease. She moved out here to get her head on straight, get away from the drugs, but she still misses acting."

"As you could tell I'm a bit of an exhibitionist. I always have been."

"Well that explains how natural and erotic you were on stage." Grease admitted. "You wowed the audience Gretchen. I don't think there is one man in the tent that won't dream about you tonight."

Gretchen smiled at him. "Thanks Grease you were pretty terrific yourself. You know I still have some contacts if you ever want to...."

Grease interrupted her. "No, that's not for me."

"Well if you change your mind."

Grease chuckled knowing that at least Gretchen wasn't mad at him anymore.

"We won." She said with a coy smile.

"What?"

"Yeah," She laughed. "Here's your trophy." She handed Grease a small bronzed shot glass and laughed again when she saw the silly look on his face.

"Thanks." He said feeling the cool glass burning into his hand. "And Gretchen I really am sorry that I hurt your feelings."

"We're cool Grease." She then stood up on her tip toes and gave his cheek a forgiving peck.

Dak placed his arm around her and smiled at Grease, letting his friend know that she was with him now.

Grease chuckled and turned back to Tank, who had been watching from his seat by the small fire pit. Grease tossed the small, unwanted reminder at Tank who caught it mid-air.

"You won?"

"Guess so."

"Gretchen okay?"

"Yeah." They watched her go into Dak's tent.

"So Grease, I'm going to leave tomorrow and I need someone to ride with me." Tank told him quietly.

"That'd be me, Tank."

"Okay settled."

It was after 11:00 and the only sounds in camp were the motorcycles and trucks making their way to the south side of camp where the men knew a cage had been erected and fights were taking place. Devils Hand was running the operation. The fights didn't start until 11:00, because they didn't want to attract unwanted attention from the police.

"Must be crazy back there." Grease said and Tank knew he meant the fights that were taking place.

"Yeah, maybe you should go beat the shit out of someone and let off a little steam." Tank joked.

"Yeah, but I'm so messed up right now that I'd probably get my ass kicked."

Tank chuckled. "I hear ya."

An hour later Dak and Gretchen emerged from Dak's little pup tent. Dak was all smiles and Gretchen was glowing from post orgasm bliss. They walked to the men hand in hand and Tank offered them a beer.

"No thanks." Dak said waving him off. "We're going over to the fights. You guys want to come?"

"No I'm good." Tank answered.

"Me neither, but thanks."

The happy couple got on Dak's bike and headed over the dusty road that led to the south end of the property where the cage was hidden by the trees behind a meadow.

19

Grease had stopped drinking knowing that he and Tank were going to be heading home tomorrow, and knowing Tank like he did, they wouldn't be stopping too often. A cycle roared in the distance and the men saw that one rider was flying towards them. As it got closer they saw that it was Dak and he was alone. Dak fish tailed to a stop, sending dirt and grass flying and Grease knew immediately that something was wrong. His first thought was that Gretchen was in trouble, since she wasn't with him.

"It's Sadie. She's in the cage with a huge woman. I think something's wrong with her."

"What? Christ."

Grease started running for his Harley as did Tank. "Get Sweets, Dak!" Tank yelled as he hopped on his bike and he and Grease raced it towards the fights. Grease and Tank parked as close as they could and started running towards the make shift cage. They had to literally throw people out of their way to get closer and when they finally were close enough to see inside the cage Grease's heart slammed into his chest.

Sadie was stumbling around the wire enclosure. Her hands were up warding off punches, and when she'd try to throw one herself it careened wildly completely off target. She looked like she was drunk and there was something else about her that didn't seem right, but he didn't have time to figure out what it was. He needed to get her out of there. As they continued towards the front of the crowd, they saw that Dak was right behind them, and 100 yards behind him were Lolly and Sweets.

Grease was picking his way through the throngs of spectators when he saw Cage standing smugly near the cage. When Cage saw Grease he smiled nastily at him and that sent chills through Grease. Cage then held something up in his hand and when Grease saw what it was, he became very afraid for Sadie. Cage was holding her braid up laughing. Message received Grease thought angrily.

Two things were clear; Cage knew about him and Sadie despite his attempt to throw him off by his scene on stage at Poppy's, and more importantly Sadie was in imminent danger. He couldn't worry about blowing her case or preserving her undercover persona anymore. He had to get her out of that cage.

The crowd was cheering as Sadie took a punch on her cheek and hit the canvas hard. The woman she was fighting had to be over 6 feet tall and she was huge. She was taunting Sadie, trying to get her to stand back up. Cage was yelling for the woman to finish her off, meaning finish Sadie off. Grease was praying she'd stay down, but in his heart he knew Sadie would never quit. The other woman would have to hurt her real bad for Sadie to not stand up and fight.

Cage was yelling through the bars for Sadie to stand up and he shook her braid in his hands hoping to rile her up. When Grease and Tank reached the front of the crowd Grease saw the one door leading into the cage and it was being guarded by two very large and very bad ass Devils Hand members. They were both carrying guns in their jeans waist bands and he looked to Tank and Tank swore knowing this could go south real quick.

Grease got to the men first.

"Stop this fight. That girl is messed up." He said pointing to Sadie.

"Get lost ass wipe." One man said knocking Grease backwards, which was no easy feat.

Tank stepped in. "That woman has been drugged; she's going to get hurt."

The other bouncer placed his steely hand on Tanks chest and Tank glared at him. Dak, Sweets, and Lolly came running up, surrounding the four men.

Lolly screamed at Sadie to 'look out' because the Amazon, in the cage with her was about to deck her again. Sadie ducked just in time and staggered away. "You stop that fight. She's going to get hurt." Lolly screamed.

The men chuckled and Sweets had to physically hold Lolly back. Grease tried to push through the men again, and this time when one of them pushed him back Grease ducked and slammed his strong frame against the bigger man, causing the surprised biker to fall back against the cage. The big man launched himself at Grease but froze when he heard a whistle. Grease saw that a man sitting in a lawn chair, very prominently, near the cage door had whistled and that single whistle had stopped the man cold. Both Grease and the Devils Hands member looked to the man who motioned for them to come to him.

Grease looked at Tank and Tank nodded that he should go. When they got to the man Grease saw that the man was the Vice president of the Northwest Chapter of Devils Hands. Holy smoke this was a VIP and Grease worried that he may have just dealt his beloved motorcycle club a death blow by mixing it up with the notorious motorcycle club.

"What's the problem?" The Vice president asked. His voice was raspy like he'd been smoking cigarettes forever.

Lolly, Sweets and Tank strained to hear what the man was saying as they kept one eye towards the ring and Sadie and the other on Grease.

"That's my woman in the ring and she's been drugged. It's not a fair fight."

"I paid good money for her to fight." The man told him.

"I'll double what you're getting." Grease told him quickly.

"No, I need a fight. The crowd wants to see a fight."

"I'll fight the bitch." Lolly hollered as Sweets held her back with both hands around the waist.

Grease couldn't help but smile. He held his palm up to Lolly. "I'll give you a fight." Grease told the man.

"Oh yeah? How do I know you can fight?"

Grease stood up and smiled. He hoped his reputation preceded him.

"I used to fight professionally, in Miami. I'm Romeo." Grease told him hoping for a hint of recognition upon hearing the name.

The older man seemed to be contemplating what he had said and then a wide grin broke across his face.

"My old man saw you fight. He talked about it for days."

"So stop this fight and you get me."

The Vice president chuckled. "Who's going to be stupid enough to fight the famous Romeo?"

Grease grinned and pointed at Cage who was still screaming through the mesh wire for the Amazon to finish off Sadie.

"See that man right there?"

The older man nodded. "The one I paid for the small chick?"

"He was the man I was supposed to fight next before I left. He's still pissed about it. He'd love a chance to get me in a ring."

"No shit? Cage was supposed to fight you? I heard he used to fight."

"Yup."

The Vice President thought about what he had just been offered and then he smiled. "Okay deal."

The man nodded at his men and they opened the door to the cage allowing Grease to walk in. Sadie was bruised and she had a cut under her eye that was swelling. Seeing her physically hurt wrecked him and anger blossomed like a nuclear bomb plume inside of him.

Sadie was off kilter, she didn't recognize him immediately, but when she did, she shrank away from him. She may have been messed up, but she definitely remembered what he had done earlier that evening.

One of the Devils Hands bouncer's was explaining to the other woman that her fight was over and she was cussing loudly until Sweets pulled out his wallet and waved a couple of hundred bucks at her through the screen. The Amazon walked out of the cage in a snit, and swiped the money from Sweets hands as she passed them.

Grease walked over to Sadie, who was running away from him, and when she ducked under his grasp it was apparently comical because the crowd laughed. He finally cornered her and the fear he saw in her eyes broke his heart. She began swinging at him with closed fists, landing soft blows on his shoulders and chest. He pressed his big body against hers, her back was against the mesh of the cage, and he grasped her hands firmly, but gently, ending the wayward punches. "Sadie, sweetheart stop." he whispered in her ear. "I'm sorry. I'm so sorry I hurt you baby."

Sadie stopped trying to wrench free from Grease's grasp and finally sagged against his chest. She was trembling and he knew she was afraid. Whatever Cage had slipped her had affected her physical capabilities, something he knew she prided herself on.

Grease rubbed her wrists with his thumbs waiting for her breathing to return to normal. It took a few seconds but it dawned on Sadie that he was in the ring with her. She peered cautiously over his shoulder looking for the woman that had been beating on her. Sadie looked back to Grease.

"Grease, there's a woman that's trying to hit me, you better get out of here." She told him in a serious but drunken whisper.

Grease smiled at her sadly, "She's not going to hit you anymore, I stopped the fight."

"You did?"

"Yes Sweetheart, now lets get you out of here."

Sadie remembered the beautiful Gretchen. "I'm not you're sweetheart anymore." she slurred hastily, her breath warm on his neck.

"You are." He told her more confidently than he felt. "Are you drunk Sadie?"

"No Cage gave me pills." She said slurring her words together.

"Do you know what drug Cage gave you?"

Sadie cocked her head thinking about his question and then she shook it back and forth.

"I don't know what it was. I'm seeing double and I can't move the way I want to." She chuckled and in an intoxicated sing song voice she whispered, "Can you imagine if there were two of you in one bed. Wow." Grease sighed praying silently that his one self would get a chance to be with her again.

Grease swung her up into his arms and the crowd cheered seeing the romantic gesture. He strode out of the cage to the safety of his friends, where he placed her between Sweets and Tank. Using a tone that neither man had ever heard before, Grease told them to guard her with their lives. Grease turned and walked back up the steps to the cage. Sweets and Tank shot each other a look over Sadie's head and then they both grinned. Grease was so in love.

"Finally, the tough guy falls." Sweets said quietly.

The event announcer, wearing jeans, his Devils Hands vest and a bow tie entered into the ring and using a microphone that had been rigged to speakers got the attention of the audience.

"We want apologize for cutting that last fight short folks. All bets will be reimbursed." The crowd grumbled, many feeling that Sadie had forfeited and that the Amazon had won.

"Or you can roll them over to cover this next fight." Grease stood, just inside the cage, taking off his shirt and chained wallet. He opened the door tossing both to Dak.

"Some of you may remember this next fighter. Back in the day, when cage fighting was in its infancy there was a premier fighter by the name of Romeo, an unbeaten heavy weight."

A murmur went through the crowd. Romeo had been a big name in the new sport of cage fighting. Many biker clubs held local fights, but the ones he had participated in were big and covered by newspapers and a few times his fights had been televised as a pay per view event. Romeo had been well known, not only for his fighting prowess, but also because of the public relation antics that his manager had come up with involving woman's underwear.

Grease stepped into the center of the ring and a few chants of Romeo, Romeo floated across the crowd. Yeah, they remembered. If they hadn't seen him fight, their fathers, brother's or uncles did.

"Who's he fighting?" Someone yelled from the crowd. Grease turned and stared at Cage who was visibly blanched.

"Well my friends you are in for a real treat. It turns out the man that had been slated to fight Romeo next, before his forced retirement...."

Grease heard a few snickers in the crowd. If they knew who he was then they also knew he had testified against a known crime boss and then disappeared. Motorcycle clubs and mobsters didn't do business together. It was like an unwritten code. Grease wasn't worried that the crowd were going to shred him because he had testified. He was one of them; he was a Steel Horse Cowboy and rode Harleys.

Grease was staring at Cage now who still had Sadie's braid clutched in his hand.

"Fighting against Romeo will be Cage, Vice President of Satan's Army." The crowd gasped and then cheered, they knew they were going to see a good fight. Cage had not told anyone who he had ever met that he was a big time cage fighter. This fight was also between two large men, one outlaw, one not. Grease saw Shooter push his brother towards the cage and Cage sneered at Grease while he took off his chained wallet and shirt before walking to the door.

When Cage passed near Sadie he leaned towards her and Tank had to pull her back when she tried to drunkenly punch at him.

"You're boyfriends gonna die tonight bitch." He spat at her before entering the ring.

The announcer continued, "Romeo..." Grease whispered something to him and the announcer chuckled.

"Romeo here asks to be called Grease. He's the Sergeant at Arms for the Steel Horse Cowboys!" The crowd loved that and they cheered that Grease was honoring his club.

Cage walked into the ring and the crowd cheered him as he raised his fist to the crowd displaying his large muscular arms.

The announcer motioned for the two men to meet at the center of the ring with him. What he said was broadcasted over the speaker system.

"Fighters this match is over only when one man can't get up. If he's moving he's fair game."

The crowd went berserk upon hearing that. "There are no rounds, there are no rules, you fight until one of you isn't moving. Got it?"

Grease and Cage were staring at each other and Grease saw the hate in the other man's eyes. Hate was a powerful motivator and Grease knew he had to be cautious, but it also caused many men to make stupid mistakes. Grease was banking on the latter.

The announcer moved out of the ring and locked the door with a padlock, which the crowd loved.

Tank was uneasy. He knew Grease could fight, but anything could happen and he knew who ever lost this fight would never be the same. He was holding Sadie up against him and he could tell she was trying to follow what was happening but she was fried. What ever was in her system, had her slurring her words and unable to hold herself up.

"Sweets I'm scared." Lolly whispered to her husband. Gretchen joined Dak at the side of the cage and when Sadie saw her she whimpered in distress causing Grease to look over at her. That's when Cage took his first shot.

Grease's head rocked back and he stumbled backwards. He was able to regain his balance just as the next punch came and Grease was fortunately able to block it. Shit! He had to focus. The two men circled each other warily. One would jab and the other would counter. A few punches landed but they were veteran fighters and they both knew a single punch wasn't going to end this fight in the first few minutes. Cage release a series of kicks and Grease blocked most of them. One had landed on his thigh and Grease knew if that had landed a few inches lower on his knee he'd be down on the canvas. The fighters were exchanging powerful hits. Sweat poured off both men and Grease wiped his brow quickly.

The crowd was clamoring for blood. Grease was waiting for an opening and as Cage lifted one knee for a kick he dropped his right hand low enough that Grease was able to punch over it, hitting his chin hard, causing Cages head to snap back. Blood spilled from Cages mouth and the crowd went wild at the first letting of blood.

Cage wiped the blood from his mouth and Grease saw the loathing in his eyes that Cage had for him. Then Cage let out a banshee like yell and charged at Grease, wrapping his muscular arms around Grease's waist and taking him down to the canvas. Grease twisted as he fell and landed hard on his shoulder, but Cage's large body landed on top of him, and the crazed man wailed furiously on him, landing hard blows to his face, neck, and chest. Grease blocked most of the blows, but to the crowd it appeared as if he was getting crushed. He let Cage get off a few more blows before he scissored his powerful legs around Cage's torso and twisted hard to put them both on their sides facing each other. Cage was gripping Grease's short hair and Grease had a solid hold of his wrists and then he kicked out hard, snapping his legs so they landed squarely on Cage's thighs causing Cage to grunt and release his hair. Grease quickly rolled away and got to his feet.

The crowd was cheering, but Grease had blocked them out. He was in a zone now, one that he had developed when he was fighting so he could concentrate when the crowds were too loud. Cage got to his feet quickly and again the men began to circle each other. Blood was evident on both men as their heaving bodies glistened under the lights. Grease could see that Cage was starting to lose it. His anger was making him sloppy and his technique became hurried and less effective. Each punch, each kick, and every combination that Cage threw was thrown with enough force that if they landed the fight would have been over.

Grease saw Cage reach into his pocket and produce a set of brass knuckles, which he slid over his right hand fingers. He could hear Tank and Sweets yelling from outside the cage that it was unfair, but the announcer had covered it all. No rules.

Grease kept to Cages left side, where his right hand could not reach him. He continued to jab and occasionally kick, patiently wait for the perfect opportunity. The one that he hoped would end the fight. Cage got lucky and caught the side of Grease's knee with a side kick. He then moved quickly so he could land punches with his steel covered knuckles. Grease received a few hard strikes that were ten times more damaging because of the knuckles. One blow to his ribs had him seeing stars it was so painful. Grease blocked out the pain and continued to trade blows with the irate man. Their blood was flowing freely now and both men had to keep wiping the red liquid away from their eyes.

Grease could tell that Cage was beginning to tire. One of the fighting tactics Grease had learned was how to conserve energy. Grease had won many matches by patiently waiting for his opponent to tire from their forceful barrage of punches. Grease use to wait for the opening and then lay out his then limped armed opponent. Cage was now throwing full weighted punches that Grease would block and then answer with a jab, keeping Cage off balance.

Grease knew precisely when Cage decided he wanted the fight to end. He watched as Cage faked a kick and planted his weight on his back foot. Grease knew exactly what Cage was going to do next. The son of a bitch was going to throw the exact combination that Grease had purposely walked into back at the rest stop parking lot all those weeks ago.

Cage lifted his front right leg trying to sweep Grease of his feet, but this time, instead of Grease stepping into the deadly combination, he spun to Cage's left side kicking the back of his weight bearing knee buckling the big man. Before Cage had a chance to recover Grease elbowed him hard in the ribcage and then he swiftly moved in front of him again and grabbed the back of Cage's neck with both hands pulling downwards. Cage had been slightly off balance because of the combination he was planning to throw his massive body followed the inertia Grease had created resulting in Cage being bent at the waist. Grease quickly took advantage and slammed into his exposed jaw with a powerful uppercut, and as Cage was reeling from that blow Grease lifted his right leg and as Cage was staggering back wards he performed a perfect round house kick that landed on Cage's temple. The look on Cages face was priceless as he tried to ward off the devastating blow with his hands. Cage fighters did not normally wear shoes when fighting, but today Grease had on his size twelve biker boots, and he knew the second the hard kick landed that Cage wasn't getting up.

Cage fell to the canvas with a thud and the crowd cheered. Grease stood over Cage making sure he was out. Grease could see his chest rising and falling so he knew he hadn't killed him, but there was no way he was going to be getting up.

Grease leaned over and placed his hands on his knees as his adrenaline ebbed and the exhaustion slammed into him simultaneously. Sweat pored down his shirtless chest and blood dripped off him onto the canvas. He filled his lungs with a needed breath and stood up under the ring lights as thunderous applause filled the wooded area.

The crowd was on their feet. They had certainly gotten their moneys worth. Grease watched as one of the Devils Hands bouncers unlocked the door and held it open for the MC.

The smiling MC walked to the center of the ring and grasped Grease's hand thrusting it up to signify that he was the victor. He then handed Grease a huge wad of cash and happily slapped him on the back congratulating him.

Grease was tired and his thoughts returned to Sadie and the mess he had made. He thanked the man and headed towards the door when he heard two gunshots ring out. Grease felt a sting blast against his upper arm and he slammed to the ground for cover. All hell broke loose.

Tank and Sweets made good on their promise and had been holding Sadie protectively between them throughout the fight. When they heard the gunshots they dropped to the ground. Tank covered Sadie's smaller frame with his own. Sweets was over Lolly, and Dak held Gretchen safely underneath his body. Grease slapped his hand over the painful slice that the bullet had left on his bicep and watched as the crowd dispersed. Devils Hands members swarmed the cages perimeter and when they discovered who the shooter was, they quickly wrestled him to the ground. It was a Satan's Army member, a man that Grease recognized from McDives as one of Cage's cronies.

Two Devils Hand's men held the gunman between them and Grease watched as Shooter approached him, punched him in the face, and then stripped the unconscious man of his colors. That was huge! Holy crap Shooter was pissed!

Grease was still in the cage with the MC who had also dove to the mat, and Cage who was still unmoving on the canvas.

Tank stood up keeping Sadie's head low and when he saw that it was clear he told the others they could stand. He stood up just in time to see Shooter strip the club member of his colors.

Shooter looked through the cage to where Tank stood and saluted him in a gesture of respect. Tank knew the man had not acted under orders from Shooter and this was Shooters way of letting him know this, one club president to another. Tank saluted him back.

Grease began putting his tee shirt on that Dak had thrown him as the Devils Hands Vice president approached the cage. Grease stepped down from the door and the VP shook Grease's hand.

"Haven't seen a good fight like that in years."

Grease handed the Vice president the wad of cash that he still had in his hand and the Vice President looked at him to explain. Then Grease nodded at Sadie and the man understood.

"She must be something special." He said quietly.

"You have no idea." Grease answered.

Grease had fought for one reason and one reason only. He had fought for Sadie.

His bruised body was throbbing, but all he wanted was to feel Sadie in his arms. Tank released her from his protective grasp and Grease pulled her to him. Sadie was still unaware of what had happened and Grease was worried about her.

"We have to take her to clinic guys. I don't know what Cage gave her."

"Wait a second." Tank walked around the other side of the cage and spoke with Shooter who called over another club member. When Tank returned he told them that she's been given two Quaaludes. Grease didn't know the quality of the pills and he hated that Sadie was almost rag doll limp.

"I need to get them out of her system."

He lifted a limp Sadie into his arms and carried her to the edge of the tree line. With help from Lolly he forced his finger down her throat triggering her to vomit. Sadie was swearing up a storm, but Grease didn't care how mad she was, if he could get some of the barbiturate out of her stomach she'd feel better and so would he. He held her tightly, bending her so none of her stomach contents got on her and Lolly held back what was left of her hair trying to calm her down by talking softly to her in a maternal way. Sadie was able to dispense with everything in her stomach and Grease hoped the rest of the barbiturate was purged and unable to get into her system.

Grease rode his Harley slowly back to camp because his damn rib was killing him and because he was holding Sadie in front of him. His one arm held her to his chest while he steered with the other. Tank had offered to take her, but Grease shook his head, which made Tank chuckle. Yeah, the tough guy had fallen. Back at camp Lolly made Grease shower in the trailer while she tended to Sadie. She tucked Sadie into one of the beds that folded down from the wall in the trailer. When Grease got out of the shower he quickly changed and then sat near Sadie as she slept. Her pretty face was marred with a bruise and a small cut. Her eyelids were puffy from crying and the tug on his heart knowing how much he had hurt her was crippling. He placed a kiss on her forehead sadly thinking that might be the last time he ever touched her with his lips again and retrieved a bottle of water from the refrigerator placing it near her. She was going to need it.

When he stood to leave Lolly cornered him and made him sit back down so she could bandage his ribs and tend to his cuts. She carefully smoothed antibiotic ointment over the wound that the bullet made on his arm and she butterfly bandaged the small cut on his face. His forearms were sore from fending off the blows he had taken and he knew they would be an ugly blue tomorrow.

When she finished doctoring him he went outside and found Tank and Sweets sitting by the glowing fire that had died in their absence.

"You okay?" Tank asked him seeing him grimace as he stepped down from the trailers steps.

"Yeah, I'm good."

"That was a hell of a fight Grease." Sweets praised him.

"I wasn't too happy to see those brass knuckles come out." Tank added.

"Me neither but the rules were that there were no rules." Grease reminded them.

"Still, you fought smart. People are going to talk about that for a long time."

"I did it for Sadie."

"Yeah, we know bro." Tank said smiling.

Lolly walked out of the trailer and sat on Sweets lap. Grease looked up from watching the smoldering logs in the fire. "Tank we're leaving tomorrow still right?"

"Yeah, I just talked to Sweets about it. Dak is here, so we're still represented. They'll explain things to the Border Bandits since we're scheduled to ride home with them."

"First light Tank?" Grease asked as he started for his tent.

"Yup. Grease!"

"Yeah." Grease turned back to his friends.

"You still want to go with me?"

"Yeah." Grease said quietly.

"Why don't you stay in the trailer tonight Grease?" Lolly asked, worried that her friend was hurting far worse than he was letting on.

"Sadie hates me Lolly. When she wakes up I don't want my stupid mug to be the first thing she see's."

"Honey she'll forgive you." You have to tell her why you did it."

"If I get the chance I will, but it doesn't matter. I made her cry. I bet she never cries." He said solemnly. "I hurt Gretchen too. Hell, I could have gotten Sadie killed tonight. I'm sure that's why Cage cut off her braid and drugged her. It was a pay back. If I hadn't tried to pretend that I didn't care about her, if I had just left the bar like you told me too, Sadie would be all right. She wouldn't be laying here all drugged out, and God knows what happened with her case." Grease was beating himself up and Lolly felt sorry for him, but everything he said was true. Lolly admitted to herself that she wasn't sure how Sadie would react if she saw him in the morning. She handed Grease two Advil that she'd brought out for him and told him to get some sleep.

"Hey," Grease said looking at the three best friends he could ever have. "Thanks for being there tonight. I was an ass at the bar and you hung with me. I know I would have landed in jail for putting a hole in the bars siding too. I owe you. But standing up with me against Devils Hands that was crazy, and you did it anyway. Tank, I know they were carrying. Do not tell Tess, she'll never talk to me again." He said seriously.

Tank chuckled. "Yeah, that could have been dicey. You handled it Grease. We're proud of you. The whole club is. The shit back in the bar, honestly if I hadn't seen how hurt Sadie was I'd been thumping you're back along with everyone else."

"Yeah, that was hot Grease." Sweets admitted.

Lolly laughed, "Gotta say it torqued me up a little too." Her hand feathered through Sweets graying locks.

Grease smiled sadly. "Well thanks for everything. Tank see you in a couple hours." Then Grease disappeared into his tent.

Lolly looked at her husband. "That man's hurting."

"Yeah, but there's not a damn thing we can do for him. Sadie's the one that has to forgive him."

"You know not for nothing," Lolly continued, "but she isn't all innocent here either."

"What do you mean?"

"If she really cared for Grease she would have never gone on stage with Cage. I mean honestly, I know she had a job to do, but she basically chose finding the contents of a truck over a good man."

"It's probably not that simple Lolly." Tank told her.

"Well no matter, Grease was crazed seeing her with Cage like that."

"I would have killed him." Sweets admitted.

"Well let's hope that Sadie understands what he did for her tonight."

"I may just tell her." Lolly said snuggling into Sweets warm chest.

"Now woman don't go getting involved." Sweets warned his wife with a knowing chuckle.

20

Sadie woke up and only vaguely remembered what had happened the night before. She had no idea where she was and her mouth was ash dry. She perched up on her elbow and looked around. She was in a camper and then she remembered Lolly tucking her in. Then she bolted upright as she hazily recalled that Grease had been there too.

Sadie sat up and reached for the water bottle someone had kindly left for her. A curtain opened and Tank appeared wearing unbuttoned jeans and no shirt. Shit, that was a sight. The man was built.

"Morning." He said unaware of how his shirtless body was effecting her.

"Morning." She said as Tank shuffled towards her.

"Some night, huh?' He said wondering how much she remembered.

Sadie teared up immediately thinking about Grease and Gretchen.

"Shit." Tank whispered, not wanting to wake up Sweets and Lolly. "Don't cry."

Sadie heard a soft voice coming from behind another curtained area.

"Tank I swear if you upset that poor girl." Sadie knew it was Lolly and then Lolly pushed open the curtain and walked out wearing a tee shirt that fell to her knees.

"How you feeling Honey?" She opened the Advil bottle and handed two pills to Sadie who washed them down her throat immediately.

"I have a little headache. What happened?"

"What's the last thing you remember?" Lolly asked.

"I remember Poppy's." She said with a hitch in her voice. Lolly patted her hand.

"Yeah, that wasn't fun was it?"

Sadie shook her head as tears sprung into her eyes again. "Then I remember Cage yelling at me and he..." Sadie reached behind her and when she didn't feel her braid she swore. "That damn bastard chopped my braid off. Son of a bitch." Tank chuckled at her colorful language.

"It will grow back." Lolly said gently. "What else do you remember?"

Cage forced pills down my throat and I wanted to throw it up but I couldn't. The next thing I knew I was in a wire cage and some big ass woman was beating on me."

Sweets walked out of the curtained room as Sadie continued talking, "It's a little hazy after that."

"Want us to tell you what happened?" Lolly asked her seriously.

"Yes, tell me, please."

The three of them began explaining everything that transpired after they had left Poppy's. Tank told her how Grease had lost it seeing her up on stage with Cage and that he hoped that being in the shooter contest with another woman would lead Cage to think that he wasn't interested in her. The problem was, Tank explained, was that he took it too far. Sadie interrupted.

"Yeah, too frigging far. I couldn't stop crying and that's when Cage knew there was something going on between us. He became irate and I lost it. I was thinking that I was choosing a damn truck over Grease, and I knew I had hurt him by going on stage with Cage."

"Smart girl." Lolly interjected.

Sadie went on. "I knew my cover was blown, but I didn't even care. I was so mad at Cage, at Grease, but mostly with myself. I told Cage that Grease was more man than he would ever be, and that he was dreaming if he thought I would ever be with him. Cage was laughing like a he was deranged. It was scary. He pointed out that Grease was no way into me. That Grease's new woman was beautiful and sexy and that I was dreaming to think I could ever compete with her. God that hurt." Sadie said quietly.

"I remember that I was trying to get away from Cage. He had me tossed into a truck bed, but I was able to get in one good swing. That didn't go over too well. He climbed into the truck with me and with the help of his minions he forced a pill down my throat and washed it down with whisky. They were laughing and I was helpless. They tied me to the truck bed and I remember thinking that I was so dead. I was still putting up a fight; I think I got in a head butt, so Cage had his men hold me down while he chopped off my hair. Then they covered me with a blanket, stuffed a rag in my mouth and tightened the straps even more. I couldn't move. We were bouncing along a dirt road and I wanted to purge the pill, but I was flat on my back and it had already started to effect me. The next thing I remember I was in the cage."

Tank picked up the story from there, "Dak was at the fights and he rode back here to tell Grease that you were in the cage and that you didn't look right. We raced over there and Grease jacked up one of the men who were guarding the door. It was turning ugly, but the Vice President of the Devils Hands got involved. He was the one running the fights. Grease talked him into letting you out of the cage and in your place he would fight Cage."

Sadie let that piece of information sink in.

"I kind of remember him taking me out of the cage. Did Grease win? He did, right? Is he all right?"

"Yeah, he won, but he took some good hits."

"He got shot, too." Lolly reminded the guys.

"What?"

"One of Cages followers shot him after the fight. It only grazed him. Shooter ripped the colors from the guy."

"I'm telling you, Shooters not bad." Sadie told them.

Lolly took over telling Sadie the rest of what had transpired. "So after everything calmed down Grease had me help him make you toss your cookies. Tank had asked Shooter what Cage had given you and Shooter told him it was two Quaaludes. Grease didn't like that it was in your system so he stuck his fingers down your throat and purged your stomach."

"Wow."

"Yeah, the man cares for you Sadie."

Sadie hung her head. "I saw him with Gretchen remember?"

Tank chuckled. "Honey why don't you go talk to the man? He's right outside in the pup tent. He may have taken a bit of a beating last night from fighting Cage, but trust me, it's nothing compared to how he has been beating himself up since Poppy's."

"I don't know." She said tentatively.

"Sweetie, I'm asking you as a friend. Please go talk to Grease." Lolly implored her.

Sadie asked to use the bathroom first. She washed her face and pushed her hair back behind her ears hoping to tame the uneven edges. She thanked Grease's friends and headed towards the pup tents.

She wasn't sure what she was going to say to Grease. She knew she should thank him for getting her out of the cage, but visions of him with Gretchen danced in front of her as she walked and she wasn't sure if she could handle seeing him. He had moved on and she had stupidly thought he would wait for her.

As she neared the two tents she saw the zipper moving on one of flaps and out stepped Gretchen looking morning sexy in a just fucked kind of way. Sadie froze in her tracks and tears stung her eyes. How could she be so foolish? Of course she was sleeping with him. Why would Grease ever want her if he could have someone as gorgeous and sexy as Gretchen? Her stomach lurched and she couldn't stop the anger that coursed through her thinking that his friends had sent her out there on purpose. That was just mean! Well message received!

Sadie turned and began walking away in the opposite direction.

"Hey, hey, wait a second." Gretchen shouted at her. Sadie couldn't turn around. Was she going to rub it in her face that she had just slept with Grease?"

"Sadie stop." Gretchen pleaded. Sadie sighed, wiped her damp eyes and turned around. Gretchen was standing outside of the tent looking upset and then Sadie saw the same tent flap move again and this time Dak stepped out. He wrapped his arms around Gretchen sleepily and nuzzled her neck.

Whoa, what was she doing with Dak?

The tent next to them unzipped and Sadie watched as Grease lumbered out of the small tent opening. He didn't have a shirt on and his jeans were unbuttoned at the top. She saw that his ribs were bandaged his arm was also wrapped with gauze and that he had a cut on his face. He looked so virile and badass handsome that her breath caught in her throat.

Sadie stared at Grease and Grease stared at Sadie. Grease was afraid she was going to scream at him and Sadie wasn't sure as to what was going on. She heard the trailer door slam open.

"Oh for the love of Pete! Sadie, Gretchen was with Dak." Lolly yelled to her.

Grease was looking at Sadie with a concerned look and Sadie saw the immense sadness in his eyes.

"I saw Gretchen come out of the tent." She stammered. Grease began slowly walking towards Sadie until he stood about a yard away from her. She was so confused and a zillion different emotions were flying through her.

"Are you okay?" He asked her, running his eyes over her face and down her body.

"Yes, are you?"

"Yeah."

"You're friends told me what you did for me last night. Thank you."

"I was so afraid I wouldn't get to the cage in time. We were pushing through the crowd and I kept seeing the woman pull back her fists to hit you. I knew if she connected, you'd be really hurt. I felt so helpless. Sadie, I'm so sorry I hurt you."

"Grease, I hurt you too." She admitted to him. "I should have never gone on stage with him."

"I only wanted to help you. To make Cage think I didn't care for you, but when I saw him kiss you and touch you I lost it."

"Yeah, I wasn't too happy seeing you with Gretchen."

Grease stepped closer to her and was relieved when she didn't back away. "When I saw you crying it destroyed me. My tough girl was crying. I thought you'd see through the ruse, but I was out of my head. I lost it."

"I was devastated Grease." She admitted with her eyes on his. "I didn't think it was an act, you and Gretchen. I thought I'd driven you to her by being with Cage. I looked up on that stage and saw the first man that I had ever loved performing an intensely erotic act with a beautiful woman not only in front of me, but hundreds of other people."

"Loved?"

"What?"

"You said loved. You used the past tense."

"Grease." Sadie whispered as tears spilled down her face.

"I know I don't deserve your love." His voice trembled thinking she was going to say good bye.

Sadie looked up at him. Her beautiful green eyes swimming in emotional tears. She wiped away the tears that wouldn't stop rolling down her cheeks.

"Don't you know that you're my happy evermore?"

"Evermore?"

"Forever. My mom used to tell me I'd find a good man and instead of saying Happily Ever After she'd say I'd Find my Happy Evermore."

"I know what it meant Sadie, I just." Sadie interrupted him looking flustered.

"I can't hold this inside me anymore, and I know it's more than you bargained for, but I'm going to lay my feelings out for you." Sadie sighed knowing her honesty may cost her big time, but she might as well tell him. If he wasn't thinking the way she was it would be better to cut the ties now. She'd still hurt but she couldn't imagine the pain that she'd feel if she was with him for a few months and then they called it quits. That would be even harder.

"Grease, I can't imagine me ever loving anyone more than I love you. Present tense." She finished with an anxious smile.

"You still love me? After Gretchen? After probably blowing your job? Getting your hair chopped off? Getting you drugged?"

Sadie smiled gently at him and she nodded unable to speak.

"Are you sure?" He asked unable to believe what he just heard.

Her eyes twinkled mischievously, through the shimmer of fresh tears. "Well losing my hair, that could be a deal breaker." She teased him gently punching his one arm playfully with a closed fist. Grease pulled her to him and kissed her breathless. Then he cuddled her gently to him.

"No. I heard you woman. I'm your Happy Evermore." He reminded her. He kissed her tenderly and then found her eyes with his.

"I have missed you so much Sadie."

"I've missed you too."

From behind them they heard Lolly say, "Finally." and Tank and Sweets started laughing.

"Grease, man you said we could go home today." Tank yelled to him. "Tell her you'll see her back in Happy. I want to see my family."

"You're leaving?"

"I promised Tank I'd ride home with him today. What are your plans?"

"I need to find CC. I'm not sure what happened with the case."

"Will you come back to Happy when you're done?"

"Yes." Sadie looked at him and he saw a cloud of despair pass through her beautiful green eyes.

"What's the matter?" His voice caught unsure of what she was going to say.

"I can't believe I finally get to see you and you're leaving." She admitted sadly.

Grease smiled at her. His heart was pounding wildly against his ribs he was so happy that she still loved him.

"I promised him and I'd never let him make the trip alone. Dak and Sweets are going to stay with everyone else."

"I understand that. I only meant I wish I had more time with you."

Grease kissed her tenderly. "You clear that calendar of yours love. We need to spend some quality time together. I've never been in a relationship before but if I have to drive to Helena everyday to see you, I will."

"Uh, Grease about that."

"What?"

"Liam's retiring at the end of the summer. Joe's going to be the new Sheriff and I've applied to be the new Deputy." She waited for the news to sink in.

Then Grease got the biggest smile on his face that she had ever seen and he picked her up, twirled around and when he put her down he planted little kisses all over her face.

"That's the best news I ever heard."

"Really? Oh that's a relief. I was worried that if we were still together you might feel like I was butting in on your new life in Happy. You know having your girlfriend around all the time?"

Grease got a thoughtful look in his eyes and nervously looked away from Sadie and down at the grass before looking back up at her.

"About the girlfriend thing." He hesitated awkwardly and Sadie felt her stomach pitch uncomfortably.

"Sadie." Grease sighed anxiously. "Before I leave and so there are no misunderstandings. I don't want you in my life as a girlfriend."

Sadie's heart plummeted and her face turned crimson she was so embarrassed. Wow, she had really miss read him. What an idiot she was.

"I, I'm sorry Grease I didn't mean to assume anything. I, uh."

"Darlin." Grease interrupted her seeing how she had misunderstood his last statement. "I want you in my life as my wife, not my girlfriend."

At first Sadie just stared at him. She was so upset about him not wanting her to be his girlfriend that it took a couple of seconds for her to process what he had just said.

Then she got a huge grin on her face. "Grease!" Sadie laughed. "You did not just propose to me here in Sturgis after the worst night of my life, looking like hell?"

Grease still a little worried that she may not accept his unplanned impromptu proposal

"Yes, I did. I don't want to waste any more time not being with you, Sadie. I love you. I think I have since the day I saw you in your Mom's office, and for the record you will always look beautiful to me. Now, answer me woman."

Grease got down on one knee and Lolly, Sweets and Tank watched on from the window inside the trailer and again he proposed to his Sadie.

"Will you honor me by becoming my wife, and please tell me you want kids?"

Sadie knelt down and wrapped her arms around Greases broad shoulders.

"Yes, I'll marry you, and yes I want children."

Grease hugged her to him and when he stood up he brought Sadie to her feet as well.

Tank, Lolly and Sweets came rushing out of the trailer. They had all been watching from the small kitchen window. Hugs and congratulations were given to Grease and Sadie and after a few minutes of rehashing the way Grease had proposed Tank let himself be heard.

"Now can we go Grease? I miss my Tess!" Everyone laughed at their fearless leader's child like whine.

Sadie helped Grease roll his tent and sleeping bag and put in the back of Lolly's truck. It took them longer than usual since Grease kept kissing her.

As Tank and Grease sat on their bikes ready to head out Grease couldn't stop holding Sadie, He couldn't stop smiling either, and Tank told him he was going to eat bugs the whole ride home if he didn't shut his mouth.

"You'll come as soon as you can?" Grease asked her again hating to let her go.

"Yes, promise."

"You'll stay out of the bars?"

Sadie laughed. "Yes, Grease I'm sure CC will find me soon."

"You're going to marry me?"

"Yes." Sadie laughed.

"And have babies with me?"

"Yes. Now go. Poor Tank is losing his patience."

"One more kiss." Grease said pulling her to him.

"For goodness sakes Grease!" Tank clamored as he roared off.

"Love you Sadie." Grease said, following behind his President. "Hurry home!" He yelled over his shoulder.

21

The entire ride back to Happy Grease was a happy
man. They pulled into a motel after a good five hours
of riding to sleep and before the sun was up they
headed home. Grease drove right to The Pen and
Grease'd Hogs. His small work force was glad to have
him back and Bitsie and Ivy made him two grilled
cheese with bacon sandwiches and a vanilla milk
shake as a welcome back lunch.

The store had done well in the days that he had been
away and Polly was already looking through catalogs
to replenish their stock. Ed had become somewhat of
the host for the luncheonette. He would greet
customers at the stores door and if they wanted to look
around the store he would welcome them and if they
wanted to eat he would show them to a table.
Everyone seemed content and the business was
flourishing so Grease was beyond pleased.

After eating, Grease went out back to the barn. Justin
Brent was the man Tank had hired to sell his Harley's.
Justin was in his late twenties and knew every little
thing about Harley's. He often was found reciting the
history of how Harley's came to be to would be
buyers. Justin was relatively new to the Steel Horse
Cowboys and had been a real asset to the club since
he'd been given his leather vest. He was also one of the
men that had accompanied Grease when he'd gone and
brought back Sadie. Grease liked the man. He didn't
have family that anyone knew of and he kept to
himself. It reminded Grease a little of himself years
ago. The two men got on well since neither were the
talkative type, yet both were hard workers.

Justin was all smiles when he saw Grease and Grease
soon found out it was because he had sold two

Harley's while he was gone and had lined up a rebuild for Grease. Grease thanked him and then began working on the new motorcycle that he was outfitting for Brett Phantom, who he had bought his tailgate lift from.

Grease put in a good days work before leaving. He stopped at Pete's for some food staples and then headed up the mountain to his cabin. He ate a peanut putter sandwich and it reminded him about Sadie. Everything was reminding him about her; his bedroom where they'd made love, the patio where he discovered how compatible they were, his Harley, and how she put her hands under his shirt while riding behind him. Grease wished he could call her and it dawned on him the only thing he didn't like about living in Happy was not being able to use a cell phone. He already missed Sadie and he had no idea when he was going to see her again.

After a good night sleep Grease felt great. He had two things he wanted to do that day, so after a shower and cup of coffee he headed down the mountain. First he drove to Sadie's parents' house. It was only nine in the morning at Grease hoped to catch her parents at home. When he drove in he saw that both their cars were there. After knocking Nancy let him in and she introduced him to her husband Randy. Nancy poured a cup of coffee for Grease and after a few minutes of polite conversation that centered on Grease's businesses in town Grease got right to the point.

"I love Sadie. She loves me. I would like to marry her and it would be a good weight off my mind if you'd give us your blessings."

Nancy must have had some idea why Grease had dropped by because she had a small smile on her face and remained quiet. Randy, who was a large man, with a mustache and strands of gray threading through his light brown hair and the same eyes as Sadie, green with brown flecks, rubbed his chin before speaking.

"You love her?"

"I do."

"How do you know?"

Grease smiled picturing Sadie's beautiful face. "I can't think straight when she's near me and I'm crazy when she's not. My insides ache when I'm not with her and when we are together I feel like I'm going to combust I'm so happy."

Randy started chuckling. "Yup, Nancy the boys in love alright. That's exactly how I felt when I first started dating you."

"Felt?" Nancy said teasing her husband.

"Still do Darling and you know it." He said giving her a wink, which made Nancy blush.

"So son what's the plan?"

"I have to talk to Sadie, but if I had my way we'd marry tomorrow."

"Now Grease I want a nice wedding for my only daughter." Nancy told him.

"And son, I plan on walking her down the aisle." Randy added.

Grease's face fell. He'd been given their blessing but he really didn't want a big affair.

"Why don't we let Sadie decide what she wants." Grease said diplomatically.

Sadie's dad grinned widely. "Smart man."

After Grease left his soon to be in-laws house he headed for Helena. He wanted to buy his woman the best ring ever. The next time he saw her he planned to get down on his knees again and this time when he asked her he'd have something to put on her finger.

At the jewelry store Grease found the perfect ring. The engagement ring had a round diamond that wasn't set too high and on each side it had emeralds and smoky quartz gems. The ring reminded Grease of her beautiful eyes. He then bought a silver wedding band that complemented the engagement ring. Under the band he asked that 'My Tough Girl' be engraved. With her job he knew she wouldn't wear the engagement ring, everyday but she would wear the wedding band. He wanted everyone to know she was spoken for. The sales person was complimenting his taste and she boxed up the engagement ring. She told him the man that did the engraving was working in the back, but she didn't think he could do his ring right then so she asked Grease to come back in a week. Grease pulled out two hundred bucks and laid the two bills on the glass counter top.

"I'd be very appreciative if he could do my ring now." Grease told the woman.

The woman picked up the bills and went into the back room. When she returned she told Grease his ring would be done in an hour.

One hour later Grease returned to the store and left with two cushioned white ring boxes. One had her engagement ring and the other contained her engraved wedding band.

Grease couldn't wait to see her again; it was killing him not knowing when she'd arrive. He pulled into

Grease'd Hog and saw a white Subaru parked in the back. He hoped Justin had another customer.
When Grease walked into the small dealership his mouth dropped. Sadie was sitting up on Justin's desk in a little yellow sundress and cowboy boots. She'd been laughing and her legs were swinging gently as she listened to Justin's Harley history lesson.
Grease now walked into the small show room, and the second Sadie saw him she jumped from the desk and sprung into his arms. She wrapped her tan legs around his hips and kissed him solidly. Grease had his hands on her thighs anchoring her to him and his world completely righted again just because he was holding her. A small cough from Justin reminded them that they were not alone and Grease gently let her slide down his hulk like frame.
"You're here." Was all Grease could choke out.
Sadie was all smiles and leaned into his side. "I am."
Grease thanked Justin for keeping her company and then he led Sadie into his shop and closed and locked the door they walked out of and Grease made sure the barn door was locked as well.
"I'm glad your home." He told her with a husky voice. His cock had responded immediately to her sweet kiss and he planned to put it to good use. He'd missed his woman.
Grease lifted her up onto the clean work table. He couldn't believe she was there. He threaded his fingers through her hair and that's when he noticed that she'd had it shaped.
"I like your hair cut."
Sadie was smiling coyly she hadn't taken her hands off of him and she loved how his body felt under her hands. "Thank you."

Grease leaned down and kissed Sadie tenderly. "I love you Sadie Hawkins." He whispered with his lips almost touching hers.

"I love you too Grease Prentiss." Her warm breath tickled his lips and he pressed his mouth against hers. What started out as gentle and unhurried turned frenzied and hot with in seconds.

Grease had his hands under her dress and skimming up the sides to cup her ample breasts. Sadie moaned as he found her nipples with his thumbs. Grease pulled his hands out from under the confining material and lowered the dresses thin spaghetti straps. The dress did not have a zipper, just a little elastic under the breasts and Grease pulled the top of the dress down freeing her round globes of flesh.

He immediately lowered his head and latched on to a rose bud and twirled his tongue around the erect flesh. His cock was throbbing and he stood and quickly undid his belt and his top button and lowered the zipper on his jeans to relieve the pressure.

Sadie reached for him and Grease loved feeling her slide her soft hands up and down his manhood as he bucked gently into her hand. Then he took her hands in his and placed them on his shoulders. Sadie looked into Grease's beautiful eyes and saw such love staring back at her that she mouthed the words, 'I love you' to him.

Grease helped her to stand and then he quickly took off her dress and little thong. He kept the cowboy boots on, she looked hot in them.

Grease then plucked her up and she circled his hips with her legs while Grease held her rear in his hands. He walked them to a back wall and leaned Sadie against it. He then took her hands and placed them on the small beam above her.

"Is my man going a little dom on me?"

"If that means am I going to make love to you until you scream then yes."

Grease was so strong that Sadie didn't even have to hold herself up she just held her hands above her head and grasped the beam. The erotic position had her breasts positioned perfectly for Grease to enjoy with his mouth. Grease took one hand off her rear and pulled his cock free from his drawers.

Sadie could feel the dampness already coating her folds and when Grease's satiny domed head slid through her needy lips she moaned. Grease moved his cock up and down her wetness as he held her possessively with his large hands. His eyes were locked on to hers and Sadie felt the ripples begin as his head pressed against her engorged clit.

Grease sucked one of her breasts into his mouth and Sadie moved her hips against his rock hard length. She was going to cum and she quickened her pace to get herself there. Grease felt her start to quiver and hiked her slightly higher onto the wall. He then found Sadie's eyes with his and slowly sank into her molten core.

"I need to touch you." She whispered.

"Touch me." He whispered back not breaking the eye contact that was cementing their souls.

Grease began to work himself deeper into her heat and Sadie's walls clutched him. She was euphoric loving how aroused she felt, how deeply he was inside of her, and how much she loved this man.

"Grease. Please, please. "Sadie uttered.

Grease moved his hands so his finger tips could gently opened her backside allowing his length to forge even higher. Sadie moaned it was such an exquisite feeling. He was deeply seated and his powerful surges into her had her vibrating, but it was the way he pulled out of her that had her coming unhinged. He'd drag himself out of her tight channel slowly, and when his thickly edged rim rubbed against her cushiony g-spot she physically trembled.

Grease knew she was close and so was he. He'd already bitten his tongue twice to keep from shooting early. Grease ran his finger tips through the wetness near her core as he continued to press in and out of her. Then he ran one lubricated tip around her small virgin rosette pressing into her gently. Sadie moaned loudly and Grease felt his balls pinch tight. He continued to dip his one finger in and out of her while he increased the pace of his love making. With his hands on her backside he leaned his forehead on her forehead and pressed her so that the firm skin above his wide base massaged her clitoris.

Sadie began to shake. Her breasts bounced, her hips flexed and then she completely unraveled crying his name out over and over as pulsating waves of pleasure rolled through her. Grease felt her tighten on his thick cock and when her core wept for him he found his own sweet release.

Grease had cum so hard that his knees were weak and his ribs were now hurting so badly from her legs being wrapped so vice like around him that he sank to the floor bringing her with him. Sadie loosened her grip on him but remained on his lap with him still wonderfully burrowed deeply inside of her. They were both breathing heavily and Sadie rested her head against his now damp tee shirt.

Sadie's arms were wound around his massive chest and she moved her hands under his shirt and that's when she felt the wrap he had on to support his ribs.

"Grease? What is this?" Grease tried to push her hand away gently.

"Nothing. Don't worry." He never finished his sentence as Sadie pushed his shirt up and saw the wrap.

"Is this from the fight?" She said gently unwrapping the bandage.

Grease did not reply.

When Sadie saw the large ugly purple mark on his rib cage she gasped.

"Oh my gosh! What happened? No fist would leave a mark like that."

Grease tried to put his tee shirt back down but Sadie was stubborn and was not going to let this drop.

"Grease tell me now!"

"Brass knuckles. Cage used a pair of brass knuckles."

"Oh baby." Sadie had tears in hers eyes. "I'm so sorry."

Grease wrapped her tightly in his arms after getting her to put his shirt down and held her. They sat like that for a few minutes and then Sadie kissed him so tenderly that Grease choked up.

He was still inside her but softening until Sadie pressed him backwards. His jeans and boxers were around his thighs now and Sadie took her dress off and tucked it under his head. She then bent down holding him inside of her as she dragged her large breasts gently across his face. His response was swift and stiff. Sadie took his hands and placed them over his head as she gently rode his hardening manhood. Her breasts were tingling as he sucked and twirled her nipples into two sensitive hard points. Sadie worked her mans flesh into a hot thick rod. He tried to press up into her, but she clucked her tongue at him giving him a saucy smile. She wanted to make love to him and Grease let her. She moved slowly at first until he was solidly set inside of her, then she moved faster and when she felt him tighten she lifted off of him completely and roll her slippery wetness over his broad shaft. Sadie was feeling the pulls of an orgasm herself so she guided his satiny head back inside of her and twerked her hips rapidly so that his sizeable length slid in and out of her.

"Sadie, Sadie that feels so good baby." Grease was beside himself. She was so wet and hot and his cock was fisted tightly inside of her. Grease felt the heat begin to shoot through his rod. He untangled one of his hands from Sadie's grip and strummed her clit hard sending her careening into a shattering orgasm. Grease rocked into her hard as his love jetted out his body and into her warm core.

Sadie fell on top of his chest being mindful of his rib. "I can't get enough of you." She said against his rising chest.

Grease chuckled. "Ditto baby."

After a few minutes Grease decided they needed to take themselves to a bed. He helped Sadie to stand and they walked to the bathroom off the work room together. They washed up using the paper towels and Grease helped her put her dress back on, but not until after he had kissed her in a few delicious places first. Sadie placed a tender kisses on the swollen purple welts surrounding his ribs before she rewrapped him. When they were presentable Grease unlocked the door and they walked up to The Pen.

Grease introduced her to Polly, Ed, Minnie and Peach. He didn't refer to her as his fiancé and Sadie felt a tug of disappointment in her heart. She knew he loved her but she wanted it all with him. He was her happy ending and she prayed he still wanted that too.

Minnie and Peach fed them and after they ate Grease locked up the barn and they drove on his Harley to the spot that he had taken her on their first date; the one that looked over the town of Happy.

Sadie knew where they were headed and she simply enjoyed being behind him as they rode. She snuck her hands up under his shirt and leaned close so she could talk to him. "I love touching you when we ride."

"It's funny, but I was thinking about that just the other day."

Grease parked his big bike and helped Sadie off and they stood looking out over the town as the sun changed into a glorious orange ball heading towards the mountain range.

"This is a special place isn't it?" Sadie asked.

"It is. When I joined the club it's where Tank told me I was no longer a Prospect and that I would be getting my vest that night."

"That's a good memory."

"Yes, but I want an even better one." Grease said stepping away from her. He got down on one knee and looked up at his beautiful woman.

"Sadie, I love you. I know I already asked this but I wanted to do it proper. I asked your parents this morning and got their blessing."

Sadie interrupted. "You did?"

"I did." He said smiling. "I want to make this official. I want you in my life as my wife, my friend, and hopefully soon, the mother of my children. I love you woman. Marry me?"

Sadie was misty eyed with the beautiful proposal and she nodded happily, but what he did next floored her. Grease stood and opened a white ring box and inside was the most gorgeous ring that she'd ever seen.

"Grease it's beautiful." Grease placed the ring on her finger.

"It reminds me of your eyes. Beautiful, brilliant, green with brown flecks. I'll never forget looking into them for the first time."

"It's lovely. I love it! Thank you."

Sadie leaned up and kissed him and they kissed tenderly so content to just hold each other.

"Okay, now it's official! I still haven't had enough of you yet so how about we take this back to my cabin?"

"Um Grease I can't just start living with you." Sadie laughed.

"Why not?"

"Well my parents for one reason. I'm sure I can spend a few nights with you but until we are married I'll have to stay with them."

"Oh come on Sadie! There is no way I'm sleeping apart from you ever again. Ever!"

Sadie started laughing and Grease looked at her like she was nuts.

Finally she confessed. "Yeah, I feel the same way too."

"So what are we going to do? Your dad already said he wants to walk you down the aisle and your Mom wants a nice wedding."

"Come on. I'm going to put my big girl pants on and tell them I'll be staying with you while we plan the wedding. A small wedding."

Grease sighed and looked out over the beautiful vista still holding Sadie's hand.

"Baby, I don't want your parents upset with you or with me. I'm dead serious about not sleeping apart from you. I've never needed anyone in my life before, yet when I think of you not being with me... Well let's just say it isn't a good feeling."

Sadie leaned up and gave him a tender kiss.

"I love you Grease. We will be together. I promise. Your giving me this ring today it means more to me than, well, it just happened to be perfect timing that's all. I want to be your wife. I want that more than you can imagine. I actually would prefer that we make it official as soon as possible. Let's go reason with my parents."

Grease smiled at his beautiful fiancé and kissed her palm sweetly. Then they got on his Harley and rode to Sadie's parents' house.

Grease had a knot in his stomach the entire ride. He had done right by going to talk with her parents, but now he knew they may not be to happy that while waiting for them to pull a wedding together they were going to live together.

When they arrived at Sadie's house they saw that Liam's Sheriff's car was in the driveway. Grease gave Sadie a little look wondering what was up and Sadie simple shrugged. "They're good friends Grease. He's my Godfather. Maybe it's good that he's here."

Sadie took her Tough Guy by the hand and they walked into the house ready to face her parents.

The first thing they noticed was that Nancy was wiping away tears with a tissue and Randy had his arm around her. Before they had a chance to ask what was up they heard another car pull into the drive. Sadie went to the door and opened it up to CC and another woman she didn't recognize, but she was wearing a US Marshal Badge. Sadie noticed that another man wearing a badge remained outside by the car.

"Sadie, this is US Marshal Amanda Holt." Sadie didn't have time to react because Liam came in from the other room.

"We haven't told her yet."

Sadie got a knot in her stomach. "Told me what?"

Liam took Sadie by the elbow and walked her into the living room.

"Everyone needs to sit down." Liam told the group. Grease did not like what he was seeing. He knew all too well what US Marshal's did and he became uneasy. He still hadn't told Sadie about his past. Was this about him? He had no idea and it scared the ever loving crap out of him.

When everyone was situated CC took hold of the conversation.

"Sadie, you did a great job in retrieving the stolen truck and its contents."

Sadie nodded. "Thank you." She said quietly looking nervously around. Her mother was still weeping.

"We have been given information that Cage has been working with a network of outlaw bikers, not just here, but in Mexico. A very reliable source has informed us that he has put a hit out on you. It's a sizable bounty and we are worried."

Sadie's mom began weeping harder and Randy looked ashen as he tried to comfort her. Grease took hold of Sadie's hand knowing what was coming next. His stomach had dropped and his mouth went dry as he physically began to feel sick.

"Sadie we want to put you in Witness Protection until Cage is caught."

Grease looked at Sadie who was sitting very still and if not for the way she was gripping his hand so tightly he would have wondered if she had actually heard what CC said.

"Baby?" He leaned towards her and whispered softly. No one spoke as they waited for Sadie to react.

"Do I have to go?"

"The hit includes your parents Sadie. They know who you are. Cage had one of your coworkers killed at Ship It Good and tortured her for your personal information. How did he know you worked for them? We have no idea. The only thing we can figure is when they were processing the men that we caught one of our Agents let slip that Sadie and Ship It Good were going to be stoked."

"Well shit." She said softly.

"Yeah, he's been suspended. Young kid, too exuberant. We're sorry."

"So you really think I need to be protected?"

"We think you and your parents do, just until Cage is caught. You can testify about some things regarding him, but honestly it's more of a vendetta against you."

"Should have killed the ass hole." Grease muttered to himself uneasily.

"We can place you and your parents together and I promise we will get him Sadie. It's for your safety and your parents."

Sadie looked at Grease his lips had formed a tight line. She could tell he was reigning in his emotions. His eyes had turned a dark blue gray. Those were his troubled eyes.

"How long do I have?" She asked knowing she had to protect her parents.

"You're leaving now, as soon as your Mom and Dad can pack a few things. We know you have most of your stuff in Helena. Your place has probably been staked out by Cage or one of his club members so we aren't even going there. We will buy you all new stuff."

"Satan's Army is involved?" Grease asked tightly.

"No Cage has broken off from them, but a few men went with him."

Sadie stood up and pulled Grease up with her. "I need a few minutes with Grease. Mom go pack."

Grease smiled sadly seeing how his Tough Girl was handling everything. He had been in her shoes once, and he admired her and loved her even more for protecting her parents and making the difficult transition easier on everyone. He followed behind her as she pulled him into the kitchen. He knew what was coming. He was about to become unengaged and maybe even lose her forever. He felt his heart aching with agony.

"Grease, I'm sorry about this." She was facing him and had her arms around his waist as she looked up at her man.

"I know Honey."

"Do you want me to give you your ring back?" She asked hesitatingly.

"No. I love you Sadie. You're it for me. Do you want to break it off?"

"No, actually I was hoping you would marry me before I leave?"

What? It was as if he heard the brakes skidding to a stop on asphalt.

"What?"

"Would you marry me before I leave?" She repeated.

"Sadie I love you, but I can't go into Witness Protection with you. My businesses and well I just can't. I'm sorry."

"I know. I would never ask you to come with me. Well, I would if I thought you could, but that's not practical. I understand that."

"So you still want to marry me? Even though we won't be together?"

"Even more so. We can't tell anyone though. Well, you can't. I don't want you to become a target, but I would like to take your name before I leave." She stood on her tip toes and kissed his sweet lips. "I'm coming back Grease. I'd like to come back to my husband. If you still want me?"

"I'll always want you, Sweetheart. Always. How can we do this?"

"Liam's an ordained Preacher." She told him with a sad smile.

"Okay then. Let's do this."

Sadie went upstairs telling Grease she wanted to change into a dress and Grease felt very under dressed but Sadie recognized this and quickly kissed him telling him the way he dressed was part of the many reasons she loved him, which put him instantly at ease. While Sadie was changing Grease had gone back out to his Harley and retrieved the white box containing the wedding band. He put the box back in the pack on his bike and pocketed the band.

When he returned Sadie was already back downstairs. She had changed into a white summer dress and despite her sad face she looked gorgeous and once again Grease admired her strength. She must have said something to her parents because they had no problem with the quick nuptials. Sadie took his hand and walked him away from the small waiting group.

"This isn't too fast?" She asked quietly. "I'll understand if you want to wait."

"Shhh." He said laying a finger across her lips. "Let Liam make you mine lawfully."

"Lawfully?" Sadie giggled.

Grease looked her in the eyes and cupped her cheeks with his large hands. "You're already mine Tough Girl. I've been waiting for you my whole life."

Sadie got tears in her eyes.

"Sheesh, and I told myself I was not going to cry!" She admonished Grease lightly for his sentimental declaration.

Grease leaned in and whispered, "We'll do it up right Sadie when you get back, okay?"

"There's no need Grease. Just getting to marry you before I go, that's what I care about. I love you. Evermore, remember?"

"I love you too. Evermore."

Grease gave her a gentle hug and they walked back to the center of the living room. Liam asked for everyone's attention and within five minutes Grease and Sadie were declared husband and wife. CC took pictures with her iPhone and fifteen minutes later Grease and Liam stood outside and watched the Marshall's car drive away.

22

It had been eight months since Grease had married
Sadie. Eight long and lonely months had passed, but
he had endured his first winter away from his club. No
one except Liam and CC knew he was married. When
their paths crossed they always asked how he was
doing. He knew they were concerned for him. No one
knew why Sadie had all of a sudden vanished from
Grease's life. Tank had tried to talk to him about it and
Grease just shook his head and gave him a look that
warned Tank off the subject.

Bettina had tried to get him drunk during the Labor
Day picnic hoping to rekindle their 'friends with
benefits' status, but Grease let her know very quickly
that he was not interested. He wished he could tell her
that he was a married man and that he was
permanently off limits but he knew that couldn't
happen. His friend's left for Townsend the next day
and a comforting peacefulness settled over the small
mountain town.

Grease had thrown himself into his work and rarely
left Happy. His friends had made the drive north to
visit him a couple times and Grease knew Tank was
worried about him because Toby had dropped in on
him for no reason at all. Joe had tried to get him to go
out to dinner with him and CC, but Grease had
declined those invites. Grease didn't want to be around
other people. He missed Sadie. He had no idea where
she was or even what was happening with the case.
CC had hand delivered a few letters from her. In the
letters Sadie said she was well and that she missed him
terribly. She couldn't tell him where she was or even
what she had been doing so the letters were cryptic but

they did give him a small piece of mind that she still loved him and that she was missing him too. He had written her a letter a week. When CC gave him her letters he would hand her a stack to give to Sadie. In his letters he gave her a detailed account of what was happening in Happy, with his businesses, the people in town that he was meeting. He always wrote that he missed her and that he loved her and couldn't wait for her to get home. He always signed them with, Your Tough Guy, and she always signed hers Your Tough Girl, since they were not allowed to use names.

Sadie had been correct that Grease and his businesses would have become a target of Cage's had he found out that they were married. He knew he was personally shielded from Cage's hit, because to anyone around it looked as if Grease and Sadie were not together. She'd been gone for eight months. Grease knew that the last time he had seen Cage, besides the fight was when he had been in Poppy's with Gretchen.

The Pen and Grease'd Hogs had also survived its first winter. People traveling through Happy on their way to and from the nearby ski resorts stopped for food and some even purchase things from the retail shop. Justin had sold a couple Harleys around Christmas, but nothing since then and he was bored, so Grease was showing him how to do rebuilds. Fortunately Grease'd Hogs was doing a brisk business. Everyone wanted Grease to work on their bikes now, while the weather was cold and they couldn't ride them. So Grease was keeping his two businesses afloat and more importantly he was keeping busy.

The sun was starting to stay up a little longer each day since it was now April and Grease could feel the warmth on his face as he headed for his truck. One more month and he would break out his Harley for the season. Justin had already gone home for the night and the store and luncheonette were closed for the day as well.

As Grease reached his truck he heard a car pull into the lot. He looked up and saw a black SUV with tinted windows moving slowly towards him.

Ready for anything, and that meant opening his truck door and making sure he had access to his gun, which was stowed under his seat, Grease watched as the SUV stopped and the back door opened.

Sadie emerged from the back seat remaining behind the open car door. Grease saw her green eyes were shining brightly however her smile was tentative and although her pink lips had a small upwards tilt gracing them Grease knew this was her nervous smile.

"Sadie." he said quietly under his breath.

A man got out of the front seat and opened up the back hatch of the SUV. Sadie remained where she was so Grease headed towards her nervously, wondering why she wasn't walking towards him. His stomach clenched anxiously, but her eyes were calling him like lighthouse beacons to a lost ship, guiding him home. The US Marshal placed two suitcases on the ground near her and then got back in the car. Grease was a few yards from her. He watched her duck her head and heard her say thank you and then good bye, and then she shut the door and stepped away from the car as it moved away.

Grease froze in his tracks. Beneath Sadie's shirt was a very round swelling sitting low on her frame. She placed one hand on her protruding bump and held out the other hand to Grease.

Grease couldn't speak. His emotions were burying him while he was quickly doing the math in his head.

He took her extended hand and stepped closer.

"Mine?" He whispered.

"Of course it's yours." She told him gently smiling at his reaction.

"When? How? Are you okay?"

Sadie laughed. "Grease you know how." She teased. "When? Well my guess is July." She could see his mind was reeling.

"I had a feeling that I was pregnant when we got married Grease. Well, I was pretty sure anyways. That's why I wanted to marry you before I left. If I had your baby while I was in Witness Protection, I wanted him or her, to have her daddy's name."

"Sadie." She could see his eyes had gotten a little misty and she stepped closer to him and wrapped her arms around him. Her large stomach prevented her from a full contact hug.

"I have missed you so much." She heard him say softly, almost as if he still could not believe she was there.

Grease was embracing her very gently and Sadie chuckled. "You're not going to break me Tough Guy. Hug me good."

Grease hugged her a little tighter, but not much.

A small tap poked against his stomach and Greased backed up wide eyed. Sadie rubbed her belly. "Hey, you recognize your daddy already little one?" She spoke to the baby. She reached for Grease's hand and held it on her stomach. The baby cooperated releasing a few small kicks and Grease looked up at Sadie with his eyes filled with amazement. He then got the biggest grin on his face and let out a loud whoop, causing Sadie to laugh happily.

"There's my Tough Guy." She said sounding relieved. "Is it over? Are you home?"

"It's over. I'm home. Cage was killed in a shoot out near Mexico. That was a month ago. We had to wait until we heard from an undercover agent in another club to confirm that the hit on me and my parents had died with him. As soon as we got word I demanded be to flown here."

"Where are your parents?"

"They're home."

"So it's really over? You can come with me? Now?"

"Well, that's usually where a wife stays, with her husband." She chided him.

"You are such a toughie." He teased.

"So husband, take me home."

Grease took his sweet Sadie home and even though he tried to feed her and discuss the pregnancy, his Sadie wanted none of that. She wanted her man.

"Sadie, can we? I mean should we?"

"No intercourse, but everything else is on the table." She was naked and laying on their bed. Grease marveled at the changes that had taken place in her body. Her breasts, which had been perfect before were rounder and heavier now. Her nipples were larger and he felt his cock move just looking at them. Her stomach stretched upwards and she had hair growing on her usually bare mons.

Sadie saw what he was looking at and grinned. "I couldn't see to shave there."

Grease smiled and after taking off his clothes he stretched out carefully along side of her. Sadie saw a new tattoo on his chest. A red heart, similar to the one she had drawn so many months ago. She traced it gently with her finger.

"I like it." She said softly, repeating the words he had said when he had first seen it.

Grease was running his hands along her body, sometimes stopping to kiss a spot. His hands played over her sensitive breasts and she moaned loudly causing his cock to come to attention. He leaned over her, careful not to put any weight on her and sucked a taunt ripe nipple into his warm mouth. Grease felt her back bow as she greedily held his head to her breast.

"Grease, yes, oh God, yes."

Grease slid lower on her body kissing his way to her sweet pussy. He could smell her arousal and he felt his pre-cum dripping down his thick primed shaft. Slowly he worked his mouth lower and lower, his hands and fingers explored her new form. When he reached her feminine lips he moved between her bent knees and gently pulled her soft pink folds slightly apart. He saw that she was lusciously wet and he immediately lapped up her musky creaminess.

"Yes, yes, yes." Sadie whimpered. She was moving her hips upwards and her hands were on his head trying to guide his mouth to where she most needed him.

"Please baby, now."

Grease slid his masterful tongue through her sweet folds and then twirled it seductively around her engorged clit. He didn't want to hurt her or the baby so he decided to pleasure her with out any teasing. Normally he would have drawn it out to give her a stronger orgasm, but he had no idea how a women's body reacted being pregnant and he did not want to do anything to his wife or his unborn child that would hurt them.

He placed his lips over her exposed small pearly clit leaving enough room so he could gently rub the sides of the small piece of flesh with his fingers.

Greasssssseeeeee!" Sadie hissed at the mind blowing sensations that her man was treating her to and she immediately convulsed as an explosive white hot earth shattering orgasm ripped through her body. Grease continued to hold her open and when he knew she was still sensitive he gnawed gently on her quivering bud and she detonated again, raining sweets juices on his mouth and chin. He licked her sweets bits gently as another smaller tremor quaked through her writhing body and when she was quite finished he crawled back next to her body, planting tender kisses as he went until he was face to face with her.

She was breathing heavily and her hand rested on her baby bump.

"We okay?" Grease asked a little concerned.

"We are great." She told him in a husky sated voice. Sadie pulled him to her so she could kiss him. She tasted herself on his lips and swept her tongue through his mouth loving how he tasted with her on him.

"Your turn." She said as she got to her knees.

"No baby, it's okay. You don't have to do anything." Sadie was kneeling and she placed her hands on her hips. With her stomach all out in front of her and her skin glowing from the orgasms she'd just enjoyed she had that 'just fucked fantastic' look on her face.

"Listen here husband. I know you don't know this so I'm just going to spit it out. Pregnant women like sex. Lot's of sex. I have been satisfying myself for eight months now, but now that I have you in my bed I want to do some of the things I've been fantasizing about. Got it!"

Grease smiled widely at her. "You fantasized about me?"

Sadie laughed. "Oh yeah. Did you think about me when you were, you know touching." Sadie leaned down and licked his satiny dome.

"Ahhh." He groaned.

She took her lips from him. "Your."

She sucked the dome back into her mouth causing him to moan again.

Sadie straightened up, still on her knees and ran her fingers through her still wet folds.

"Big." She said just barely taking her mouth from him. Grease couldn't take his eyes off of her. She wrapped her hands around his thickset shaft and leaned down to suck on his shiny knob. She lifted her wet mouth from him again.

"Thick."

She bent again and licked around his entire head teasing his rim with her tongue. Grease's entire body tightened from the incredible pleasure she was giving him. Once again she removed her moist mouth from him.

"Cock." She said finally finishing her sentence.

Sadie lowered her mouth to completely cover his bulbous head and pumped her hands up and down his meaty shaft while twisting her lubricated hands in opposite directions. She worked him hard for about a minute before taking one hand off of his shaft to fondle his heavy sacks. She felt them tighten in her fingers and his cock shook as his body t-boned and warm spurts of her man jetted into her mouth. When she felt him stop trembling she kissed her way back up his body like he had done, and lay down on her side placing her head on his shoulder.

"Baby that was hot." Grease was finally able to stammer out.

The baby chose that moment to kick and Sadie grunted and Grease almost jumped from the bed he was so shocked at the force of the kick.

"Oh my gosh. That was hard. Are you okay?" He asked her Sadie.

"Boy or girl Grease this baby is definitely going to be strong like its father."

Grease was beaming he was so proud.

They spent the rest of the night talking about everything from baby names to what they had been doing.

Grease was asking a million questions and Sadie was starting to tire so she padded out to her suitcases, which were still just inside the door, and came back with a book. What to Expect When You're Expecting.

"Here." She said handing him the thick paperback.

"All your questions are answered in this book." Grease looked crushed that she didn't want to answer him anymore.

"Oh no baby, I'll answer every question you have, but I'm exhausted. I want to take a nap."

"A nap. Sadie it's Ten o'clock at night."

"Exactly. If I rest I am hoping we can fool around some more."

"Oh. Okay. I'm going to make a sandwich. Do you want one?"

"Peanut butter!" she said.

"Peanut butter." he confirmed with a smile.

By the time Grease came back into the bedroom with sandwiches for both of them and glass of milk for

Sadie she was already fast asleep. Grease put her sandwich and milk on her bedside table, got under the covers with her, and started reading the book.

Sadie woke up just once around one in the morning to find Grease still reading the book. She was ravenous for food, which Grease had left sitting near her, so she consumed it immediately, and then after relieving herself she got back on the rumpled bed and kissed her way down her husbands' fabulous body. She had poured some lotion, that she had found in the bathroom, into her hands before returning to her husband, and within a few short minutes with his rock hard cock sliding easily in her lubricated fists he came hard, moaning her name over and over again.

Grease recovered quickly and pulled Sadie to the edge of the bed. He knelt on the floor and placed her legs over his shoulders. He then proceeded to make love to her with his mouth and fingers. When he gently slipped his thumb into her warm bum Sadie exploded pressing herself into his mouth and grinding against him until another orgasm tore through her.

Once again they lay facing each other each other. Sadie's stomach was so large that she was never really comfortable any more, no matter how she lay, but rested her head on Grease's shoulder and threw her top leg over his. Grease could not have been happier. Grease gently trailed his hand along the swell that his child inhabited.

They talked for a while and Grease asked her a few questions like; what had the doctors told her? When was the predicted due date? Had she had an ultra sound? Did she plan to breastfeed?

Sadie smiled and hugged Grease to her. "I'm in good health and the baby is too. My due date is in two weeks. I had an ultra sound. I'll show you the picture in the morning. Yes, I plan to breastfeed."

He had so many more questions but he knew she was tired.

"Grease?"

"Umm?" He said softly against her hair.

"Are you okay with this?"

"The baby?"

"Yes."

"Honey look at me." he tilted her chin upwards. "I'm more than alright with this. I'm so happy Sadie. My only regret is that I wish I had been with you the whole time. I wish I had been there when you saw the doctor. Were you sick?"

"Yes." She admitted.

"I wish I could have taken care of you when you were sick and rubbed your back, the book said you would like that, and I would have taken such good cared of you." He kissed the top of her head gently and sighed. "But I'm grateful that you're with me now. I'm going to see my baby born in the next couple weeks. I'm a little nervous, but Sweetheart I'm ridiculously happy."

Grease stopped talking and Sadie knew he was itching to say something.

"Spill it Tough Guy."

"Would you have had the baby without me?"

Sadie kissed his chin. "No Honey. It had become a bit of an argument between the US Marshals and myself, but I have no doubt that I would have prevailed. I told them that if they didn't fly you to me when it was time that I was going to call you myself."

That made Grease feel better. "We need to get some sleep Sadie, but I have so much to tell you." Grease was thinking about his past.

"I love you Tough Guy."

"Love you too Tough Girl. Thank you for taking such good care of our baby."

Grease heard Sadie sniffing and felt wetness on his chest. He quickly pulled her back to see what the matter was. "Sadie?"

"Sheesh Grease you always say the sweetest damn stuff and it makes me cry." She mumbled. "I'm not a crier you know." She said almost indignantly making Grease smile.

Grease folded her into his big arms and they fell asleep together, relishing their first night together as husband and wife.

Epilogue

Grease was busting to tell all his friends his good news. When he finally tore himself away from Sadie he drove down to Happy and told his employees that he would be taking the next two days off and why. They were absolutely delighted for him. He then stopped at Pete's and used his phone. Having to drive to Pete's to use a phone now became completely unacceptable, and after he called Tank, Sweets, and Dak, he called the phone company and told them he needed a phone line put in at his cabin. He was surprised that they could start on it within two weeks. Tank, Tess, Lolly, Sweets, and Dak made the short trip to Happy after Grease had called them. Grease hadn't said why he wanted to see them he just asked them to come. Grease was so excited to tell them that Sadie was back and that they were married and expecting. They had been his family for the last fourteen years and he wanted to share his good news with them. They met at Happy Endings and an impromptu party to celebrate their nuptials ensued. Toby and Breezy came, and so did CC and Joe. Grease's employees showed up, and so did Pete and his wife, Liam and his wife Bethy, and Sadie's parents. Grease had no idea how everyone knew about it. He thought he was only meeting up with his club friends, but he did not care. He was a happy man. When everyone saw Sadie's rounded belly for the first time they were quiet for all of a few seconds before they started congratulating the happy couple. The party lasted into the night and Grease and Sadie rarely left each other's side. Grease noticed that his wife was yawning and rubbing her back and he realized she should not be on her feet so much. He quickly and politely thanked all his friends for coming, and then he and Sadie were leaving explaining because he wanted to get his wife home so she could get some rest. Sadie protested mildly, but Grease smiled at her tenderly and told her to 'hush.'

It was Memorial Day weekend and camp was gearing up for its first pig roast of the summer. Grease drove his truck into camp with Sadie sitting beside him, her hand resting lovingly on his knee. Grease looked in the rearview at the car seat where his son lay gurgling happily. He had been born on April 27th via a c-section and it had been one of the scariest and happiest days of Grease's life. His boy was big, 9 pound 3 ounces and the doctor did not want the large baby to tear Sadie, so he suggested the c -section. Grease let Sadie choose what she wanted; he just wanted them to be safe and healthy.

Grease had been allowed to cut the cord, which he thought was awesome. The recovery would be a little tougher for his Sadie but he knew she would handle it like a champ, which she did. They named their son Mac, short for MacPhearson, which had been his biological surname.

He had finally told Sadie about his past and she asked if he had wanted to take his old name back, but he said he was all right with his new one. He added that she was Sadie Prentiss and he joked that he didn't want any confusion about who her husband was.

Grease helped Sadie from the truck cab and then he plucked the car seat out of the back seat like a pro. With one arm around his wife and the other hand holding his son's car seat carrier Grease walked to where all his friends were sitting. This was their first outing as a family and Grease thought it was perfect that it was at a club picnic.

Tank was holding his daughter Isabelle who was three months old against his shoulder. Tess was contently sitting next to him sipping a beer watching Tommy. Lolly was sitting next to Sweets and she was all smiles. She considered herself to be the matriarch of their group and with everyone gathered around her she was at her happiest. Tanks son, Tommy, and Josie, CC and Joe's daughter were playing in the horseshoe pit and were filthy dirty. Grease loved that no one was crazed about how dirty they were getting. Dak was looking a little out of sorts with everyone being coupled off. Grease had heard that Gretchen had gone back to Hollywood. She missed the limelight. Sadie confessed that she was glad that she wouldn't be seeing her. The show she and Grease had put on at Poppy's still haunted her.

Grease could empathize with Dak. He remembered when he had felt a like he was missing something, with all his friends, finding their happy, with wives and now children.

Grease could remember the exact moment that he knew that he wished he could find a good woman to love. It was that awful day when Tess had been shot and they had all been at the hospital. Grease had looked around the waiting room at the couples who were just as stressed as he was about Tess, and he watched as they talked and touched one another, and drawing comfort from the one they loved.

Sweets unfolded two more chairs as they neared their extended family and Lolly begged to hold little Mac, so Sadie unbuckled him and lifted him into Lolly's arms.

The barbeque was fun and Grease couldn't remember one he enjoyed more. He thought back to the one the year before, when he had bedded both Bettina and Gretchen, and how happy he was now compared to back then did not even come close. He reached for Sadie's hand and she gave him a knowing wink. They had just come from the doctor's office and Sadie had been given the all clear to have sex. Grease was a little apprehensive, but Sadie was so happy that she had tried to get him to stop home first before going to the barbeque.

Grease loved that she was so sexual. He had already pleasured her quite a few times orally after Mac had been born, but they hadn't had sex yet, and he was more than ready. They were not pit stopping at home first though, he had told her with a laugh, because they'd never end up leaving. His Sadie had sighed, pretending to be upset but he knew she was only playing with him.

That was just one of the many reasons he loved Sadie so much, she was fun. He loved being married to her. She was easy going and happy. He loved watching her with Mac. She was a wonderful mother. Watching her breastfeed was one of his favorite times at night. He'd retrieve Mac out of the cradle that Sweets had built him, and hand him to Sadie, who would lower her gown, exposing her swollen breast. Then he'd get back under the covers and they would talk while she fed their son. When she finished he'd change him and put him back to bed and then they'd wrap their arms around each other and fall asleep, until the next feeding.

There was no adjustment period for Grease and Sadie as they began their life together as man and wife. Their bond was so natural and so easy that they were even surprised. They had settled into a wonderful routine and Grease loved coming home to his wife and baby. Sadie was impressed with The Pen and Grease'd Hog and after she finally talked him into going back to work full-time, she and Mac would meet him for lunch every day at The Pen. The four women running the luncheonette were already spoiling Mac. Justin was talking about making his first mini bike for him, which Grease laughed at, and good naturedly told him that his son would not be riding for a bunch of years.

The only time they had quarreled, if you could even call it that was when Sadie talked to Grease about returning to work as a Deputy in Happy. Grease couldn't bear to think of her in harms way and even though he knew she would be great at her job, he had a knee jerk reaction and had immediately loudly protested. It took him less than a minute to apologize and then they sat down and talked it out. Sadie was going to go back to work when she was ready, which the doctor guesstimated would be at the beginning of August. Liam had pushed back his retirement so that when he left, Sadie would be able to step in. It was a very selfless act on his part and Grease was happy that even Bethy, Liams' wife was on board with it. She had confessed to Grease one afternoon, while at the luncheonette, that he was just going to drive her crazy being home all day anyway.

Day care arrangements turned out to be easier than they expected. The four women running the luncheonette offered to watch Mac, at their homes on their days off. Grease would drop him off in the morning and pick him up at night. Sadie loved the women and she thought it was a great idea. Everything was falling into place.

The food had been served and most everyone had eaten. Grease was thinking about taking his beautiful wife, home and making love to her and Sadie must have been reading his mind because she smiled at him and then started to say good bye to everyone. The rumbling sound of loud motorcycle engines coming down the camp drive had the men standing quickly. It was déjà vu for the group of friends who had experienced the same uneasy feeling when Tank and Tess were dating and Satan's Army had made a trip to their camp to return Tank's vest that had been taken off him when he'd been kidnapped and beaten. Tank looked at Sweets who shook his head, letting Tank know he had no idea who it could be. It sounded like about ten bikes. One or two bikes wouldn't be a worry, but ten could mean trouble. Big trouble. Grease covered a sleeping Mac with a blanket and watched as Tess took Isabelle from Lolly while Lolly captured little Tommy by the hand, even Tommy had stopped squirming feeling that something was wrong. CC had Josie in her arms and Joe pushed them behind him. The motorcycles were too close for the women to find shelter. Grease began to step towards Tank who was foremost in the group when they saw Satan's Army riding into camp. He felt Sadie grasp his wrist. He turned to her and gently unclenched her hand from his wrist. His eyes told her everything she needed to know. He looked to Mac and she knew he was imploring her to keep their baby safe.

Joe pulled Tess back behind where CC was, really déjà vu now, because he had done the same thing two summers ago. They watched as Shooter led a group of Harley's into their camp. They were not wearing their colors and that was a good sign.

Shooter and another man pulled up and got off their bikes walking towards Tank and Grease. Sadie was holding her breath. She didn't realize that Satan's Army was not wearing their colors was a show of respect to the Steel Horse Cowboys.

"Tank. Grease." Shooter said sticking out his hand to shake. The men shook hands.

"You guys keep coming to my camp without warning and someone's going to get hurt." Tank joked.

"Yeah, well if you got cell service and I had your number I would have." Shooter joked back.

"Passing through?" Tank asked. Back before Tank was kidnapped Tank had stood up to Shooter and asked him the same question when they were at The Pen, the bar.

Shooter started laughing. "Good one. Actually, yes, but I was hoping we could set up a meet?"

Grease looked away from Shooter and surveyed the other eight riders. One of them was an absolutely stunning raven haired beauty with porcelain skin. Shooter noticed Grease looking at her and chuckled.

"We are letting women pledge as members. She's our first female Satan's Army. She's pretty selective, but I can put in a good word for you." Shooter chuckled.

"I'm married." Grease said stoically. He glanced back at Sadie and saw that she looked upset. He saw that everyone else was relaxed, recognizing that Shooter showing up was merely a social call. Dak was staring openly at the beauty on the bike.

"We can meet." Tank said. "But not here and not at your place."

"That's fair. I'm inviting the Border Bandits, too." he informed Tank.

"Want to share what this meet's about?"

"Sure." Shooter said and then right before he began to talk he saw Sadie.

"Sadie? What the hell are you doing here?" He began to move towards her and Grease stepped in front of him quickly.

"Don't even think of going near my wife." He said it so harshly that Tank had to put his hand on his friend to still him.

Shooter looked over Grease's shoulder.

"Sadie?"

Sadie motioned for Lolly to watch Mac then she walked to where the men were standing. She looked from Grease to Shooter nervously and then to the amazement of everyone she hugged Shooter. Grease stepped backwards upset, and once again Tank steadied his friend.

"Hi Shooter."

"I haven't seen you since." Shooter looked at Grease. "Since you were in the cage in Sturgis."

Grease was fuming and Sadie saw that she needed to calm her man down.

Sadie stood so she was against Grease's side. "Shooter I'm married to Grease. We have a baby."

"You are? You do? Oh Sadie that's great. I'm happy for you." Grease's mouth dropped open at his response.

"I always knew you were too smart for my dumb ass, RIP," Shooter made the sign of the cross over his chest tattoo, " brother".

"Shooter I might as well come clean while my husband is here and I know he would never let anything happen to me." Sadie chuckled, half joking half not. "I was working undercover when I was in Norwalk. I was looking for the truck that Cage had stolen."

"Well that makes sense." Shooter laughed. "I swear I could not figure out what the hell you were doing there. That really wasn't my place, it was Cage's."

"So what are you doing here?" Sadie asked nudging her shoulder under Grease's arm and placing her arm around his waist. Grease finally responded and placed his arm firmly around her shoulders holding her possessively. She knew he had just had a little shock and she felt badly, but she loved how he had been ready to take Shooter down for just talking to her.

"I'm setting up a meeting."

"You're doing it aren't you?" She said giving Shooter a little smile, which Grease wasn't happy with and his slight squeeze to her shoulder let her know it.

"Yup. Red and I had been talking about it for a long time. Tank did it. I want to pick his brain."

"What are we talking about?" Tank asked.

"He's trying to take Satan's Army out of the Outlaw business." Sadie told them.

"That right?" Tank asked.

"Yup. So how about we meet at Sturgis, in August? That's neutral ground."

All the crap that Grease had faced in Sturgis rushed back to him and he didn't know if he could ever handle going back there. He would if Tank went though. He would have to. The other thing was, the way he was feeling right now, there was no way he wanted to leave his wife and son behind for week.

"I'm not sure if I'll be going this year." Tank told Shooter, much to Grease's relief.

"Yeah, I guess if I had what you had I wouldn't want to leave either." Shooter said looking over at Tess.

Grease reached into his wallet and took out his 'Grease'd Hog' card. He looked to Tank who nodded. Grease handed the card to Shooter. "Call us in a week. We'll arrange something."

"Sounds good. Didn't mean to break up your party."

"You go legit and we'll be inviting you to our parties." Tank told him seriously.

Shooter and his men mounted back up and the ten bikes left camp.

Tank left Sadie and Grease to check on Tess. She had never met Shooter, but he knew she still wasn't completely over her kidnapping in which Satan's Army had unknowingly been a part of.

Sadie turned and placed her hands on his hips.

"Honey, remember I can take care of myself." She teasingly scolded him giving him a little toothy smile.

"As long as I'm around woman, I will take care of you." He said seriously. "He likes you Sadie. Like a man likes a woman like you."

"Yeah, I kind of thought he did, but he never made a play for me because Cage had claimed me. Now he knows I'm yours."

Grease ran a hand through his hair as if to push away an unpleasant thought. Sadie knew just bringing up Cage's name had filled her husband's head with images of her with Cage.

"Grease look at me. You're my first love, my Happy Evermore. You know that. Even if Shooter had tried anything back then, I was never interested in him. I acted like I wanted Cage for my job, and even that was hard after I met you." She rubbed against him suggestively. "Now how about we take our son home and we make love forever?" She said exaggerating the word forever huskily.

"Don't you mean Evermore?" He said giving her a teasing grin. Grease placed a tender kiss on his wife's lips before pulling back. "I love that you know." He repeated the words she had spoken to him ten long months ago. "Your first, your Happy Evermore." Sadie smiled softly. "Come on Tough Guy. Let's go home."

***

I hope you liked this story. I would love and appreciate reviews posted to Amazon and Goodreads. Reviews generate sales and sales mean I can put out more books!

Thank you for reading The Tough Guy Falls. As a self-published author I do review my work fastidiously before publishing, however I realize that there will be an occasional spelling or grammatical error. Ugh! Please know that I want to put out a good product, so if you find an error please feel free to email it to me at zannesweeney@gmail.com so that I can fix it.

Just an FYI: None of my books are cliffhangers! I do recommend reading The Happy Montana Series in order.

Other Zanne Sweeney Books:

Neighbors
A Chance For More
Someone To Come Home To
Finding Happy - A Happy Montana Book 1
Silver Lining Summer - A Happy Montana Book 2
Now It's Perfect - A Happy Montana Book 3
The Tough Guy Falls - A Happy Montana Book 4
One Tough Love

My website: www.zannesweeney.com
Facebook Zanne Sweeney/author

www.ingramcontent.com/pod-product-compliance
Lightning Source LLC
Chambersburg PA
CBHW071300170626
46809CB00001B/296